HAVOC

JANE HIGGINS

TEXT PUBLISHING MELBOURNE AUSTRALIA

The Text Publishing Company
Swann House
22 William Street
Melbourne Victoria 3000
Australia
textpublishing.com.au

First published by The Text Publishing Company, 2015

Design by W H Chong
Cover illustration by Sebastian Ciaffaglione
Map by Bill Wood
Typeset by J & M Typesetting

Printed and bound in Australia by Griffin Press, an Accredited ISO AS/NZS 14001:2004 Environmental Management System printer

National Library of Australia Cataloguing-in-Publication entry:
Creator: Higgins, Jane, author.
Title: Havoc / by Jane Higgins.
ISBN: 9781922147295 (paperback)
             9781922148339 (ebook)
Subjects: Young adult fiction.
Dewey Number: NZ823.4

The paper this book is printed on is certified against the Forest Stewardship Council® Standards. Griffin Press holds FSC chain of custody certification SGS-COC-005088. FSC promotes environmentally responsible, socially beneficial and economically viable management of the world's forests.

Jane Higgins was born in New Zealand and lives in Christchurch. She is a social researcher at Lincoln University, specialising in projects with teenagers. She has worked on many human rights campaigns and is interested in astronomy, mathematics and classic science fiction. She won the 2010 Text Prize for Young Adult and Children's Writing for her first novel, *The Bridge*.

janehiggins.co.nz

Teaching notes at textpublishing.com.au/resources

For Pamela and Douglas

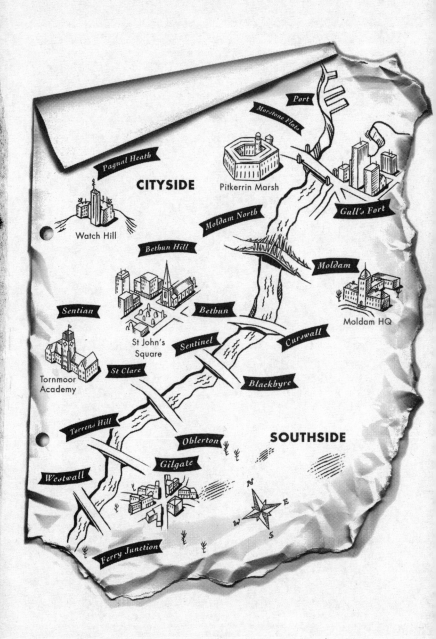

PROLOGUE

There is no marsh at Pitkerrin Marsh, but there is a memory of one. It seeps through stone floors in underground rooms, mottles walls, and hangs stinking in the heavy air. There's no warmth in those rooms, and no true light, no glimpse of sky.

The Marsh is no place for a Dry-dweller.

But that's where I was. Four days I'd been there, four days shaking the wire of my cage shouting in all the languages I knew, four days hallucinating about escape. Sometimes I woke up on the floor, fingers and toes red-marked, back and shoulders black-bruised, and I knew I had climbed that cage in my sleep.

My name is Nomu. At home in the desert that's a word for rain. My mother chose it, though whether she meant it for a prayer or a joke, I do not know. Three gifts she gave me: my life, my name, my brother Raffael. Now, in the Marsh, I had lost my name and my brother, but I would not lose my life, not without a fight.

I watched the girl in the cage next to mine. She was brown skinned and half starved. Breken, I thought. That's what the people living in squalor on the south side of the river are called: Breken, for the broken Anglo that they speak. The girl was dying. There were fifteen of us in that room and by my count twelve were very sick, but she was dying faster than the rest. Her sheets were tangled around her legs and arms, and her cough had become a retch. The blood-dark rash was spreading on her body as if she was charred black by her fever. Soon her eyes would turn bloody and sightless, but by then she would be too weak to scream at the horror of it. I would though. I would scream. I would make the whitecoats standing at the observation window take notice.

When she lay quiet and breathless on her bed I sat beside the wire mesh between us and talked to her. It calmed us both. I told her that when I was her age I used to climb the watchtower of our settlement hub at day's end and sing the sun down. I told her how peaceful it is up there that time of day; the old chains clank in the breeze and the tower sways and groans as if complaining to its brothers across the rock and sand. They do not answer. They lurch out of the dunes like giant buzzards with broken wings, straining for the sky. Dry-dwellers, you see, I told her. We stretch our bones to the sky.

Settlements squat at the feet of those watchtowers, small satellites of our own great hub, each one as shattered and dark as a husk pecked open by some gigantic beak.

But our hub remains; in fact it prospers.

From my perch beside the watchtower's tiny cockpit high above the ground, I can feel the thud of the water pumps, the heartbeat of the hub, feeding the meadows and orchards with water from deep beneath the Dry. Trees are heavy with dates and limes and oranges, honey bees crowd their hives, the leafy tops of greens push through the black earth. Ahead of me, the desert at day's end is amber sand and tall black basalt, and the horizon is a shadow of dusty red.

Sitting in the underground of Pitkerrin Marsh, I ached for that old watchtower so much I could smell its ironwork hot in the sun. But you know, I told the girl, it was not put there for my dreaming. The ancestors built it when the world began to go dark so that they could see trouble a long way off, before it reached our door. And trouble came—bands of desert raiders crept insect-like across the plains, hoping to surprise us, and storms grew from dirty, far-off smudges into surging, billowing, mountain-high monsters of sand and dust that scoured the Dry and left us gasping. But always, we were ready.

Then, in my seventeenth year, the year that I began

my apprenticeship in the laboratories, a threat came from a city in the north. It came thundering towards us worse than any storm or desert raid, and our watchtower stood its tall and lonely ground and did not see it.

I stopped my story. The girl was past hearing it, so I began to sing to her instead. I sang the Drum chants in the old language of the desert. Why choose a warrior chant for a dying girl? Because we die fighting when we die young. And because no one should die in silence.

I knew she would be gone soon, for I knew this disease. I'd seen my own people die of it. We knew it as HV–C6: Hemorrhagic Virus–Class 6.

The whitecoats called it Havoc.

CHAPTER 01

Southside laid down its guns.

At noon on midsummer's day, Breken squads all along the south side of the river stepped down from an attack footing, and a one-sided ceasefire went live. It was supposed to be an act of good faith. It felt like defeat.

I worked late that night at the hilltop HQ where Moldam township's militia squads were barracked. No one there was leaping for joy or sighing with relief. Maybe some fingers were crossed; maybe some prayers were said. The whole place was deathly quiet, as though we were holding our breath. Up and down the south bank of the river seven Breken townships, about a quarter of a million people, had just handed Cityside the chance to do things differently: to end the war, unlock the bridges and let Southside be transformed—no more, the gigantic detention camp and reservoir of slave labour—transformed, renewed, restored to what it used to be: the other half of a single, great city.

Dreams are free. Also pulverisable.

At 11pm when the power went down for the night I left for home. Moldam was sleeping, except for a couple of guards on the bridge gate, a squad on patrol and a few stragglers on the streets. Walking down River Road I stopped beside a stuttering streetlamp and climbed onto the riverwall. The wind was up, blowing cold from Port and promising the open sea beyond the rank air of the Moldam alleyways. I breathed deep and looked across the river to Cityside. There was nothing to see—Cityside was blacked out—but you could feel it lying there, like some huge wild beast from an old fairy tale, half asleep, tail twitching, eyes slow-blinking, watching across the water.

Friends were over there. Fyffe with her parents up at Ettyn Hills. Dash, now an agent with Security and Intelligence based at Pitkerrin Marsh. Lou and Bella lying half a year in their graves, their bodies pierced with shrapnel from the Breken bomb that had put them there. Sol's grave was there too, but his ghost was here. Right here, at my shoulder. He never left me and why should he? He was dead; I hadn't saved him. He'd be eight years old forever. There were a thousand ways I could have done things differently and he might have got home. I'd thought of all of them, planned them, executed them perfectly in my head, and at the end of every one of them he came straight back to me, the dead weight of him in my arms on the bridge, the bloody tunnel of the bullet through his chest, his eyes staring at the sky.

There was a scrabbling noise behind me.

'Nik, hey there.' Lanya kissed me cheerily on the cheek, sent a shiver and an ache right through me. She studied my face and read my mind. 'Saved him yet?'

I made a face at her and she smiled.

'You won't solve it,' she said. 'For once, your brain is not your friend.'

We were always having this conversation. I was stuck in 'if only' territory. If only I'd stopped Sol being kidnapped and brought to Southside in the first place; if only I'd convinced the militia here that they should let him go, no strings attached; if only the exchange they'd set up, of Sol for Suzannah Montier, a Breken leader held hostage on Cityside, hadn't been sabotaged by a Breken faction opposed to her return...then he would be home free, instead of buried back on Cityside, having done nothing, ever, to deserve that.

I said, 'Okay. Here's another way.'

'What?'

'Revenge.'

Lanya nodded slowly. 'Revenge.'

'Yes. Why not? Everyone else is doing it.'

This was true: for every assassination, rocket attack and mass imprisonment perpetrated by Cityside, some group on Southside struck right back with its own murder, bombing and kidnapping.

'No one wins,' I said. 'So rationally it's no answer but you said not to use my brain.'

She gave me a lopsided smile. 'Any word on the ceasefire?'

I shook my head. 'Waiting.'

'There's a surprise.'

Southside was used to waiting on Cityside. It had tried not waiting, that's what the uprising was all about—trying to push back, to drive both sides towards talks and a less murderous future. Right through winter, Lanya and I had met on the riverwall and exchanged what news we had about how it was going. By the beginning of spring, things were looking grim. Cityside's security and intelligence service and its army had quit squabbling with each other; the two had joined forces and hit Southside hard. The uprising faltered and stalled. By late spring people on Southside were talking surrender. Then came some good news at last: One City was back in business.

Southside had allies on Cityside and One City was the strongest of those allies. Activists, urban guerillas, extremists—they came with various labels depending on who was doing the labelling. Some of them had been years in Pitkerrin Marsh, but when Breken forces had taken control there six months before—only for a day or two before losing it again—they'd broken the politicals out. Now those people were spreading a shedload of chaos through the well-ordered Cityside streets: cyber attacks gridlocked trains and traffic, maxed out the phone network and crashed the electronic payment system in shops downtown. Graffiti was splashed across City Hall, churches and banks, and the news channel was being intermittently hacked.

It all sounded a whole lot more fun than going quietly crazy in Moldam HQ propping up a computer system that could have come off the Ark, which is how I spent my days.

Now Lanya and I were on the riverwall again, standing close—as close as you can get when you're wearing big old army coats, which is not nearly close enough. Lanya looked across the water. I looked at her. In the half-working streetlamp I could see her wide eyes and long lashes, the curve of her cheek and all those beaded braids spilling out from the twisted red scarf around her head.

Some people look at Cityside like it owes them. You can see it in the way their lip curls and their eyes narrow. Not Lanya. When she looked across the river she saw a new city where there was space for everyone. She dreamed it, and she wanted to build it too—to muck in, get her hands dirty, raise a sweat and make it rise up whole on both sides of the river. Me, I didn't see how that could happen. And anyway, no one was building a new city yet, not without a lasting ceasefire.

Lanya said, 'On with the lesson. What are we up to?'

She wanted to know what life was like over the river. I made up lists for her: we were up to H.

'Heating in winter,' I said. 'Hot showers. Halfway decent chocolate.'

She looked sideways at me. 'You said chocolate already, under C.'

'And I'll probably say it again, under 'R' for really-good-if-you've-got-enough-money chocolate.'

She laughed. 'Cheat.' Then she pointed towards Cityside. 'Oh, look!' A light flashed there. Then a series of lights—laser-bright—arced across the bridge. All in silence.

I got as far as 'Holy sh—' when the shock wave slammed us off the wall and the roar rolled over everything.

CHAPTER 02

The roar didn't stop. It slammed us into the ground, stomping through our bodies and shaking our insides to water. Rockets shrieked overhead and smashed into the hillside, breaking it open in jagged bursts of light. We clung to the cobblestones, blinded, deafened, frozen with fear.

The rockets pounded.

Kept pounding.

Then stopped abruptly. There was quiet, except for the ringing in my ears.

We lifted our heads, bodies shaking, breath gasping. The old street lamp above us flickered. Moldam held its breath. One minute. One twenty, one forty. Two. Lanya and I looked at each other and breathed out cautiously. People appeared from all around us, calling out, organising; sirens multipled. My eyes began to clear after the blinding glare of the explosions. I got to my feet and put a hand out to Lanya. She grasped it and stood up, and we hugged each other fiercely.

I wanted to stay there, letting the world go off, spinning around us, with Lanya alive and breathing in my arms, but someone touched my shoulder and said, 'You kids okay?' and we broke apart and nodded. Tears smeared Lanya's face. I kissed her forehead, tasted salt and dust.

'Bastards,' she said. 'Bastards, bastards—'

She broke away from me and yelled across the river, 'Ceasefire, you bastards! What d'you think that means!'

The air was gusting with smoke and sour with the ammoniac stink of explosives. It made me sick at the back of my throat, but that's not all that was making me sick. I looked up at the hilltop.

Lanya saw where I was looking and said, 'Did you just come from there?'

'Yeah.'

'Who's up there?'

'Everyone. Levkova, Vega, Jeitan…'

'Your father?'

'I don't know. Probably. Didn't see him today.'

She looked back across the water, then ahead of us into the blaring night. 'Is it over? Do you think it's over?'

'Maybe. They've made their point: no rules, and to hell with your act of good faith.'

She took a deep, ragged breath and blew it out. 'That was terrible. That was…terrible.' Then she nodded towards the hill. 'We have to get up there. Come on!' She put on her best 'don't mess with me' face and we joined the crowds on River Road.

We were heading along the edge of the shantytown, now a mess of flattened wood and iron sheeting that was starting to burn in a scatter of fires. The shacks around the bridge gate were flimsy patchworks that shuddered in the everyday breeze off the river. The rockets had flattened them without touching them. People were shouting to hear each other above the sirens and screaming kids and bellowed instructions from evacuation officers. Turns out that Moldam was well prepared for this kind of attack, which surprised me but shouldn't have. Evac officers stood along the road under the few remaining streetlights bawling to everyone, 'This is an evacuation!' They must've been picked for their voices: they could have woken City-side coma patients. Small groups of people pushed past us heading into the shanty: evac teams on the move, hunting for the injured in collapsed and burning shacks.

'Let's get to the bridge gate,' said Lanya. 'We'll take the road up the hill from there.'

Between the cookhouses and makeshift market stalls on one side of the road and the riverwall on the other, a crush of people emerged from their flattened homes and streamed out of alleyways. Some had kids wrapped tight around them, others were hauling whatever they'd grabbed before the fires took hold, the precious stuff like cooking pots, rugs, the family mattress. The clamour and smoke and sharp fear took me right back to the bombing of Tornmoor—my school on Cityside. That had been a Southside attack. This was a Cityside one. Difference when you're in the middle of it? Nil.

Then I lost Lanya. One minute she was holding tight to my hand, the next our grip was broken and she disappeared into the crowded dark. I dived after her, yelling her name, but I couldn't even hear myself in the noise. I stood for a second being jostled, then sped on, watching for her red scarf and beaded braids. Lanya would marshal an army better than most; she didn't need me playing nursemaid. In fact, in this whole mess of a war, she didn't really need me at all. She had a plan: she wanted to dance, and on Southside the way to do that was to be a Pathmaker— a dancer in ritual ceremonies and celebrations. After tonight, the Makers would be busy with funerals, but she wouldn't be one of them. She was on probation after breaking the rules six months ago. I'd said to her once that being seen with me didn't exactly square with her probation conditions, especially since I was the reason she was on probation at all, but she'd grinned and mentioned the army coats. Now her probation was nearly up and she had to decide, soon, if that's what she was going to do. So she was thinking. And I was watching her think.

Makers don't partner. She'd told me that as soon as she knew she had a chance to follow that future again. We could be friends, yes, close friends even, but there it stopped. She wanted to know if I was okay with that. Sure, I said. No problem. Which was mostly a lie, but I was trying not to get in the way of her doing what she most wanted to do.

I arrived at the bridge gate—or where it used to be. There was nothing there except the remains of the gate uprights: they were splayed out as though something giant had marched through, pushing them aside, and stormed off into the township.

Moldam Bridge was gone.

It had been ripped from its moorings, broken in pieces and hurled into the water. All that was left were its ragged beginnings jutting towards the river. People grew quiet when they came near it. They stood and looked, then hurried back into the mayhem. I thought of Fyffe and how we'd walked over this bridge for the first time only half a year ago. That stupid nursery rhyme arrived in my head:

> *Over the bridge it's dark not day,*
> *Over the bridge the devils play,*
> *Over the bridge their souls are black,*
> *Go over the bridge and you won't come back.*

No one was going back over the Mol ever again.

The gate had been a square steel frame, taller than me, with bars running top to bottom. Now it was lying in a mangled heap across the road. People were dead. That was why everyone who came near went quiet. The two guards on the gate had been blasted to the other side of the road. The medics hadn't arrived yet, but someone had stopped to care for the bodies: they'd been moved out of the foot traffic to lie side by side near the remains of the gate and had been partly covered by a couple of coats.

A kid sat beside them. He was a few years younger than me and he wore the red bandana of the Breken uprising around his head. People hurrying by nodded to him. Some said a word of greeting or prayer, recognising that he was doing what someone needed to do: sit with the dead. There was no sign of Lanya so I crouched in front of this kid.

'Did you know them?' I said.

He shook his head. 'My sister's gone to get the medics. I said I'd stay.'

'Have you seen a girl about this tall?' I stuck a hand in the air. 'She's wearing a red scarf in her hair and a baggy dark coat and boots that are too big for her.'

'I haven't been lookin' too close. It's dark, you know? And I've been saying the Charter to—'

He stopped.

I nodded. 'Good idea.' To keep the ghosts at bay.

'Yeah. So I haven't seen a girl like that. She hasn't stopped here.'

Not what I wanted to hear. 'Okay, thanks.' I stood up.

He said, 'You can wait for her here, if you want.'

He seemed really young and not liking what he was there to do. I couldn't blame him. I sat down.

'What's your name?'

'Teo.'

'I'm Nik.'

'You from Gilgate?'

That made me smile. 'You'd think so, wouldn't you. But no.'

'Sure sound like it.'

'Yeah, well, the man who brought me up came from Gilgate.' That was Macey. He'd been a security guard at Tornmoor, a Southsider, and as close to a parent as I'd had for the last decade.

'Where you from then?' Teo asked.

'Different places. You?'

'I'm from here. Are you Nik Stais?'

That shut me up for a second. 'Yeah. I am. How'd you know?'

'Heard of you. You were on the bridge with Suzannah.'

Suzannah Montier. Southside's leader-in-waiting. She'd achieved first name status with everyone. Much loved. Lost. Even the stain of her blood on the Mol was being washed away right now at the bottom of the river.

Teo was saying, 'It was supposed to be a swap, wasn't it: Cityside were gonna give us Suzannah back.'

'For my friend, Sol, yeah.'

'But they both died.'

'That's right. How did you hear about that?'

'Everyone knows. You were the last one that seen her alive.'

I shook my head and looked at where the bridge had been. 'I found her. After. I sat with her—like you're doing now.'

Teo was watching me. 'You're from Cityside.'

This wasn't a conversation I wanted to have. I looked around wishing Lanya would turn up, hoping she was okay, but everything shantyside of us was still going off with sirens and fires and yelling, and everything riverside of us was quiet. Almost everything.

'Listen!' I said. 'Do you hear that?'

A sound, high pitched and wordless, pealed out of the dark.

'It's a cat,' said Teo.

I wasn't so sure. It was coming from the bridge, but it couldn't be, because there was nothing there—only mangled iron and yawning blackness. And this sound: something was yowling from the ruins.

I stood up. 'I'm going to look.'

CHAPTER 03

'It's just a cat,' Teo called after me. 'You should leave it. Leave it!'

He meant, stay off the riverbank. No one goes there, except the scavengers, and them illegally. It's forbidden ground, officially, because it's littered with river mines and sometimes with the bodies of people who have tried to swim or row across. But that's also why, unofficially, it's out of bounds. Lost souls wander there—that's what people will tell you and they're dead serious.

I needed a torch, but all I had was half the moon riding a rim of cloud low in the sky upriver and even that was disappearing behind a haze of smoke. I walked over to the bent uprights that had held the gates. The short strip—ten or so metres—of what was left of the Mol gleamed in the moonlight. Beyond it the water shone black and disturbed, sucking at the gravel on the bank.

The creature sound got louder. I dropped flat and peered underneath. I was looking through a jungle of bent and broken iron beams and piled-up concrete slabs. Right in the middle stood a thin stick of a figure. It was lifting its face to the moon and calling out over and over as if all that was left of the bridge was this ghost howling at the city.

But it wasn't a ghost, or a cat. It was a girl.

I leaned further out and called, 'Hey! You! Grab my hand. I'll pull you up.'

The howling stopped, then started up again.

Behind me came a clatter of activity: the medics had arrived. One of them came over to look at the remains of the bridge and swore softly. Then he saw me.

'Oi! You! Get off that!'

I peered over my shoulder at him. 'There's someone under here. A girl. I'm going to get her.'

'This whole lot's gonna go! Listen to it!'

'I'll be quick.'

I scrambled back off the bridge, clambered over the broken stones and wire of the riverwall and slid down the bank. I peered into the crisscross iron jungle: the girl was dressed in something long and dirty white and she shone faintly in the moonlight. 'Hey,' I called. 'Come out of there. The rest of the bridge is gonna fall.' She stopped calling out and looked at me, but she didn't move. I tried in Anglo as well as Breken, but no joy. I was going to have to go in and get her.

I talked as I moved, in both languages, trying to give off this air of nothing-to-worry-about, but my heart was going for it.

'Don't be scared, okay? We're gonna climb out of here, you and me.'

Water dripped off the wreckage, freezing cold, on my head and down the back of my neck, which made me shiver, and I tripped, smashed my shin on a concrete block and came to halt, gasping. I knelt there for a second, sick and swearing, listening to the weight of the bridge creak and graunch above us. The girl watched me. I got up and moved on and when I thought I was near enough I crouched down and held out my hand to her. She opened her mouth and howled. Scared the life out of me. The sound of it made the ironwork ring and I thought she was going to bring the whole lot down on top of us.

Someone on the bank yelled, 'Get out of there!'

A chunk of iron girder thumped into the ground by the water's edge. I jumped and swore, but at least it made the girl stop and look at me. She was older than I'd thought—about my age. I held out my hand again but she backed away, deeper into the wreckage. I kept talking, quietly, like we were just having a conversation on the riverbank on a summer night and weren't about to be crushed to a painful death any second now. She gave no sign of understanding any of it, but she stopped moving backwards. Progress.

She stood still, gripping the iron and whispering her word, the one she'd been howling. It sounded like 'fire' in Anglo. I kept my hand held out, wanting to tell her that enough people had died on this bridge, but fear had dried up my throat. I had no more words.

We looked at each other for about an hour—it felt like an hour, it was probably about ten seconds—then she held out her thin, brown hand. I wanted to grab her and run like mad, but I made myself take it gently. I edged towards her, crouched down and put her arms round my neck. She climbed on my back and clung there like Sol used to, no weight at all.

I said, 'Hold on, put your head down, close your eyes.' And we started to crawl out. Every time I put a hand on a piece of iron I could feel it vibrating like someone was slamming it with a hammer. The girl started to sing softly in my ear in a language I'd never heard—a small whispered voice. It was a chant, like a lullaby or a hymn. I tried to listen to that and not to the creaking of the Mol a few handspans above our heads.

She was still singing as we came out under the sky. We breathed air that was alive with sirens and shouting and smelled of smoke and ash and river sludge. I lifted her off my back, and she gripped my arms, eyes wide in her thin face, and rattled off something incomprehensible. It might have been her version of 'thank you' but it sounded too urgent for that.

Lanya clambered down the bank. 'Hey!' she said breathlessly. 'That was crazy-brave.'

The medics took the girl and behind us the bridge groaned mightily. Lanya grabbed my arm and pulled me back from it. We watched the last of the Mol smash down onto the bank, jolting the earth all the way out to Port and beyond.

Lanya shuddered. 'You could have been under that.'

I managed to say, 'You would have done the same thing.'

She looked at me and put a hand on my cheek. I held it there and kissed her palm. I knew she could feel the tremor in me.

'Cold,' I said.

'You're soaking wet.'

'Where's the girl? Is she all right?'

'She's up with the medics. What about you? They should take a look at you.'

'No. What for?'

She gave me her lopsided smile. 'Nothing flaps you, is that the idea? You were under the bridge—you're allowed to be a wreck too, you know.'

We climbed back up the riverbank and stood on the edge of operations: people were gathered around the girl wrapping her in a patched grey army blanket. She was sipping from a plastic mug, but now and then she threw back her head and cried out her word. Someone said,

'She's calling on the angel.'

'Angel?' I said to Lanya.

'Shh,' she said, 'This is not good company to be a heathen in.'

'She sounds like she's saying 'Fire.'

Lanya shook her head. 'She's saying Raphael.'

'Oh,' I said. 'Who's Raphael?'

'An angel worshipped by some bands in the Dry. Do you think she could be from the Dry? Did she say anything to you?'

'Yeah, she did, but I couldn't understand her. Except…'

'What?'

I looked at her. 'She said two words—she kept repeating them—that sounded Anglo.'

'What were they?'

'Havoc,' I said. 'And Marsh.'

We left the girl and the remains of the bridge behind and sped on towards the hill, fearing—knowing, really—that up there the destruction would be much worse and the death toll higher. There were no guarantees that the people we knew had survived.

At the bottom of the hill we met a roadblock and three smoke-streaked guys from a squad, all of them on a short fuse. One pulled the bandana from his face.

'Either of you a medic? Didn't think so. Then you're not getting through. Get back to town. They need you. We don't.'

But behind them I spied a friend. 'Jeitan! You're okay!'

Commander Vega's go-to guy was not looking his usual shiny self. He had an arm in a dirty sling and a bloodied bandage round his head. He was smoking a cigarette with his good hand and leaning on a concrete wall plastered with peeling posters from the glory days of the uprising just a few months ago—all the bridge names were there: Port, Mol, Bethun, Sentinel, Clare, Torrens, Westwall. And across every one of them a thick stroke of black paint announced a Southside victory. Short-lived victories, as it turned out.

Jeitan waved us over.

'You're a mess,' I said. 'How are you even standing up?' I looked up the hill. 'Is it bad?'

'Yeah,' he said. 'It's bad.'

'Vega? Levkova?' I asked.

Commander Vega was Moldam's head of military operations; Levkova was the sub-commander who let me bunk down at her house as long as I never mistook her for the helpless old granny she looked like but most certainly was not.

Jeitan grimaced. 'Vega's not good, but he's upright so still in charge. Levkova's still standing, last I saw. And she's cross.' He almost smiled. 'You wouldn't believe how cross.' He waved his cigarette at the fires burning across the settlement. 'So much for our magnificent ceasefire!'

Sparks and glowing ashes spiralled in the wind off the river. The riverwind is supposed to be cool and fresh on your face: it wakes you up, makes you move, makes you run to keep warm. Right now it gusted hot. Which felt wrong, unholy wrong. A cloud of smoke made us turn away coughing.

'You heading up there?' Jeitan asked. He nodded us away from the guys on the roadblock. 'You know your father's not there?'

'Oh,' I said.

'There's word about that he went across to Cityside yesterday.'

'Oh.'

He frowned at me. 'You didn't know?'

Now they were both frowning at me and I realised they were expecting me to say, 'Oh, yeah, I remember now, he told me x, y and z about his plans'. Which he hadn't. Because, why would he? I was his kid, but I'd been brought up in a Cityside school run by his enemies—the same enemies that had killed my mother and thrown him into the Marsh as a political prisoner. I didn't know what had happened to him in there, and I didn't expect him ever to tell me. Jeitan and Lanya were still watching me, waiting.

'No, I didn't know,' I said. 'I've seen him maybe six times in the last month. He's busy. He doesn't have time to, you know, talk.' I looked back across the settlement. 'At least if he's Cityside he's out of this.'

'Good for him,' said Jeitan. 'Tricky for you.'

'Yeah, I guess.'

'What?' said Lanya. 'Why?'

Jeitan raised an eyebrow at her. 'They don't really

know him here, do they. He's kept a low profile for a lot of years, and he hasn't lived in Moldam. But suddenly he turns up and people discover that he had a kid Cityside and now he's disappeared into the city just before they land the biggest strike on us since '87. Doesn't look good. People will wonder.'

'People might need a lesson in opening their eyes,' said Lanya.

Jeitan gave us a grim smile. 'Good luck with that.'

Lanya and I climbed the hill, past a procession of people being carried down it on stretchers and in body bags. Lanya, always a Pathmaker at heart, reached out as each body bag went by and touched it with a whispered prayer for a safe path from the land of the living. When we got to the top she wiped her face with her sleeve and said, 'Did you count them? You always count.'

'Sorry,' I said. 'Stupid thing to do.'

'How many?'

'Twenty-eight body bags. Twenty-three stretchers.'

She nodded, and we walked up to the gate. We were challenged for ID by a guard; there was order in the chaos. That meant Commander Vega—Sim to a very small number of people, not including me—was still in control. A rocket attack and a nearly totalled HQ were just a signal to him to get on with sorting everything out again. Not the panicky type.

Inside the compound the firelight and smoke turned the ruins of the buildings into a lifesize old movie, flickering and hazy in front of us. Fires were burning in the rambling brick admin centre and in a scatter of barracks and workshops. Generator-fed floodlights lit the bending backs and reaching arms of people clearing rubble, pulling out the dead and injured, laying them carefully on stretchers or blankets. Voices called out now and then, but the place was deadly quiet so that rescuers could hear people under the wreckage.

We found Commander Vega batting away a medic who was trying to bandage his head wound. The guy had got as far as getting him to sit on a wooden bench, but not as far as getting his attention except in the form of being waved at as though he was an annoying insect. Vega was coordinating rescue efforts in three directions at once, but he stopped when he saw us and beckoned us over.

'Your father's not here,' he said to me. 'He's not in Moldam right now.' He squinted at me from under the bandage. 'That's all I can tell you. But he's not in the middle of this, so he's probably better off than we are. All right?'

Not really, I thought. 'Yes, sir.'

We ditched our coats, tied bandanas across our faces to keep out the dust, and joined a team clearing the smashed remains of the dining hall. CommSec—Communications Security where I worked for Sub-commander

Levkova—had collapsed into it from the floor above. There'd been no one in CommSec when the rockets landed but a whole shift from the infirmary had been in the dining hall. It was so random—if you just happened to pull the first night shift and you just happened to be hungry when you knocked off, then you were in the dining hall when the upstairs floor came through the ceiling.

We edged forward in the light of two floodlamps, heaving aside rubble by hand, drawn by the sounds those people made. Eight—that's how many we found. Five, we stretchered out to treatment down the hill. The others were dead. They were two nurses and the chatty receptionist who was always asking how you were and laughing about her kids doing nutty things. Lanya closed their eyes and arranged their bodies carefully, then sat with them until time came for them to go down the hill as well. I carried on clearing rubble until the squad leader in charge called a halt. 'Right, everyone! We can't do more without the heavy lifting gear.'

I pulled off my bandana and wiped my face.

The guy said, 'You're the City kid, right?'

I nodded. There was no point saying, 'I am, but you know what—it's more complicated than that.' People don't like complicated. Early on, I'd tried to explain but no one was interested in explanations so then I'd tried to leave it at 'Yeah, that's me,' but they seemed to expect more than that, I don't know what more. I'd tried, 'Yeah.

So?' but not for long. Now whenever anyone said that to me I nodded and waited, because they'd usually made up their mind already. For the ones who wanted to pick a fight, I'd perfected the 'shrug and walk on', which usually worked, though it gave me a great education in Terms of Abuse: Breken.

This guy looked at me and then nodded, clapped a hand on my shoulder and said, 'Thanks.' Which was good enough for me.

As the last body was stretchered away, Lanya followed the bearers, and I walked with her. Out east, over the sea, the sky was starting to pale and a fresh breeze, cooler now, drifted in. There was a stillness in Lanya that was maybe exhaustion but maybe more than that. It reached me, standing beside her, and slowed me down.

She said, 'I've never done that before. Not with people killed like that.'

A sharp whistle came from over by the gates and a voice called, 'Food! Choose it or lose it!' We queued at a water pump to wash off the soot and dirt, shocking ourselves into wakefulness with the cold of it. Then we queued again at the remains of a bonfire, where a team was cooking sausages in the coals and handing them out wrapped in thick-cut bread. No one spoke much: we all stood near the fire and ate, realising how hungry we were. There was billy tea too, black and bitter, but welcome for being hot and chasing away the taste of smoke. Jeitan arrived with reports from down the hill that things were going okay, considering, and someone said, 'Any bets on what Vega's thinking right now?'

I thought to myself: Vega's thinking, 'Where the hell is Nikolai Stais when I need him?' My father was AWOL, that's how it seemed to me, and probably not only to me; maybe he was playing politics over the river, but the game had changed and he needed to be back here fast.

Jeitan said, 'He's thinking: why now? Why destroy the bridges now?'

We all looked at him and he shrugged, carefully.

'They've always needed the bridges,' he said. 'And they've always needed us. Who else will do their shit jobs for shit pay? How are they gonna organise us going over there to work and back if they destroy the bridges?'

'They taken down any others?' asked someone.

Jeitan shook his head. 'Just us, so far. But the night's not over yet.'

CHAPTER 05

Commander Vega, Sub-commander Levkova and some senior staff arrived and the chat died down while people made room. I went over to Levkova and asked, 'How are you? Are you okay?'

She gave me a curt nod, then on an afterthought, as though she realised that surviving the night was probably worth more than that, she almost smiled. 'I am, thank you, Nik. You?'

'Yes, thanks.'

Lanya appeared beside us. 'Sub-commander? Something happened down by the bridge that I think you should know about.' She nudged me. 'Tell her.'

Levkova's eyebrows lifted and she gave me a steely stare. 'It'll have to wait,' she said. 'You're wanted.'

Jeitan came over. 'The commander wants comms up. We need to talk to people upriver.'

Easier said than done, but we scavenged functional bits and pieces from different places and set up in one of the still-standing sleeping sheds. I spent an hour jury-rigging the system into something operational: it would work as long as I hovered over it and doctored it the whole time. I was trying to contact Curswall, the next township upriver, when the screen flickered.

'Incoming!' I called.

'Ah!' said a voice from the screen. 'There you are.'

'Commander?' I said. 'We've got audio.'

The feed stuttered. 'Commander Vega? Are you there?'

Then we had visual, but it wasn't coming from upriver at all. It was coming from across the river. A woman peered out of the screen. She had grey-streaked dark hair pulled tightly back, a sharp pale face, bird-dark eyes and a tiny, tight mouth. Frieda Kelleran, the woman who'd taken me, aged four, to the Tornmoor Academy after my mother had been killed by Cityside security agents and my father thrown in the Marsh. She'd been promoted for her efforts, and now she was a high-up for that same outfit—Director of Security in fact.

The reception was blurred and crackling, and Frieda's voice, speaking Anglo, was blaring one minute and indecipherable the next. But it wouldn't have mattered if she'd been invisible and speaking ancient Croat—we'd received her message loud and clear about seven hours earlier. I glanced around. Not a muscle moved on any face. They watched, impassive. Listened. Someone nudged me to translate so I murmured along with her to a small group gathered close.

'I don't have visual on you,' she said. 'Perhaps your equipment is damaged. I'll assume you can hear me.' She waved a hand towards us. 'What do you think of our handiwork? We haven't touched the township but those of you on the hill may have casualties.'

The guy standing next to me opened his mouth as though he was about to yell at her, but Vega held up a hand for quiet and he subsided.

Frieda said, 'What we've done tonight is a small thing—a shrug. See how you shake when we shrug?' She leaned forward, her head filled the screen. She was so pale that she kept disappearing into the static, except for her eyes, black beads in the white. 'I have this to say. Listen carefully. We do not negotiate with extremists. We reject your so-called ceasefire. As for what happens next…Now that I have your attention, I could ask you where your One City friends are hiding, but I know what your answer will be. We have reliable intelligence on that in any case, and we'll be acting on it shortly. So we'll skip that step, shall we, and move right along.' She smiled thinly. 'To what, you ask. Patience, patience. You'll see. I have plans for Moldam. But for now, it's been a long night so if you'll excuse me…' She nodded to someone we couldn't see then the screen went blank and the static died away.

A wave of swearing and muttering went through the room. Then someone called out, 'Listen!' Everyone stopped, and we heard it, the hum—the high-pitched hum that makes your teeth ache and your skin crawl. The hum that will kill you when it lands.

Vega yelled, 'Take cover!' and we dived under the bunkbeds. The hum became a whine, then a scream, then an almighty roar shook the building and the ground and us to our bones.

What do you think about in those moments? If you're me your brain freezes: there's no before or after, there's just fear, which isn't even a thought, it's an adrenalin rush that leaves your body ringing, like the bridge in the aftershock of its destruction. The thought comes after, once you realise you're still whole and alive, and it's this: they hate us. And in that moment, you hate them right back.

When it stopped everyone lay still and waited. And waited. Frieda would have been profoundly pleased—she was in control even of our silences. At last, we rolled out from under the bunks, coughing in the dust, picked ourselves up to stand on shaking legs and went outside to look at the damage. The rocket had struck down the hill, destroying part of an old wall that ran alongside a grave-yard, and leaving a smoking crater and a far flung scatter of pulverised bricks.

Lanya said, 'Oh, no! How dare they!' and marched off towards it, but somebody grabbed her arm before I could and started to argue with her about unexploded ordnance.

Vega spoke to Jeitan who nodded and walked into the middle of the crowd. He shouted, 'Listen up! We're moving out! Moving out! Now! That means everyone! Walk if you can. We'll find trucks if you can't.'

Then he beckoned to me. 'Nik, where's Levkova?'

I looked around and realised that the sub-commander hadn't been in the bunkhouse with the rest of us. I went round the handful of other buildings that were standing, putting my head into each one. They all looked like they'd been picked up by a toddler in a tantrum and slammed down again; clothes, bedding and broken glass lay everywhere. I called out, but got no answer. No point hunting about inside any of them—she wasn't going to be hiding under a bed. And she wasn't going to be wandering through the rubble of the main building for old time's sake either—you could never accuse Levkova of being sentimental.

Where then? Where would you go if you weren't the type to hide under a bed in the face of a rocket attack, if you were the type to stand your ground and stare it down?

I headed to the lookout near the top of the compound, a knobbly bit of bare hillside above the graveyard. It had a bench, where you could sit and ponder the dead and the city and the connection between them, and, beside it, an ancient perspex-covered stand with a profile of the view from there. I could see the early sunlight bouncing off the stand, and then I saw Levkova sitting ramrod straight on the bench, with one wrinkled hand clasping her walking stick. She was scowling across the river. A blustery wind brought the smell of smoke and the noises of the rescue effort from the shantytown below, but she didn't move. A layer of dust and flakes of ash had settled on her black uniform and grey hair and in the lines of her face, making her look like a stone statue. Except for her eyes—they were alive and fierce. I thought of Frieda and Levkova glaring at each other across the river, but then I thought of Frieda's casual nod that had sent that last rocket screaming our way. I could imagine that after she'd given that nod and a smile to her 2IC, she'd poured herself a drink and strolled out onto a balcony with her army buddies to watch their handiwork unfold. I couldn't imagine Levkova doing that.

Levkova noticed me. 'Nik,' she said. She got stiffly to her feet.

'Ma'am, the commander's moving us out. All of us.'

She nodded. 'Tell him I'm on my way. Oh, wait a minute. You wanted to tell me something about the bridge.'

'Yeah. Sure. Later. We need to leave.'

Her eyes narrowed, but she said, 'All right. Go and

tell him I'm coming.'

I hesitated and got the full force of her glare.

'Go! I'll be there shortly. I don't need young things hovering over me.'

I went.

Down by Shed 14 the exodus was underway. Vega was sitting on an upturned crate. He wouldn't go until everyone was safely out. He must have decided that if he sat down he could direct proceedings for a bit longer, but the way he braced himself—hands on knees, hardly moving—you could tell he was mainly focused on staying upright. I told him Levkova was on her way, got a nod and was told to get off the hill. I went looking for Lanya but I couldn't see her in the crowd.

A woman in a squad uniform came pounding through the gates, struggling against the tide of people going the other way. She saluted Vega. 'Sir, a Cityside convoy has crossed the bridge at Curswall—' she checked her watch '—half an hour ago. Heading this way. About thirty of them.'

Vega glanced at Levkova, who'd just arrived. 'Thirty,' he said. 'They coming in?'

'Don't seem to be, sir. Looks like they've stopped on the Curswall boundary road.' Vega rubbed a hand over his face, smearing dirt, dust and sweat. He stared at his palm and wiped it on his jacket. I wanted badly for my father to be standing beside him, shouldering some of the command and not off over the river having, for all I knew, a nice break from all this dust and destruction and counting bodies and trying to defend the place with practically no resources at all.

Still no Lanya. I asked Jeitan, but he shook his head and turned back to allocating people to trucks and loading up whatever remained of the HQ—equipment, documents—that couldn't be left behind for an enemy to find. I was pushing through the crowd, searching, when a truck came through the gate and a man jumped out, saluted Vega and pointed downriver towards Port.

'Sir! Army trucks from the city! They've crossed the bridge at Gull's Fort and halted on the boundary road. Setting up checkpoints, looks like.'

Vega chewed his lip and looked at Levkova again. I swear those two could read each other's minds.

Vega said, 'You say they're not coming in?'

'Didn't look like it, sir, but I couldn't guarantee it.'

I stopped searching. Lanya wasn't there: not in the crowd, not helping get people into trucks, not loading up boxes of stuff. Then I realised exactly who she'd be helping, and I ran for the graveyard.

If the Cityside army was coming in, we needed to get out fast. If they were only setting up checkpoints, that wasn't so bad. Checkpoints were nothing new. Set up on the borders between the townships on Southside, they made life difficult for everyone because you had to stop and queue and explain your reasons for travelling. That's what they called it—travelling—when all you were doing was trying to go a few blocks down the road. It could take hours to get anywhere. We had to explain ourselves, at great length and in insane detail, but the checkpoints came and went with no explanation. Cityside usually did things with no explanation; it was part of keeping Southside off balance.

And now we were seriously off balance, because we didn't know what Frieda had in mind. What was the 'next step' that she was so pleased with herself about? And when was it going to happen? Chances are she had Moldam Hill in her sights, either for a takeover or for smashing, finally and completely, to dust.

CHAPTER 06

I found Lanya walking down the aisles between the graves doing Pathmaker work. Her arms were stretched out across the riverstones that they used for grave markers here, and she was chanting prayers for the peaceful journey of the souls whose bodies had been disturbed. That last rocket had blasted a crater in the western section where the older graves lay. The air there was still thick with the smell of explosives and upturned soil. I stood in the gateway and listened to the rising-falling chant in its long-ago language. I wanted to shout at her to hurry— we had to get out—but she was so calm and intent that I stopped and watched instead.

When she had walked the last aisle and was heading back, I went to meet her and we walked towards the gate. She stopped before we got there.

'Wait.'

'We have to go!'

'Wait.' She went over to the edge of the graveyard to the old house and peered into one of the lichen-covered stone urns that stood on either side of its front steps. She dipped her hands into the little pool of rainwater inside one of them, then flicked the water off her fingers and said to me, 'You too.'

I did the same. 'Why?'

'We're leaving the dead behind, moving back to the living. At least I hope we are.'

'Not if we hang around here much longer.'

We ran up to the others; Jeitan was helping Levkova into the last truck. He would have given Vega a hand up too, but you just can't help some people. Vega hauled himself up and sat beside Levkova on the front seat: staunch, both of them, but Levkova was old and showing it, and Vega was hurt. Jeitan closed the door with a grunt and leaned on it for a second, his own injured shoulder giving him grief. Then he climbed in the back, calling to us, 'Want a lift? We can squeeze you in.'

'No, thanks,' said Lanya. 'We'll walk.'

'Get some sleep,' said Jeitan.

'Sure,' I said. 'You too.'

The truck drove away, and we walked out the gate after it, leaving the HQ abandoned behind us.

Back down in the heat and clatter of the township we

stopped at a makeshift cookshop—a tarp awning rigged off the end of a lorry where an entrepreneurial type was selling the bitter black stuff that passed for coffee here, along with hot slabs of bread, semi-charred on the grill and piled with the salty little fish so beloved of Southsiders. We pooled coins, found enough to get some, and sat on a couple of old crates beside the truck.

Lanya yawned. 'I'd better go home. They'll be wondering.'

'I'll go with you, if you like.'

'We'll have to queue.'

'Oh, yeah. Checkpoints. Because we haven't been awake for long enough.'

'Thank you,' she said. 'You can have many börek for your trouble.'

'Promise?'

It was a standing joke: her grandma made these fantastic spiced meat and cheese pastries but in a household always full of kids and their cousins and friends we never got to eat more than one or two in a plateful.

She smiled. Salty oil shone on her lips and I wanted to kiss her. Her eyes did this slow, heavy-lidded blink.

'Was Jeitan right? Did anyone give you a hard time about your father being on Cityside?'

I shook my head. 'Nah. They hardly noticed me. You were great, by the way. You were senior Pathmaker-in-residence.'

She sighed wearily and drank the last of her coffee. 'I hope no one minded I was only an apprentice Maker, and on probation.' She smiled at the thought. 'It'll either get me in a lot of trouble or taken back immediately with acclamation.'

I knew which I'd pick but I said, 'They'd be mad if they didn't take you back.' I took her empty cup and, briefly, her hand. Pathmakers wear a thin silver band on their right hand, third finger, but hers was bare while she was on probation. I ran my thumb over where it would be and let go.

By the time we began our trudge back through Moldam the sun was high and blazing and the breeze off the river had given up trying. On River Road people sat about in groups, bleary eyed and slump shouldered, keeping an eye on their kids and guarding the little piles of belongings they'd managed to salvage.

Once we were past the remains of the shantytown and into west Moldam, the crowds began to thin, but River Road was still noisy with people—everywhere in Moldam is always noisy with people. Everyone seemed to be stocking up: the roadside stalls hawking water and vegetables were frantically selling out of everything; bicycles loaded with provisions wobbled down the streets and people had that hunted, hurried look, like they thought there was more to come.

We met a few people Lanya knew, and got a variety of greetings ranging from, 'Are you okay?' to 'Say hello to your mother for me,' to 'You're not still with that boy?'

The west is the 'better' part of Moldam, but the only thing it's better than is the shantytown beside it. There's row after row of crumbling terrace houses with windows boarded up, laundry hanging from balconies, and ancient cars squatting wheelless and windowless on the side of the road. Curswall, where we were headed, is more or less a repeat of Moldam. They're treated like separate townships but they're not. That's because Southside and Cityside were once a single city that crowded the river-banks, sprawling back on both sides towards the hills, and linked by ferries crisscrossing the river and by the seven bridges. Dividing the south bank into Moldam, Curswall, Gilgate and all the rest was Cityside's attempt, years ago, to turn Southside into a giant detention camp for refugees who flooded in from countries south and east escaping failed harvests and war and persecution by tin-pot generals. They arrived starving, with no money and the wrong papers or no papers at all. They crowded into cheap boarding houses and when those overflowed, the shantytowns mushroomed down by the bridges. At first, Southsiders worked at jobs that no one Cityside would touch, and they got paid almost nothing. Once they started asking questions about that, things became inconvenient for Cityside, and its own tin-pot general put them back in their place.

And so here we were, generations later, with the whole rocket attack and checkpoint thing still going on, and no end in sight to any of it.

Lanya and I were near the intersection of River Road and the Moldam–Curswall boundary road when we heard yelling up ahead and saw a crowd of people. Some were hefting stones and bits of rubble and hurling them towards the checkpoint, some waved sticks and iron bars. But no one was moving forward.

'Dammit,' said Lanya. 'We'll never get through while people are throwing stones. Can't they just queue and get it over with?'

Then shots slammed into the air—the rapid fire of automatic weapons. Everyone ran for cover, and that's when we saw what they were shouting about. They weren't rioting out of frustration at having to queue at a checkpoint. There was no queue because there was no checkpoint. There was a fence, two metres high, of coiled barbed wire.

CHAPTER 07

The burst of shooting stopped, and we peered back around the corner of the house we were sheltering behind.

'Come on,' I said to Lanya. 'Let's try Hurrin Street.'

'Won't do you no good,' said a man crouched on the ground beside us.

'But I have to get to Curswall,' said Lanya.

He looked up at her, then back to the soldiers pacing beyond the coils of wire. 'Then, girl, you are shit outta luck. They've fenced us in all round. I've looked, so I know.' He hefted an iron bar. 'But if they think they're lockin' me in they got another think coming.'

He got to his feet, gave us a grin and jogged away up the road.

Lanya watched him go. 'All round?' She looked at me. 'All round!'

'Let's find out,' I said.

At the intersection of Hurrin Street and the boundary road it was the same story. The way through to Curswall was blocked by steel bars resting on big steel X's that had been rammed against the buildings on each side of the road. Great rolls of vicious-looking barbed wire were looped along the bars. The road was impassable.

There was a crowd here but they were mainly standing about, quiet and curious, like they were waiting for it all to be over. On the other side of the wire were three soldiers in full battle gear—sunglasses, helmets, combat rifles slung over shoulders, the works. They were talking to each other, joking about, not paying much attention to us.

Lanya chewed her lip and watched them.

I said, 'I'm gonna ask.'

We shouldered our way through, and when we got to the wire I called out, 'Hey!' and waved my arms at the soldiers.

They stopped talking, and one of them sauntered over to look at us.

I said, in Anglo, 'She needs to get through. Her family's in Curswall.'

He jerked his head riverwards. 'Piss off, kid.'

'Come on!' I said. 'She lives there. We're not armed. We just want to get her back home. It's only a few streets away.'

People were starting to gather round.

The guy glanced back to his mates and said, 'Get a load of this. They talk proper here now.' He lifted his gun off his shoulder and looked back at us. 'You talk it. Don't you understand it? Piss. Off. *Now!*' He stabbed the gun at us and laughed when we flinched.

Lanya tugged at my arm. 'It's no good. Let's go.'

I pulled away. 'No,' I said. 'Why? It's just a simple ask. I want to know what's going on.'

The guy with the gun watched us from behind his shades and his riot of wire. 'You're still here,' he said. 'Do I have to spell it out? P. I.—'

'No,' I said. 'Just tell us what's going on. What's the deal? Why the lockdown?'

The soldier called back to the others. 'Hey! We got trouble.'

Lanya pulled at my arm. 'Don't do this, Nik. Let's go!'

'We're not trouble,' I said to him. 'We want to visit her family, that's all.'

'You thick or something?' he said. 'You're not leaving, right? You're stayin' put and doin' what you're told. All of you. Until…'

All right, I thought, I'll play your stupid game. 'Until when?'

He smirked. 'Further notice.'

I ignored Lanya's unspoken resistance and said, 'When will we be able to get through, then? How long are you going to be here? This an overnight stay or are you settling in?'

'Talk a lot, don't you,' he said. 'You know what I think? I think you should quit talking Anglo. It's not yours to talk. You got your own shitty language. You talk that.'

'Look—' I said.

'Nope,' he stepped back. 'Ask me in Breken-speak. Go on! Ask me in Breken and I might tell you.'

'He won't,' said Lanya. 'You know he won't. He's just a grunt. He doesn't know why they're here or how long for. C'mon. Let's go.'

'See?' said the guy. 'The girl talks it. Now you try. Or is it such a crap language you're 'shamed to?' He came closer to the wire and stuck his head forward. 'Go on! Do as you're told, you little shit. Say something!'

His mates were taking an interest, so I called to one of them, 'Hey! How long are you gonna be here?'

The gun jerked up level with my face.

'Say it in Breken or I'll blow your fucking head off!'

People scattered like a flock of starlings. I held up both hands and backed away.

'Okay, okay,' I said in Breken, 'Going now.'

He lowered the gun and put a hand to his ear. 'What'd you say?' he asked. 'Can't understand you. Crap language.' He laughed like a maniac at how hilarious he was.

I said, 'Moron,' in Breken and the gun came back up.

'What'd you call me?' he yelled. *'What'd you call me?'* But we were backing away faster now, and then his mates must have told him to chill because he lowered the gun a millimetre. We turned and dashed back around the corner to safety.

Lanya was stooped, hands on knees, staring at the ground like she was going to be sick.

'Why did you do that? That was mad.'

'Yeah,' I said.

I picked up a stone from a pile of broken building on the roadside, turned back round the corner and hurled it hard as I could. It landed in the wire. The three of them spun towards it, guns coming up, and I ducked back to safety.

Lanya threw up her hands. 'What are you doing?'

'I'm being hacked off, all right? They've just built a wall round us! A wall! We're trapped. Doesn't that freak you out? We're trapped and they can do anything they like to us now.'

'Like they couldn't before?' She looked around. The people who'd been standing in the intersection had gone. The place was suddenly empty. 'Let's go to Levkova's,' she said.

I shook my head. 'I'm going to check the other boundary intersections first. See if they're the same as here.'

'So you can get yourself shot properly next time? Not with my help, you're not.' She set off east, walked a few paces, then looked back at me. 'Coming?'

She had a point. But I didn't want to go and sit at Levkova's kitchen table and talk sensibly about strategy and tactics. I wanted to throw stones and take to the fences with an iron bar and wire cutters.

'I told you,' I said. 'I'm going to check Battleby and Cafford. Maybe Enders too. They might not all be like this.'

'They *will* all be like this. You know they will.' She walked back to me. Her face was shining with sweat, and tight round her mouth and eyes. She gave me a little shake.

'Nik, we don't win these fights. People really do get shot. I'm going to Levkova's. Come with me.'

She turned and walked away.

I called after her, 'But you need to get home!'

'I can wait,' she called over her shoulder.

'And we need medics from Curswall. What about them?'

She turned round but kept walking slowly away. 'You think you're going to get them here by throwing stones and getting shot at?'

She didn't wait for me to answer.

I watched her go, told myself I needed to know more about what was going on, and jogged away towards the Battleby intersection. I didn't see much as I ran, except

Frieda. I kept seeing her in my mind's eye, planning at her desk, smiling to herself as she signed off on…what? Once, when I was four, she'd held my hand and taken me to school. I used to be able to escape school though: climb the wall and slip away into the city for a wander, breathe the night air, find some space to think.

I looked up at the sky: blue-white, washed out in the heat. The cordon they'd built might as well reach that high; our chances of getting through it were nil. Something was on its way here—something that needed soldiers and barbed wire to make sure we got it full in the face. We don't win these fights, Lanya had said. Wait it out, she meant; we'll get another chance.

Maybe we would. But maybe not. What if this was new, a whole new wargame, and only Frieda knew how it would play out?

I heard the blare and whistling feedback of a crap sound system ahead, and when I swung round the corner into Battleby Road I plunged into a crowd. Hundreds of people were surging around a guy standing on some steps. He was yelling into a battered megaphone about rights and freedom of movement. Everyone was shouting, angry, throwing stuff at the fence that was locking them in. I couldn't see the soldiers on the other side through the crush of bodies pushing forward, arms raised, fists pumping. Battleby Road is narrow and overshadowed on both sides by five-storey tenement blocks. The noise was huge, ringing off those buildings so I barely heard the guy next to me yell, but I saw him point to the roof at the end of the row, above the barbed wire. There was movement up there.

'Sniper!' he yelled.

'Whose?' I yelled back.

'Theirs!'

Snipers. Barbed wire. No one was going to get through.

What if you know you can't win so you just want to run at your enemy in a rage and hurl yourself at them and do as much damage as you can before they do damage to you? That's what that crowd felt like. That's what I felt like in that crowd.

A single shot ahead of us shut everyone up for a second. Then came an explosion in mid air and billowing clouds of pale smoke. The guy with the megaphone yelled, 'Move back! Keep calm!' There was no room to scatter. The crowd surged back towards where I was standing, and I turned with them, but the smoke got to us before we could get out and suddenly I was inhaling fire and my brain was dissolving in acid and streaming out of my eyes and nose.

It wasn't smoke, it was gas. Skin-flaying, lung-scorching, eye-scalding gas. We were running—trying to run, not seeing properly, trying to escape and not fall over people, dragging up those who fell and stumbling on, retching, crying, coughing, gasping. I slung my coat over my head as a shield from the gas and ran with the rest of them. Then we were out of Battleby, and jostling, hunting for clean air.

I kept moving. I couldn't see where I was going but I stumbled along on feet that seemed miles from my head, with my hands grabbing at whatever would hold me upright: buildings, fences, bollards, walls.

After a few minutes the air stopped burning. I found a street lamp to lean against and coughed my lungs out. Realised I'd lost my coat. I wasn't going back for it.

CHAPTER 08

Lanya was sitting on the steps of Levkova's house. She watched me walk up the street towards her, and when I got near she stood up.

'Gods, look at you. What happened?'

'Some kind of gas,' I croaked. 'At Battleby.'

'Do you know what to do?'

I shook my head.

'Come with me. Quick.'

We went round the back to the washhouse.

'Go in there, put your clothes in the washtub and pour a lot of water over yourself. Water and soap. Lots of it. It'll hurt even more for a while, but you've got to wash it all off. And watch out for your eyes. Don't take your T-shirt off over your head.'

'What do you want me to do? Cut it off? I've only got three.'

'And you've only got two eyes. Come in here, I'll help.' She went in and hunted through a pile of clean washing, found a pillowcase and held it out. 'Stick this over your head. I'll get the shirt off.'

She was all business getting my T-shirt off, lifting off the pillowcase, holding them both at arm's length and dropping them into the big washtub. When she'd done scrubbing her hands with soap and water she turned back to me, arms folded, face unreadable.

'Thanks,' I said.

My skin still burned and my eyes were watering like crazy. I didn't ask her how she knew what to do—I guess it came with growing up on Southside. 'Do this often?' I asked.

Her mouth was a thin line. 'Once or twice. That's often enough. Put all your clothes in the washtub. You'll have to wash them all really well, but do that later. Wash yourself first. Will I get you some clean clothes?'

I shook my head. 'There's some in that pile there.'

'Right. I'll go then.'

'I didn't get shot,' I said as she reached the door.

She turned back and gave me a glare. 'I'll be out on the steps.'

Lanya was right about the water—it made it burn worse than ever at first. But I managed to slosh enough over myself to get rid of most of whatever chemicals were clinging to me. By the time I went back round the front and sat down beside her, I was starting to feel human again.

'How are you now?' she asked.

'Better,' I said. 'Thanks.'

She handed me a piece of flatbread folded round some mini spiced sausages called merguez.

'Sorry it got squashed,' she said. 'I've been holding it a long time.'

'Levkova made merguez?' I said with my mouth full.

She looked at me sideways and snorted a laugh. 'Somebody came in with a pile of them, but I don't think they made it as far as the kitchen.'

'Full house, then?'

She nodded. Levkova kept an open door for CFM, the Campaign for Free Movement, which meant that the place was on the go all hours with people having impromptu meetings in every available room as well as in the hallway and on the stairs, and when they were done with those, they worked or napped on the couches in her study and living room.

Lanya said, 'How far did you get?'

'Battleby. The gas sent us running. I didn't look any further.'

She grimaced. 'You sound terrible.'

'Coughed a lot, I guess.'

'Levkova's in the kitchen with some CFM leaders. You should tell her you're here.'

I shook my head. 'She's busy. I just want to crash.'

'She asked where you were.'

'What did you say?'

'That you were off fighting battles you couldn't win and getting pointlessly shot.'

I fired her a look. 'Did you?'

She smiled. 'No, of course not. I said you were on your way.'

I finished the merguez and stared up the street, wondering what was happening at other intersections.

Lanya watched me. 'You're not going back.'

I didn't answer.

'You're not!' she said.

'I'm not staying where they put me.'

'But—'

'I don't tell you what you should be doing, do I?'

She put a hand on my forearm. 'You need sleep. You're wound right up.'

I looked at her hand. Her skin was cool and dry and made the hairs on my arm stand on end.

I said, 'And, to be honest, that's not helping.'

She let go abruptly and stood up. 'I'm going in.'

And she was gone.

I pushed my fingers through my hair and stared down at my boots. I was going nowhere. In every sense. I got up and went inside.

I worked my way through the people in the hallway, put my head into the kitchen to say hello to Levkova and motioned that I was going upstairs, but she called me in. Lanya sat in one of the big armchairs beside the fireplace, hugging her knees, head down. I slumped into the chair opposite her. She didn't look up. I closed my eyes, thought about being an idiot, and then about Frieda and being trapped and gassed and about protests you can't win, and then, at last, about my bed upstairs and being in it.

There were six people round the table and no sign of Vega or Jeitan—I hoped someone had found painkillers for them. Levkova, presiding, looked as alert as a bird of prey. I wondered if she ever slept. They were talking about how they were going to drum up medical supplies, but Levkova called a halt and asked Lanya and me where we'd been and what we'd seen. What we had to say wasn't exactly news. Turns out it was the same story everywhere. Moldam was locked down—but only Moldam. There had been no rockets for the rest of Southside, and no barricades either.

Levkova said, 'Who heard Kelleran's broadcast up on the hill?'

People around the table shook their heads, so I said, 'I did. She's playing games. She says she has plans for Moldam, but she won't tell us what they are. She says she has enough intel on One City to move against them, but she won't tell us what it is.'

One of the older guys, grumpy looking and restless, tapped his fingers on the table and muttered, 'Plans for

Moldam. What does that mean?' He glanced at Levkova. 'Could be this Operation Havoc?'

My ears pricked up. Levkova was shaking her head. 'Maybe,' she said. 'We don't know what Operation Havoc is. Right now it's just a name fed to us by One City. And they don't know what it is either.'

The girl under the bridge had said something that sounded like Havoc. Before I could say anything, the grumpy-looking guy turned on me.

'How has Kelleran got intel on One City?' He was scowling fiercely, pulling bushy grey eyebrows together. 'She must have an agent in there. Eh, kid?'

'What?' I said.

'You heard me. Has she got an agent in there?'

'How would I know?'

He turned his scowl on the rest of the table. 'Look, no one's prepared to say it, so I will. Anyone wonder why our comms are so easily compromised these days?'

'These days?' Levkova gave a short laugh. 'We've always been leaky, you know that.'

He pressed on. 'And who's been going back and forth between here and One City with nobody even raising an eyebrow? Hell, isn't he over there right now? *Commander* Stais?' He made scare quotes with his fingers around 'Commander'. 'It's obvious where the leaks are coming from. Obvious to me, anyway.'

I rubbed a hand over my eyes, remembering too

late what a bad idea that was—they felt like they'd been blitzed with sand.

'Nonsense,' Levkova was saying. 'But we do need to take this to One City. They need to know they've been compromised. And we need to know about Operation Havoc—what it is and whether it's Kelleran's plan for Moldam.'

'How are you going to do that?' asked grumpy guy.

'Nik will go. He has the language and he knows the city.'

I opened my eyes. I should have seen that coming, but yes, as things stood, I'd go. You bet I would.

The man got to his feet. 'We'll see about that,' he said and marched out.

One of the women said to Levkova, 'That won't work, Tasia. We haven't got a dog's show of getting anyone out of Moldam alive right now.'

And away they went again, round and round the table.

I looked for an excuse not to listen and found one in the distant growl of thunder as a summer storm came rolling in from the borderlands. The wind howled in the chimney and rattled the windows in their frames and big drops of rain lashed the glass. I hoped the army guys at the wire fences were getting soaked. I hoped Battleby Road was being washed clean. I wanted to get back there, to be in a crowd that was yelling and pushing forward, shouting at Cityside that we weren't going to sit around and wait for Frieda's plans to unfold.

I got up and lit the kero lamps hanging from hooks on the walls. Their oily tang stung my nose and eyes and made my head pound. I hung one at the fireplace next to Lanya, but she waved it away. She'd hardly moved since I'd come in. Head on knees, she could have been asleep or angry or anxious or, most likely, fed up with the lot of us. I sat back down, closed my eyes and thought about sleep.

Listening to the talk at the table I realised that I missed Vega's hard-nosed intelligent risk taking. He pushed things forward, carried you along, even if it was you that ended up taking the risk.

They left at last, not much further forward than when they'd arrived. Levkova turned to me. 'Well?'

I stared at the ceiling. 'Yes,' I said. 'It makes sense. But how?'

'That's for you to work out.'

'Oh, good.' I looked at the rain on the windows and tried to think, but my brain had shut down.

'Later,' said Levkova, taking pity for once.

Lanya disappeared without a word into the little sunroom off the kitchen where she slept when she stayed over, and I hauled myself up the stairs to my own bed and crashed, fully clothed, face down on top of it.

CHAPTER 09

Options, options. Like Lou used to say, when considering an escape from school, try something so obvious they won't expect it. Try walking out the gate.

'Okay,' I said to Levkova at the kitchen table next morning. 'Let's forget about trying to go through the wire and across Curswall Bridge.'

I glanced at Lanya. She was concentrating far more than was necessary on spreading jam on a piece of bread. She'd been extra polite to me all morning.

Levkova said, 'As long as it's soon. Kelleran won't be wasting time and we can't either. What are you thinking?'

'The Mol.'

Lanya looked up. 'What?'

I said, 'What's the only bridge gate on Cityside that won't be guarded anymore? And what's the only strip of river where there are no mines because they've all been detonated and not replaced yet?'

'Oh,' said Lanya. 'Are you going to swim?'

'The girl under the bridge,' I said. 'How did she get there? What if she had a boat?'

'Are you serious?'

'What girl?' asked Levkova, and listened while we explained.

Lanya said, 'Suppose this girl did have a boat, and suppose you found it, and it was undamaged, you're talking about sneaking out right under the eye of their army.'

Levkova was watching me with a calculating frown.

'I think it's worth pursuing,' she said.

The makeshift infirmary was a cluster of dust-coloured tents pitched on land that used to be a park west of the shantytown, in the older part of Moldam. I told a medic that I wanted to see the girl who'd been found under the bridge, and she laughed and said, 'Who doesn't!'

She pointed me towards a queue outside one of the tents. About two dozen people were sitting, standing, shifting from foot to foot, patient the way people are patient in queues on Southside. 'There's not much point, though,' she said. 'Girl swallowed the river—she's got God-knows-what running through her at the moment and she's sick as a dog. You won't get any sense out of her for a couple of days at least. And even then...' She paused and studied me. 'You're that Cityside boy, aren't you?

She's got no Breken, but she does speak some Anglo, so you probably could talk to her. But not for two days. At least.'

I couldn't wait two days.

I went over to the queue and asked what they were waiting for and they said, 'A blessing.'

'A what?' I said, but all I got in answer were stares and thumbs pointing me to the back of the line. Then this guy came out of the tent. I knew him, vaguely. Sandor something. He was a couple of years older than me, and he was making a name for himself as a doer of deals. A smooth talking southerner, his dark hair cut carefully, always dressed to impress—doing well for himself, but then you looked closely and saw the mending on his clothes and how threadbare it all was. It wasn't your pockets and your wallet that you watched when you saw Sandor sliding through a crowd, more like your life savings and your hopes for the future—for a little cash, or not so little, he'd turn your dreams into schemes that couldn't go wrong. So he said.

Now he stood at the front of the queue and told the people that he'd seen the girl, that she was called Nomu, and that she'd blessed him and spoken to him from a trance-like state about the angel Raphael. They watched him, almost with reverence, and when he'd finished, people reached out to touch him. A neat trick: he'd become sacred by association. He walked down the queue talking to people and nodding like he understood their problems and was sure he could help them, for a small price no doubt.

He saw me watching him; I should have just left but when he got to the end of the queue I said, 'Why do you do that? Feed people that stuff? You don't believe any of it.'

He looked at me, sly and sideways. 'Nik Stais, right? Why do you care?'

'Did you really see her—the girl?'

'Who wants to know?'

'Me, obviously.'

He looked around and waved at someone in the queue. 'And why would you be interested in her?'

I nodded towards the tent. 'How did you even get in there?'

'Well,' he looked extra pleased with himself, 'I rescued her last night. Risked my life to do it.'

He peered at me. 'What's funny?'

'Nothing. Never mind. Did she tell you anything, apart from that she was sent by an angel?'

He turned his back to the crowd. 'Look, these people have just had the shit kicked out of them and they're locked in like it's the Marsh or something—they want to be told everything will be okay. I'm telling them. You got a problem with that?'

'No, no, you go for it,' I said. 'But I know who got her off the bridge and I know a medic who will swear it wasn't you.'

'So?'

'So, tell me what she said to you. Did she say where she'd come from? How she got here? Why she's here?'

He shrugged. 'She might have.'

I closed my eyes, which wanted to be still sleeping, and tried to get a grip.

'I'll do you a deal. Tell me what she said and I won't let on that it wasn't you who rescued her.'

He thought about it and shrugged again. 'Couldn't understand much of it. Her Breken is really stink.'

'Yeah,' I said. 'That's probably cos it isn't Breken.'

He sneered and stepped away. 'Okay, be a jumped-up little Citysider then.'

'No! Wait. Sorry.'

'You want to hear this or don't you?'

'Yes, I do.'

'Well, okay. She's real sick, so mostly she's rambling and talking gibberish—I don't think she's one of ours, I think she's from City. My best guess—she was on a boat from City and it got swamped by the wave from the bridge going up, she gets thrown out and lands near the riverbank, crawls ashore.' His eyes narrowed at me. 'Is it a boat you're after? Think you can get outta here on a boat?' He hooted with laughter. 'Things getting too tough? The City boy wants to go home.'

'Yep, that's right.' I turned away.

He said, 'You think I'm just a scavenger. You know the only thing worse than a Southside scavenger? A City-sider pretending to be one.'

I walked away, but he must have rethought the possibilities because after a minute he was back beside me saying, 'Hold up! Wait! I'll help you find the boat if I can go with you. It'll probably take two to handle it anyway.'

'Sure,' I said. 'We're under lockdown and you think we can just row away from here without being shot by a Cityside grunt or blown up by a river mine. Besides, why leave when you've got such a nice thing going here?'

'Why leave? *Why leave?* Let me count the reasons.'

He stopped and his eyes got positively misty at the thought of the pots of gold just out of reach on the other side of the river.

I walked and didn't answer. But he caught up again.

'You know, that boat'll be long gone by now. There's scavengers here that put you and me to shame. It'll be under lock and key for sure, if it's still in one piece, smashed for scrap if it's not. That's if the soldier boys didn't find it first.'

When I didn't say anything, he said, 'If it's been locked away by our people, I know where it might be.'

'Do you,' I said and kept walking.

'I'll show you. You'll never find it on your own.'

I was trying to ignore him, but my feet slowed.

'You won't,' he said and smiled.

I reported back to Levkova and Lanya. 'Two days, at least, before she's well enough to talk.'

I was standing in the back doorway of the kitchen looking out onto a riot of colour and greenery that was fresh from yesterday's rain.

'But,' I turned back to them, 'I think she was on a boat, and I might be able to find it.'

I sat down at the table and told them about Sandor. 'Only thing is, if he helps me find it, I'll have to take him with me.'

'No.' Lanya shook her head. 'He's a low-life. You don't need him. I'll help you look.'

She met my eye, at last, and gave me a small smile. 'And then,' she said. 'When we've found it, I'm going with you.'

'Yeah,' I said. 'No.' I glanced at Levkova, who was watching us thoughtfully.

Lanya leaned over the table and whispered, 'You are not my mother.' She sat back. 'Think about it. Do you really want to be a lone brown male wandering the city streets? You think they won't pick you up as soon as they lay eyes on you?'

I shook my head. 'I wouldn't…I can't keep you safe over there.'

She smiled. 'Look at you,' she said. 'You look so sad.

You can't keep everyone safe the whole time, you know.'

'I haven't been able to keep anyone safe at any time. Maybe you noticed?'

'I can take care of myself, thank you. Besides, you'll need someone to watch your back.'

I looked at Levkova again, but she shrugged and said, unhelpfully, 'She's right.'

In the half-light of dusk Lanya and I scoured the riverbank, upriver and down, separately and together. We managed not to get caught, but we didn't find a boat. As it was getting dark we admitted defeat and climbed back up the bank. On the river wall we came face to face with Sandor, sitting there, kicking his heels.

'Told you,' he said.

CHAPTER 10

The bridge girl's boat was lightweight carbon fibre, big enough for four people, and even in the narrow gleam of Sandor's kero lamp we could tell it was not in great shape.

We were standing in a hold dug deep into the river-wall about ten minutes walk downriver from where the Mol used to be: the door looked like the entrance to an electricity substation and was plastered with *Danger—Do Not Enter* signs.

We asked Sandor how he knew about it, but he just winked and looked smug.

He held up the lamp. 'Look at this thing. Will it still float?'

I gave the crushed outboard motor a kick. 'Well, we couldn't have used that anyway.' I peered at the smashed searchlight. 'Or that.'

Sandor leaned in and inspected the bent half-canopy

with its cracked windshield, then glanced at me. 'Might work. If we take off all this broken stuff.'

Lanya watched us, tight lipped and frowning. 'Can you even row?' she said.

'Sure I can.' Sandor lifted the lamp in her direction. 'How do you think I knew this was here? Boats go way back in my family.'

She snorted and walked over to me. 'It's not a trafficker's boat,' she said. 'It's too smart. It's a boat for carting important people around. Who do you think that girl is?'

'Yeah,' said Sandor. 'It's a Cityside boat, all right. You know what that means?'

'As if we care,' Lanya muttered.

But Sandor was undaunted. 'It means if they see us on the river, they won't blow us out of the water right away. They'll wait till they find out who we are.' He slapped the side of it and grinned. 'Then, they'll blow us away.'

Lanya folded her arms. 'You think you're coming?'

He stared right back. 'I have oars. Which you'll find you need. And anyway, a deal is a deal.'

'So it is,' I said. 'Now we pray for fog.'

That night Lanya and I walked to the end of Levkova's street and sat on the riverwall looking across at the moonlit spread of the city. We talked through the plan that Levkova and a walking-wounded Commander Vega had come up with. We'd find my father who was with our

Cityside allies; we'd warn him that they had an informer in their midst; and we'd tell him what was going on here so that they could work out a way to (a) discover what Frieda's Operation Havoc was and if it had anything to do with us, and (b) scuttle it. Neither Levkova nor Vega could tell me where my father was because he hadn't told them and anyway knowledge of where he was would be dangerous if we got picked up. Instead, Levkova sent an encrypted message setting up a meeting. She'd sent it electronically, which was risky on an eye-watering scale, but what else could we do—we were short of homing pigeons.

As for a meeting place: I'd put up a bunch of possibilities and they'd shot down every one. Nowhere was safe. The city was riddled with cc-eyes peering along alleyways and under bridges, monitoring plazas and parks and shops. In the end they decided that meeting in a crowd was best, so Lanya and I were going to make our way to the Friday morning market in St John's Square beside the old church where, lifetimes ago, some friends and I had hidden in the crypt after running from our bombed-out school.

In theory, it made sense. In practice, who knew? There were too many places where the whole thing could come horribly unstuck. No one mentioned the most unthinkable. Everyone was politely quiet on the fact that my father had gone over the river at a suspiciously convenient time. What if the informer in the One City ranks was him? That thought sat in the back of my brain, as deep as I could bury it, but it never went away.

Sitting on the riverwall, Lanya and I started devising backup Plans B through to Z to cover some of the holes in our Plan A, not least of which was, how do we get home to Moldam once we'd delivered our message? We gave up when we realised the complexity of it all and lapsed into 'it'll be all right because it has to be'.

Then we sat, not speaking, until Lanya said, 'Yesterday, on the steps?'

'Yeah. Sorry. I was—what did you call it?—wound up.'

'But you've always said it's okay with you for us not to be…together, except as friends.'

'And it is,' I said. I looked at her anxious face, brows pulled in, lips tight. 'I mean, it will be. Once you're back being a Maker.'

'So when you said yesterday morning that they'd be mad if they didn't take me back—'

'Did I say that?'

'You did.'

'Damn.'

She smiled. 'Do you really believe that?'

'Of course. They would be. Anyone would be mad to let you go.' Including me, I thought. I went on, 'It's what you want to do.'

She looked away. 'What do you want to do?'

'I want to get through the next twenty-four, forty-eight hours, however long it takes to get this thing done.'

'That's not what I meant.'

'I know. And I don't know.'

She thought for a bit, then she said, 'Do you ever wish you'd become an agent with the security services like you were meant to and never come here at all?'

'And ended up on the other side of the wire? No. Not when I know what I know now.'

'What do you know now?'

I looked at the moonlight on her cheek and the arch of her eyebrow and thought, there are some things it doesn't help to say out loud, so I said, 'Coming here is like being told a secret. You can't unknow it.'

'What secret?'

'That the city is hungry. It's like a kid that wants. It wants and wants and wants and it won't stop until it's got everything. It's shit hot to have everything, but to have it, you have to take it.'

She studied me. 'You would never have made it as an agent.'

'How do you know?'

She gave this small shrug. 'You're not the taking kind.'

We sat there a while longer then went back to Levkova's and prayed for fog.

Fog didn't come. Only a pathetic morning mist that would burn off as soon as it saw the sun.

Sandor was on the riverbank before us, waiting in the half-light with oars over one shoulder and a canvas bag over the other. He squinted at Cityside through the mist.

'You were supposed to pray,' he said. 'Everyone says you're a heathen, and now I believe them.' He dropped a bag at Lanya's feet and gave a mock bow. 'For you, princess.'

'What's that?' I asked.

'It's a little something her highness here asked me to bring. Can't understand it, myself, but whatever you're up to, I don't want to know. Just point me at the city and let me at it!'

Lanya kicked the bag lightly. 'Levkova's idea. In case things get sticky at the market.'

'Market?' said Sandor. 'That sounds promising. What market?'

I bent to open the bag and she and Sandor both said, 'Don't!'

'Why?' I asked. 'What is it?'

'A friendly Southside export to the city,' said Sandor. 'Rats. Three big ones. They're sedated, but they'll wake up in a couple of hours so you'd better be ready when they do. What market?'

'First things first,' I said. 'Let's get this thing on the water.'

It was, without doubt, the loudest thing I'd ever done. The evac sirens that had deafened us the other night seemed like a miserable background hum compared with our attempts to get that boat on the water. Our feet crunched on the gravel—six boots, six hundred bits of gravel grinding with every step.

Then, at the water's edge, the bottom of the boat rasped on the riverbed as we slid it into the water. Then came the slapping of waves on its hull as it rocked there, oblivious to the agonised care we were taking over it. At that point, Sandor ditched his jeans for shorts and waded in, noisily, to stand thigh deep at the front of the boat to hold it steady and guide it out, and I started to think that maybe he did know something about boats after all. He gestured for Lanya and me to climb in, which we did, the clumsiest, thumpingest falling into a boat there can have ever been. Sandor followed, just as loudly. Then the stupid oars took on a life of their own, rattling and clattering as we shipped them in the rowlocks.

Finally we were there, ready, and we'd only just begun.

We sat for a moment, looked around us, behind us, up and down the river, then at each other. Listened. Heard the slap of the water, and nothing else. We were past the point of no return: if we were caught now, we'd be taking a quick-one way trip, straight down.

Sandor and I took an oar each and Lanya knelt in the

front peering ahead for broken chunks of bridge, and we crawled, if you can crawl on water, towards the city. The oars clacked in the rowlocks and slapped the water with every stroke. Half of me wanted to race and get it over with no matter how loudly we did it, and the other half wanted to creep along so slowly that we'd never be heard, and maybe never get there at all.

But our luck held. The riverwall loomed in front of us at last.

Near the Mol on Cityside the riverwall plunges straight into the water without a riverbank, but the wall has mooring rings and ladders running up to street level. We bobbed there in the shelter of the wall for a while, listening for activity on the street above us, and looking back towards Southside. The sun had tipped over the horizon and was sending long glancing beams into Moldam and onto the water, lifting the mist.

'Are we leaving the boat here?' asked Lanya. 'What if it's not here when we come back?'

'There's a phrase for that,' I said. 'Something about crossing that bridge when we come to it?'

She gave me a tiny smile. 'Unless they've blown it up.'

'Right,' said Sandor to me. 'You lead, we'll follow.'

Lanya looked at him. 'You say *we*,' she said. 'But you're not coming with us.'

'Yeah,' he said, 'I am.'

'Aren't you going off to make your fortune?' she said.

'I intend to, princess. But you said you're going to a market, and that means food. I'm coming with you that far.' He looked at me. 'You armed?'

I shook my head. 'Are you?'

He held up his hand. A small gun sat neatly in his palm.

'Brilliant,' I said. 'If they do a stop-and-search on us and find that, we're dead, so you better ditch it fast if things go bad.' I looked at Lanya. 'You?'

'It's a very thin knife,' she said. 'They won't find it. Why do you think I wear boots that are too big for me? Don't fret. Come on, we're following you. Anglo all the way from now on.'

I climbed the ladder and peered over the wall: up the street and down, the place was empty. We'd been lucky again. We wouldn't keep being lucky—the world wasn't like that—but for now I was taking any and all the good luck that came our way. I motioned the others to follow and we scrambled up and over the wall.

We were in Cityside.

CHAPTER 11

'We're way too obvious here,' I said.

We hurried across bare courtyards that used to hum with breakfast crowds grabbing coffee before racing up Bethun Hill to the banks and trading houses or over to Sentinel to push paper for the army. Now the bars and cafes were shuttered with metal grilles and roller doors that looked like they'd been clamped down for months. They were all plastered with posters: *Lights Out After Dark!* and *Break the Breken!* and *Report Deserters: Reward!* And across all of that was a giant scrawl of commentary from people with plenty to say and plenty of spray paint to say it with.

We walked along the waterfront watching for trouble, but the place looked abandoned. Everything was shut and there was no one around except a few old guys sifting through rubbish bins. Even the remote watchers were absent because someone had gone down the river-side strip and smashed every cc-camera within reach. I wondered if there were cameras higher up, untouched, looking out across the water and whether a bored functionary sitting in a pokey little office had registered us coming ashore. I looked back to tell the others to hurry up.

Sandor had stopped.

'Sandor! We don't have time!'

'Look!' He pointed at a wall of posters. 'It's our girl.'

Lanya and I went back to see. A dozen images of a girl's face smiled out at us, with *Have You Seen Nomu?* blasting across the top and *Reward!* across the bottom and a number to call.

'Same name,' I said.

But this girl had masses of long wavy hair and a face like a model in an ad, all bright lips and sculpted cheek-bones. Hard to match her with the Nomu I'd found with the ultra-short hair, the too-thin face and the huge, terri-fied eyes.

'It's her,' said Sandor. 'Looks like she's from here, after all.'

'She's from the Dry,' said Lanya.

'Oh, yeah? How do you know?' said Sandor.

She gave him her best glare. 'Because when Nik hauled her out from under the bridge she was talking a whole other language and yelling for the angel that they worship out there, that's how.'

He glanced at me. 'So it was you?'

I shrugged and looked away, and found myself staring at Fyffe's name. The Hendry name, that is, right there on a poster.

'Let's go,' said Lanya.

'Hold on,' I said. 'Look at this.'

Beside the Nomu posters was a line of *Report Deserters!* posters stuck across a steel roller door that had seen more than a few attempts to batter it down. Someone had written over it in red spray paint: *Who are the real deserters?* Then diagonally across each poster, in smaller, more careful letters, they'd written a name, different on each one: *Hendrys, Venables, Coultens, Marstersons, Hallidays…* On it went. In the bottom corner of each one was a C with a 1 inside it—the One City symbol.

'Who are these people?' asked Lanya.

'Families,' I said. 'High-up families.'

'What d'you mean *high-up*?' asked Sandor.

'I mean, everyone knows those names.'

He pushed in front of us and peered at them, poster by poster. 'I don't. Never heard of them.'

'Everyone on Cityside knows those names.'

'Why?' he asked. 'Who are they?'

'They're the Cityside rich list,' I said, frowning at the Hendry name. What did it mean 'the real deserters'? What had they deserted? Were they the ones who'd torpedoed the ceasefire?

'How rich?' asked Sandor. He was staring at the names as though he was trying to memorise them. 'Are we talking small scale, like fancy computers, or big, like buildings?'

'Bigger,' I said. 'Computer networks and whole chunks of the city.'

He straightened up and turned to look at me. 'Are they friends of yours? Go on—say they are!'

'Sure they are,' I said. 'No, of course they're not. The Hendrys maybe. Once.'

The Hendrys, Thomas and Sarah, were uber rich and their kids—Lou and Fyffe and Sol—had been friends of mine. They'd opened up their family to me, let me spend summers at their house, sent presents on my birthday, food hampers during exams.

Then, when Sol died on the Mol in the exchange-gone-wrong, Thomas and Sarah Hendry decided that they couldn't stand the sight of me.

'I knew it,' said Sandor. 'I *knew* it.' He slung an arm around my shoulder. 'Let's go and find them.'

'Oh, grief!' said Lanya and walked away.

I shrugged Sandor off and followed Lanya, but he marched up beside us.

'Seriously, why not?' He was practically waving his arms in excitement. 'You front up to them with the whole *I've been stuck on Southside and now I've made it home and I need help to get back on my feet.* That could work. Why not?'

Lanya rounded on him. 'You have no idea why, so shut up.'

He did this exaggerated shrug at her as if to say, 'What's eating you?' and said to me, 'If you're friends with these people—'

'I'm not!' I said. 'Listen, we're about to go through Bethun. No way do we look smart enough or cool enough to be wandering around that part of town, so we're going to split up.'

'You're not losing me that easy.'

'Otherwise,' I went on, 'We'll just look like a bunch of brown kids on the prowl.'

'Bethun home to the rich list, is it?'

'Pretty much.'

He nodded. 'Sounds like fun. I'll go on the other side of the road and about half a block behind you. That do?'

'I guess. Try not to shoot anyone.'

He gave me a mock salute, 'Commandah!' and sauntered away.

Lanya and I had shed our squad gear for civvies. I wore jeans and a T-shirt and Lanya wore black leggings, a short skirt and a denim jacket—a combo that would have been an eye-opener for any respectable aunt back over the river. But, like I said to Sandor, we didn't look nearly smart enough to be where we were. Bethun's terrace houses smelled of money: their cream-coloured stone was clean, their bay windows were inviting, their solid wooden doors had heft against the outside world, and their signs— Property Alarmed: Armed Response—were in Breken and Anglo, just to be absolutely clear.

We'd got about halfway through Bethun when our luck turned bad. An army ute rounded the corner ahead of us.

I whispered, 'Oh, f—' and Lanya stopped. I gripped her hand and said, 'Keep walking. Look like you're talking to me.'

The ute trundled along the street and we pretended to ignore it, but I knew the men inside wouldn't go past brown kids on an empty Bethun street. It stopped beside us.

A soldier, middle-aged, middle-ranking, leaned out the window. 'Hey! What are you doing here? Where are you going?'

'Home,' I said, in my best Ettyn Hills accent. 'Missed curfew last night and she has to get home before her father knows she's gone.'

Lanya hung on my arm and giggled and waved at the men. Out of the corner of my eye I could see Sandor on the other side of the street a few houses back, one hand in his jacket pocket—I knew he was fingering the gun.

'Where's home?' said the solider. 'Show me some ID.'

Sandor was three houses away. I had no clue how trigger happy he might be. Two soldiers. He could shoot them both, wake the entire neighbourhood, bring any nearby patrols crashing down on us and end everything right now.

'Which home?' I said. 'Town or Ettyn Hills?'

The soldier's eyebrows shot up. Ettyn Hills was wealthy and then some. 'Just show me some ID, kid.'

I didn't have any. Cityside IDs were unfakeable unless you had access to hi-tech gadgetry, and imitations were so obvious that it was more dangerous to be found with one than not have one at all. I could see Sandor hesitating, watching.

'Look,' I said. 'I don't have it, okay? My father confiscated it to stop me going out.'

The soldier's eyes narrowed. 'What's your name, then? Whose your father?'

If you're going to lie, I thought, lie big. 'Stepfather,' I said. 'Thomas Hendry.'

'Sure,' said the driver. 'Try again.'

'It's true,' I said. 'The Hendrys adopted me and sent me to Tornmoor.'

I gave the Hendry's Ettyn Hills address and their townhouse address down to the last digit of the postcodes, then looked at my watch.

'Can we go now?' I said. Right now, I thought. Because that guy over the road is armed and Breken and he might not think twice about shooting you.

'Look,' I held out my arms wide so they could see

I was unarmed. 'I've got nothing but a heap of trouble waiting at home if I can't get back there soon. If you want to know for sure and really get me in deep, you can call him.' I reeled off the number. 'It's unlisted, so he'll get mad at you as well as me, but do it if you have to.'

I put an arm around Lanya's shoulders, said, 'Sorry, babe,' and tried to look resigned.

The other soldier said, 'Give me that number again.' My stomach churned. I said it one more time. He tapped it into his communicator and pushed a button.

CHAPTER 12

Time slowed right down until I could hold everything around us in one long moment: the street in the early morning sunlight, quiet the way Moldam never was, Sandor on the other side of it moving towards us, the two men conferring in the ute, Lanya standing close, utterly still, and in the distance the bells of St John's tolling.

The guy with the communicator leaned over and said to his partner, 'Comes up as Priority List 1. You want me to call?'

Sandor was nearly at their door.

'Shit, no,' said the driver. He jerked a thumb at us. 'Go on, get!'

I gave him a quick salute, said, 'Thanks! We won't do this again.'

Lanya and I walked away, resisting the urge to run, Sandor resumed his stroll and the ute trundled off.

Once we got around the corner Sandor joined us.

'Very cool,' he said.

I shook my head and blew out a long breath. 'Yeah, not really. Just terror, plain and simple.'

'I thought he was calling that number,' said Lanya. She peered back round the corner at the retreating ute. 'Was it real?'

'Yeah,' I said. 'But he'd be buying a lot of trouble if he called it. No one's supposed to know it except family and a few high-ups.'

Lanya turned back to us. 'You can sound very posh when you want to. I never knew. Your Gilgate accent is so…Gilgate.'

'So kind,' I said, and she smiled and relaxed a fraction.

'Right,' I said, 'We're not far from St John's. Those bells rang seven, so the market should be kicking off about now.'

On Southside, hunger nags at you the whole time; it's a voice you can't ignore, always murmuring, never entirely shutting up. You learn to live with it because you don't starve—there is food, just never quite enough. No surprises, then, that after a few months there, I'd started to daydream about the market in St John's Square: the lines of stalls and trestle tables stretching towards the steps of the big old church and piled with food: pies and pastries and crazily decorated cakes, baskets of apples and oranges and lemons, boxes of new potatoes and carrots, trays of eggs, huge round cheeses.

I hadn't been to the market since summer a year ago, and maybe my dreams had exaggerated things, but no way was I ready for what we found. We stood on the edge of it and Sandor scanned it with a disbelieving eye.

'Where's the food?' he said. 'I was promised food.'

'No, you weren't,' I said. But I had promised it to myself.

'Look, burgers.' I pointed at an open-sided caravan with a grubby awning, a chalkboard menu and a queue worthy of Southside.

He screwed up his nose and sniffed in disgust. 'Do better at home. Might as well be at home. This is a sore, friggin' disappointment, this is.'

He was right. The market had become a dumping ground. People had raided cellars and cupboards and sheds for anything that might raise a few coins and now they stood watching at their tables as other people pawed it. Worn clothes on racks hung drably above piles of battered shoes, and there were tables spread with old locks, door handles, tottering stacks of plates and cups, and drawers of blunt knives and bent forks; there were clocks all telling different times and cartons of ancient, broken-spined books: you name it, if it was second- or third-hand and done for, it was here. Snarly, underfed dogs sniffed around people's feet.

Like Sandor said, it wasn't so different from a market over the river, although, there, Southsiders would be trawling through it like it was treasure; here, people seemed to realise they'd come down in the world—they picked stuff up and inspected it at arm's length as though it smelled as bad as it looked.

It hadn't occurred to me until then that people on Cityside might be as hungry as the rest of us. It looked like money was short too; people were haggling over prices and counting coins carefully into the eager palms of stall holders. There were all shades of desperation here. The war was costing them.

You'd think that if the fighting was sending the place to the dogs they'd grab a ceasefire when we offered one. But no—'We don't negotiate,' Frieda had said.

The market was shoulder-to-shoulder busy, so we moved slowly, avoiding the outskirts because there were soldiers wandering about there, toting guns and watching for trouble and troublemakers. Sandor headed off towards the food stall and I called after him, 'Hey! The bag.'

'Oh, yeah,' he said. He slung it from his shoulder to the ground and considered it. 'What are you two up to? You don't get this till you tell me.'

'It's nothing,' said Lanya. 'Nothing you're going to be interested in, anyway.'

He smiled. 'I'll be the judge of that.' He hefted the

bag back on his shoulder. 'I think I'll hang around for a while, see what happens.'

'Suit yourself,' I said. We made our way towards the church steps wanting three-sixty vision because there wasn't just my father to look for, but also the soldiers on the perimeter and anyone else who, maybe literally, smelled a rat.

We got to the steps, and Lanya said, 'He should be here by now.'

'Might be inside,' I said. 'I'll go and look.'

'Be careful,' said Lanya.

'Careful of what?' asked Sandor.

I climbed the steps to the porch and stopped in the shelter of a column to look across the crowd. I stood there for as long as I dared, thinking that if he was down there and on the lookout he might spot me, but then I got nervous about the soldiers and ducked inside.

The marble interior breathed silence. I hurried down one side aisle then the other, peering into the small chapels and around the gigantic columns that held up the roof. Last time I was here was the night Southside had launched the first offensive in the uprising. The place had been buzzing with people who'd fled their homes. They'd piled their belongings on pews and in the side chapels and stood about arguing and worrying and waiting in vain for the army or the police or the emergency services to arrive. Now the building was empty and echoing. I reached the door of the crypt. This was where we'd camped—Dash and Jono, Fyffe and Sol, and me—before heading off on our disasterous attempt to take Sol and Fy home.

Heart thumping, I turned the handle and pulled the door open, hoping, praying even, that my father would be there and I could tell him what Frieda had told us, and he would know what to do: that it might be as easy as that.

Someone was there. Down the steps standing in the shadows by the altar. But it wasn't my father. And, no, it wasn't going to be easy after all.

'Dash,' I said, and my voice stuck in my throat. Everything was wrong with this picture.

'Hello, Nik.'

She came to the foot of the steps and looked up at me, smiling the Dash smile—so familiar that my heart almost lifted. Her short fair hair gleamed in the half-light, her eyes were dark in her shadowed face, and she stood as straight as ever in her black security-agent uniform. Behind her three candles burned in front of the altar icon, making its gold leaf flicker and shine. She saw me glance at them.

'I lit them for Lou and Bella and Sol,' she said.

I backed away, thinking, 'Run! RUN!' and at last my feet obeyed.

Dash called out 'No! Wait!' and I heard her racing up the steps behind me. 'Stop! Or I'll shoot!'

I skidded to a halt. Looked back. I was staring down

the barrel of her gun.

'Seriously?' I said. 'You lit candles for Lou and Bella and Sol, and now you're gonna shoot me?'

She reset her grip on the gun and gave me her concentrated blue stare. 'I have things to tell you.' She answered someone in her ear piece. 'Yes, he's here. Any sign of the father? Right, will do.' Then, to me, 'There are things you need to know. About your mother. Who she was. What happened to her.'

'Sure,' I said, backing away. 'Like I'm gonna fall for that.'

The gun didn't waver.

'Come on, Dash, you're not going to shoot me.'

I was almost certain of that.

I turned and ran.

She yelled after me, 'She worked for us, Nik! She was an agent!'

I charged out the door, yelling, 'Go!' to Lanya and Sandor who were standing at the bottom of the church steps. Sandor stared up at me in wide-eyed confusion but Lanya grabbed the canvas bag off his shoulder, pulled it open and upended it. The rats shot out under tables and feet. Then there was screaming and panic and fury everywhere.

Under the cover of chaos we took off.

We pushed a path through the market crowd and out into the maze of alleyways surrounding St John's. I was making for Skinners Lane where the cc-eyes were usually out of action, vandalised as a matter of pride by the local kids and as a matter of business by the local dealers in contraband and illegal highs. We swung into the lane at speed, stopped halfway down it beside an overflowing rubbish skip and collapsed, breathing hard.

'What the hell?' demanded Sandor. 'What's going on?'

'What happened?' asked Lanya.

'Dash,' I said. 'In the crypt.'

I stopped, remembering her blue eyes and her gun. And what she'd said about my mother. I parked that.

'They must have intercepted Levkova's message. They were expecting my father to show. I don't know why he didn't—maybe he thought it looked like a trap.'

'What d'you mean a trap?' said Sandor. 'A trap for who? C'mon! Tell me what's going on!'

'Shut up!' said Lanya. She turned to me. 'What now? How do we find him?'

'I don't know,' I said. 'We have to think.'

We sat there sucking in air, trying to pretend that this wasn't a deadend. On the other side of the alley a whole line of *Have you seen Nomu?* posters competed with graffiti and other posters demanding, *Break the Breken! Got Information? Support Your City and Call It In!*

Sandor eyed the posters. 'They sure want her back.'

I was trying to think. What did it mean that my father

hadn't shown? Dash and her team had been expecting to pick him up, which meant they had intercepted our comms—no surprises there—but it also meant that he was on their hit list. Which was good, in a way: if it meant he wasn't their informer. Unless he was, and Dash was trying to make me believe that he wasn't. I put my head in my hands—this stuff could turn you paranoid and send you down the rabbit hole at speed.

Lanya said, 'What do we do now?'

'You can count me out, for a start,' said Sandor, standing up. 'You people have things to do. I dunno what they are, but you can leave me out of them. I'm off. Got a city to see.'

And maybe a reward to cash in, I thought.

He stepped out into the alley and came face to face with the wrong end of a gun. An agent. One of Dash's team, almost certainly.

The agent yelled at Sandor, 'You! Hands in the air!' He edged around the skip, gun raised, aiming straight at Sandor's head. 'And you.' He nodded at Lanya and me. 'Get up. Slowly.'

We stood up carefully. The gun was like Dash's, but this one was not attached to a person I knew and more or less trusted. The man holding it was narrow faced with flat dark hair and a uniform as black and as sleek as his gun.

He smiled. 'Got you. Easy as that. Rats in a trap. Keep

your hands in the air! Right. You and you.' He pointed the gun at Sandor then Lanya. 'Turn around. Face that wall. Do it!'

I watched Sandor hesitate. His own gun was in his jacket pocket, within reach, but it was no match for the heavy-duty piece trained on us. If he even looked like going for it, he'd be dead before he got a hand to it. He turned and faced the wall, leaned on it, peered back over his shoulder. Lanya did the same. The agent drew a steady bead on Sandor. Ice formed in my gut and crept through my veins. I could rush the guy, but he was too far away. At least one of them would be dead whole seconds before I got there. On the plus side, he hadn't called for backup or reported his position; maybe the lane was a comms black spot.

'Okay,' I said. 'Who do you want? You want me? I'll go with you. Forget about them.'

The agent's eyes flicked between the wall where Sandor and Lanya stood, and me. 'Kneel down,' he said. 'Fucking kneel down or one of them's dead! I mean it!'

'Okay, okay.' Kneeling down under a gun is a scary thing: you can't move anywhere fast, you can only look up at the gun and the hand holding it and the finger on its trigger.

'You do what I tell you, right?' he said. 'Do what I tell you, and only what I tell you, you hear me?' He smiled over the gun. 'Or this happens.'

He shot Sandor.

CHAPTER 13

I yelled and he fired again, above Lanya's head. I spun back to her. She'd collapsed, screaming and weeping hysterically beside Sandor's slumped body.

The agent fixed the gun on me. His eyes narrowed and his teeth showed in a grin. 'See? That was so easy I might do it again. I mean what I say—you remember that. Now, you and the girl are coming with me. Get up.'

I stood up and went to Lanya who was still crying like crazy beside Sandor. But Lanya and hysterics didn't go together. I cleared the line between her and the agent, wondering if she'd found Sandor's gun. She looked up at me dry eyed.

Then her hand shot out, her knife whipped through the air and lodged deep in the agent's thigh.

He went down with a scream—many short screams in fact.

I ran to him, kicked him hard in the ribs and wrestled away the gun. He was yelling for backup so I kicked him again and ripped out his earpiece. The gun was heavy and smooth and my hands shook holding it. Keeping it trained on him, I walked backwards to Sandor and Lanya.

Sandor was lying horribly still, blood soaking his jacket. Then he groaned. A sweet, sweet sound.

'He's alive,' breathed Lanya.

She lifted his shirt and grimaced at what she saw. She pulled the scarf from her hair and pressed it against his side. He yelped.

'Yeah, I know,' she said. 'You have to hold it here. Press hard. Come on, Sandor. Press!'

The agent was still squealing and gasping, trying to pull the knife out and watching to see what I would do with his gun. I looked up and down the alley: agents usually work in pairs. We had to hurry.

'We gotta get out of here,' I said. 'Sandor? We have to move. Can you walk?'

'He's too heavy for me,' said Lanya.

The agent was yelling, 'You'll be sorry, you'll be so sorry, you'll be so fuckin' sorry! Help! Somebody! Agent down! *Help!*'

'Shut up!' I said, and walked towards him, still aiming the gun at him.

He went quiet, watching me.

I said, 'You shot my friend. Why don't I shoot you.'

'I…' he gasped. 'I…No!…But…'

I pointed the gun at his head. His eyes went wide. I said, 'Tell me about Operation Havoc.'

'What?' He squinted up at me. 'Havoc? I don't know. They don't tell us. I've only got Clearance Level One. I've never heard of it, I don't know what it is, I don't know, I—'

'Nik!' called Lanya. 'We have to get out of here before his buddies turn up. Give me the gun and you take Sandor.' She took it from me and stood staring down the barrel at the agent.

He was breathing heavily, almost whimpering, but he managed to get his sneer back. 'You wouldn't dare, little girl.'

'No?' she said, in Anglo. 'I want my knife back.'

The sneer vanished.

I helped Sandor stand, and hung his arm round my shoulders.

He gasped and screwed up his face but nodded, 'Okay. Go.'

'You go,' said Lanya, still watching the man over the gun. 'I'll wait here to give you a start. Wait—tell me where you're going.'

'I know a place,' I said. 'It's not far.' We were speaking Breken, hoping the agent wouldn't understand.

'Get moving then,' she said. 'Give me some instructions and I'll join you in a minute.'

I whispered in her ear and she nodded.

'Don't wait long,' I said.

'So go!' she said. 'Hurry!'

I hauled Sandor away.

'Not far' was three blocks down through Sentinel by way of dingy, cramped alleyways where, in pre-curfew days, the backdoors of theatres used to spill actors and bands into the night to join other partygoers in the tiny pubs and clubs that were the nightlife of Sentinel. It seemed to take forever to go those three blocks because I was pretty much carrying Sandor and I had to keep stopping for him to rest and get his breath, and I was desperate the whole time to hear Lanya's steps running up behind us. It had started to rain. Blotches darkened the cobbles and sent up that dusty summer rain smell. We were going to get soaked, but at least it soon became impossible to tell what was rain and what was blood on our clothes.

We came to the end of Bow Lane and I said, 'We're here. We have to wait for Lanya.'

Sandor leaned on the side of a building and I thought about leaving him there and racing back for Lanya, but he kept sliding sideways so I stood holding him up and counted seconds.

At last there she was, tearing down the alley and stopping grim faced but bright eyed beside us.

'Did they come for him?' I asked.

'Not yet.' She looked at the gun. 'I'd rather have my knife than this, but I wasn't going to try and get it back.' She walked over to a big metal rubbish skip and hid the gun behind it, kicking extra rubbish into place beside it.

'Right,' she said. 'Where are we?'

The lane opened onto Clouden Street, one block back from the river. Over the road from where we stood was a row of centuries-old riverside mansions that had had buckets of money poured into restoring them. They were four storeys high, of clean white stone with tall windows and balconies and steps flanked by sculpted trees and wrought-iron fences leading up to weighty doors.

Lanya gave a low whistle.

'That one,' I said. 'Number 11. The Hendrys' town-house.'

She stared at me. 'Are you insane?'

'They're not here. Come on, help me get Sandor up the steps.'

'How do you know they're not here?'

'They never come to town in summer—it's too hot. Plus, they'd think it was too dangerous to be in range of Southside rockets right now. And, even if someone is there, we have to stop Sandor bleeding and short of fronting up at a hospital, which will fast become a trip to the Marsh, this is the only way.' I looked at her. 'Got a better idea?'

She shook her head. 'But still…'

Sandor tried a grin and said, 'If you're gonna die, do it in style.'

'You're not gonna die, Sandor,' I said.

The rain was sheeting down and the street was deserted. Thunder clouds darkened the sky across the river and rumbled as if huge guns were firing from Southside.

We struggled across the road and up the steps of Number 11. Lanya looked at the massive door in front of us and the sign on the wall, *Monitored Security—Armed Response*.

'See this?' she said.

'I know,' I said. 'Here, help Sandor.'

'And you can get in here without alarms lighting up all over the place and people arriving waving guns and shooting?'

'Yes.'

'This is mad,' she said. 'We need a medic—'

'Shh. Concentrating.' I was loading the backup passcode into the keypad because I didn't want to go through the whole gamut of guessing shortcut codes and getting them wrong and alerting someone somewhere that a break-in was in progress. The backup was thirty-two characters long and would default to a screaming siren if I got it wrong twice. Lou had shown it to me. He wasn't supposed to know it, and I certainly wasn't. But that was Lou for you: generous to a fault and anything for an easy life as long as it was hilarious. Creeping into the town-house for a weekend of luxury when his parents were up north was frequently hilarious.

When he'd found out I could remember the backup without writing it down he'd given his best impression of an evil laugh, burned the written copy he'd bribed out of a servant and sworn me to secrecy. I kept the secret; only Lou knew I had it, and Lou was dead.

I typed in the last digit of the code, attempted a totally-under-control smile at Lanya, and pressed Enter.

CHAPTER 14

The door opened with a click and a sigh, or maybe it was us that sighed. We stumbled in and shut out the street and the storm.

'Now,' I said, looking around, 'Is anyone here?'

'What?' said Lanya in a loud whisper. 'You said no one was!'

'I did say that.' I flicked a light switch. 'And the main power's off, so no, no one is.'

We were standing, dripping, on a wide slate floor. Ahead of us glass doors opened onto the indoor pool with its river view and wide balcony, to our right was the curve of the staircase to the next level, and to our left, a double door led to the servants' apartment. The storm outside was really kicking in now; a flash of lightning lit up the pool room and the atrium where we stood. The place looked deserted—more than deserted. The floor and walls were bare where once there'd been rugs and sculptures and paintings, and the pool was empty. Maybe they hadn't just gone to the country for the summer, maybe they'd cleared out completely.

'Come on,' I said. 'Up!'

We struggled up the stairs to the first floor and stopped at the entrance to the games room. Lanya stared and Sandor raised his head and swore softly. This room, at least, was still lived in. I looked around at the luxury of it and saw it now through Southside eyes. The half-light of the storm through the long riverside windows lit up the deep sofas and leather easychairs, the giant screen on the wall, the kitchen space and breakfast bar, the rugs spread on polished wood, the artwork on the walls. I smelled its familiar smell—wood polish and leather, a clean smell, rich.

I said, 'There's a bedroom over here.'

The Hendry kids all had bedroom suites going off the games room, plus there was a spare for friends, which was my room when I stayed, and that's where we went now. Like the atrium downstairs, the bedroom had been packed up, but the boxes were still there. Thankfully, there was still a bed, a couch and a chair, and the water was still on in the bathroom. We helped Sandor lie down, and got busy getting water and finding towels and then peeling away the remains of his shirt with him trying not to shout at the pain of it and Lanya and me trying not to grimace at how much blood there was. The bullet hadn't drilled a hole in his back, but it had torn a grazing track across his side, and then it had exploded into the brick wall he'd been standing against so that bits of brick and mortar were left lodged in the wound.

Downstairs in the emergency room I gawped at the riches in the medicine cupboard: antiseptics, bandages, painkillers, antihistamines—shelves of the stuff, and all for a single family. You could fill one of those packing cartons with it all and haul it back to Southside, and if you weren't mobbed first by a bunch of rampaging medics you could do very well for yourself on the black market.

When we'd done what we could for Sandor, he lay still, eyes closed, and we didn't know if we'd done enough. At least the bleeding had stopped and the wound was as clean as we could make it. 'I'll look for food,' I said.

I found some tins of lamb-and-barley stew. We ate it cold because I didn't dare turn on the power in case that triggered a security alert and, anyway, we were too hungry to care. Then I went downstairs and cleaned up, disposed of the empty cans and tidied up the emergency room. I told myself I was doing that so no one would know we'd been here. But it was habit too; it's what Lou and I used to do when we'd crept in here for a weekend and it was time to head back to school. Most of the weekend we'd slouch about, games console in one hand, beer in the other, and the place would rapidly descend into a pigsty. Until it was time to leave, and then we'd go into this mad cleaning frenzy that would have astonished Lou's mother. I don't know if we ever fooled the cleaners or Sarah Hendry, and if Lou got bawled out about it he never told me.

I looked in on Sandor and Lanya. Sandor's face was tense even in sleep. Lanya was curled up asleep on the couch nearby. Without her scarf, now lying bloodsoaked in the bathroom basin, her braids fell over her cheek and she looked far too young to be wielding knives and pointing guns at security agents. But here she was, and I was glad and guilty in equal measure—which is to say, very glad and very guilty.

I turned back to the main room and went over to the windows. I looked across the river to Southside. Rain still hammered the river and the city in great sweeping torrents, and the clouds were low over Southside making it look gloomy and dangerous: the shadow city—that's how we'd thought of it at school, and that's what it looked like now. I thought, what if you were Breken, and Frieda offered you the chance to get out of there—provided you agreed to work for her. Why would you choose that? Why would my mother choose that? Maybe because it would be a better life for her kid. But if she'd worked for Frieda she wouldn't have been with my father.

Why should I believe Dash anyway? We'd been good friends at Tornmoor, and for a time, more than friends, really close. We knew each other well, but we were a long way apart now, on different sides, and not just of the river.

I had no answers to any of this, and no time to find them. The clock was ticking as Frieda laid her plans for Moldam, and I had to find my father.

Away west, the light of the setting sun slipped under the clouds and shone red down the river. I listened to the house, silent above and below. No one home but us intruders. Which, to be honest, is what I'd always been. Lou had tried to make it otherwise—like I said, he was generous to a fault—but it wasn't his call. If he got caught breaking curfew or skipping class he might lose a month's allowance. If I got caught I'd be on the street with the clothes I stood up in and nothing else. That always made me look two, three times at Lou's latest harebrained scheme before I jumped in; it made me study everything for the catch that would send things spinning out of control. Lou was the out-and-out loon; I was the one standing on the sidelines saying, 'but hold on a second'. On average then, I guess that made us a fairly sensible pair. But now? Now being too cautious would lose us the game.

I peered into Sol's room—what used to be Sol's room. It was all packed up: bare walls, stripped-down bed, toys crammed into boxes. Next door, Fyffe's room hadn't been packed yet, but it was almost as sparse as if it had been. There was a bed with a white coverlet, a white wooden desk and chair and a sky-blue rug on the floor, her single concession to colour. It wasn't how I remembered it. The frills and clutter were gone: no plumped up duvet and cushions, no basket overflowing with the soft toys she'd had when she was a kid, no dresser crowded with girl stuff. Fy had grown up and grown serious in a hurry.

Lou's room was tidy and packed, which felt completely wrong. I'd never seen it tidy. I wanted to go in there and toss clothes out of their carefully stacked boxes, mess up the sheets folded on top of the bed and open every drawer and door.

Every door.

I had a thought, went in and heaved aside the desk. Behind it in the wall was a small metal door. It looked like an ordinary cupboard door with a simple elock: type in the code and you'd expect it to pop open. But it wasn't a simple elock. I knew, because I made it.

Lou had wanted a place that, short of a stick of dynamite or a hacksaw, no one could get into. 'For what?' I asked. 'Stuff,' he said. I'd made him an elock with a disguised thumbprint scan that responded to his prints. He tried it out and gave a whoop when he discovered how it worked. 'You're a born spook,' he said. 'I always said so.'

I made it to respond to my thumb as well, just to see if I could, but I'd never used it. I used it now, and the little door sprang open. Lou's stuff fell out. Nothing earthshattering: a folded wad of cash, a spare phone, some pages of song lyrics he was working on with lots of crossings out and doodles in the margins, his favourite guitar pick, a photograph of him and Bella at a clandestine zombie party. They stared out at me, heads together, grinning like maniacs with stupid fake blood dripping from their lips and eyes and pretend head wounds.

'Hey you.' Lanya crouched at my elbow.

'Hey.'

She touched my cheek. 'You're crying.'

I wiped my face on my sleeve. 'Thinking.'

'Is that what you call it. All right. Thinking. Was this your friend's room?'

'Lou. Yeah.'

'What've you found?'

'Just some of his stuff. And this.' I handed her a black leather cardholder.

She flicked it open and smiled slowly. 'An ID? Your ID! I thought you lost it when your school was bombed.'

'I did. This one's fake.'

She peered at it. 'Oh, yes. Look, you're twenty-one years old.' She sat back on her heels and ran her thumb over the photo. 'You and Lou and the nightlife?'

'Me and Lou and, yeah, the nightlife, such as it was. His should be in here too.' I fished about in the safe and found it.

'Any chance Sandor looks like Lou?' she said, holding it up. 'Nope. Wrong colour.'

'How is he?'

'Asleep. It's proper sleep too, not that creepy drifting in and out and eyes rolling back in his head. I woke him just now and he grouched and drank some water and dozed off again.'

'Good.' I looked at her face, quiet and grave in the fading light. 'How are you?'

She smiled and frowned at the same time. 'Hard to know. Here I am in the city at last, and I nearly got shot today, and Sandor did get shot, and I knifed a security agent, and I've broken into this—' she looked around, '—this palace on the riverfront with someone who—'

She stopped and looked at me. 'There's a you in this city that I haven't met before. You're more at home here than you know.'

'I am not.'

'No?' Her eyebrows shot up and she smiled a ghost of a smile. 'It's like someone threw a switch. Over the river you fade into the background and try not to be noticed. Here, you know where you're going, and you decide fast what to do and then you're off in a hurry and doing it.' She looked down at my ID card then handed it to me. 'It's not a bad thing, this other you. You saved our lives today.'

I pocketed the ID and the cash, and piled everything else back into the safe. Then I closed the door on Lou's treasures and said a silent thank you. Lanya watched me and said, 'Tell me about him.'

By the time I'd finished that story, with Lou and Bella lying dead in the Breken bombing of our school, it was dark and we were standing in front of the big windows in the games room. Lanya stirred.

'I'm sorry,' she said.

I nodded. 'Me too.'

After a while she looked around. 'What else is here?'

Glad to be on more solid ground, I said, 'Above us, formal dining and entertaining and guest suite; above that, the parents' suite and roof garden.'

'Roof garden! Can I see?'

Outside the storm had cleared. The air was rain-washed clean and cool on our faces. There was a half moon and a few stars, and we could see Sentinel Bridge, the black path of the river, the classic old buildings gracing the riverbank, and the tall blank faces of skyscrapers rising behind us. It all looked as mint and moneyed as it ever had, but I wondered about that. What if those buildings were like the market, full of people squabbling over the used-up, dried-out remains of nothing much?

The daisies and lilies in the roof garden had gone crazy in their big ceramic pots and some climbing thing had taken over the walls and covered them in tiny star-like flowers that glowed eerie white in the moonlight. Lanya wandered about, brushing her palms over the rained-on greenery. The air was filled with the sharp smell of herbs and the sweetness of lilies, but the lilies reminded me of funerals, so I leaned on the railings and looked away, breathing the breeze off the river.

My father was out there somewhere, but doing what?

I decided I wasn't going to follow my paranoia down the rabbit hole. If he was a spy, I figured that he'd have shown up at the square, he'd have been a better actor, he'd have been more like a father and less like a stranger. So, supposing he wasn't a spy—what was he doing? Planning the next stage of the uprising? Congratulating himself on not getting suckered into a trap today? I felt like I was hammering on the locked door of a fortress and some-where up on the battlements he and his One City pals were scanning the horizon, busy with their battle plans and not even hearing the noise down below.

Lanya came back to me, eyes shining. 'Wow. So beautiful.'

I took her hand and kissed her palm and we stood looking out at the shadows on Southside.

'Why didn't he meet us?' asked Lanya.

'I don't know,' I said. 'He must have realised it was a trap.'

'He'd still have come if he'd known you'd be there.'

'Maybe.'

'Maybe!' She gave me a sharp look. 'Of course he would have.'

When I didn't say anything she pulled on my arm to turn me towards her. 'You don't think he would! You think he'd put his own safety ahead of you.'

'I don't know, that's all. He's been in the Marsh once. Once is probably enough.'

She shook her head. 'You're wrong. If he'd known, he'd have been there.'

'Either way, it doesn't solve our immediate problem,' I said. 'Let's give Sandor a few hours, and then we'll have to move.'

We went downstairs and stood at the end of Sandor's bed like a couple of parents fretting over their sick kid. He was breathing, and not bleeding.

'Should we stay up and watch him?' said Lanya.

'Bet we couldn't if we tried.'

'I know,' she said. 'I'm dropping just standing here. Where do you want to sleep?'

With you, I thought but didn't say. 'Chair, couch, I don't mind. You take the couch, I'll sit.'

'All right. Thanks.' She wrapped herself in one of Fyffe's blankets, curled up on the couch and slept.

After a while I did too.

CHAPTER 15

The bedroom light came on.

It took me a moment to realise why. Then my feet hit the floor and my heartbeat shot to maximum. Voices were calling out downstairs and the front door slammed.

Sandor moaned. I put a hand over his mouth and tried to wipe sleep from my fogged-up brain. Lanya was pulling on her boots, shooting me fierce glances and mouthing, 'What now?'

I put a finger to my lips and mouthed back, 'Wait.'

We looked at each other. Waited. Heard the whine of the lift door opening, closing. Heard the lift whirr, climbing slowly, so slowly, up to our floor, past our floor. The voices re-emerged upstairs.

'Can we get out?' whispered Lanya.

I shook my head. No chance, not with Sandor.

'Who is it?' she asked. 'Can you tell?'

I cracked open the bedroom door the tiniest sliver and peered through.

'I will!' called a female voice. Then there were foot-steps on the stairs coming down to our level. Booted steps. A man, thirty-something, in understated battle gear paused on the bottom stair and looked around the room the way bodyguards look, as if there's a secret assassin lurking behind every door. He'd definitely shoot first and ask questions later.

Then Fyffe came down the stairs and stood beside him.

Tears jumped into my eyes. I hadn't seen her for half a year and I stared at her now, trying to work out how changed she was. You can't lose two brothers to a war and not be changed. Outwardly she did look different: her hair was cut to a close cap; she wore a long white shirt, narrow black jeans, no jewellery, no make-up. Spare, like her room.

She tossed a pair of black boots beside a couch and said, 'Please don't worry, Alan. It'll be fine, really. You can go on down and settle in if you like.'

The guy looked unhappy, but he nodded, took a last glance around the room as he marched across it, and disappeared down the stairs. Fyffe went to the sound system: acoustic guitar chords and a woman's slow, low voice filled the room. Fyffe stood there lost in the song. She always was a sucker for a sad song. And then, I don't know, I guess she felt it, the way you sometimes do, that she wasn't alone. She turned around and looked towards the room we were in. She didn't run away. Didn't call out. She stood and looked, daring whoever was in her space to front up and face her.

I opened the door.

She clapped a hand to her mouth and we stood staring at each other while whole seconds ticked by. I should have been trying to read her—whether she was about to yell for the guy downstairs, whether we were enemies now—but the sight of her standing there put my thinking brain on hold and flooded it with the memory of her striding over the bridge on that cold afternoon when we went after Sol's kidnappers. Call it heart or courage or just plain stubbornness—whatever that quality of hers was, it was still there now, as strong as ever.

I realised she was crying and I let out the breath I'd been holding. She opened her arms, charged across the room and gave me a huge hug. Then she pulled back and put a hand on my T-shirt.

'That's blood!' she whispered.

'Not mine,' I said.

She looked relieved, and darted a look over her shoulder. 'You can't be here, It's too dangerous.'

When I started to explain she shook her head. 'Shh. My dad is here, and Alan, our guard. Go back in there.' She gave me a push backwards. 'I'll let you know when it's safe. Dad's going to a meeting. I'll get him to take Alan.' She stared at me for a second as if she was making sure I was real. 'Nik, I'm so glad to see you.'

She closed the door and I could picture her on the other side of it, squaring her shoulders as though she was a lot more solid than she actually was, getting that determined look in her eye, and then marching up the stairs. She would smile at her father and kiss him on the cheek and try to convince him that she would be perfectly fine left alone for a few hours. He wouldn't be happy; he would be horribly anxious. But in the end he would give way because Thomas Hendry would do absolutely anything for his daughter. He would, I'm certain, give away his entire fortune to make her happy. A thought crossed my mind then—about whether my father would give away his revolution for me. He wouldn't. Hadn't. I told myself to quit being pathetic. Then I turned back with thumbs up to Lanya.

We waited, jumping at every voice and every whirr of the lift. Sandor surfaced, groaning. His wound had bled in the night but not a lot, and he looked a better colour than he had the day before, but his painkillers had worn off and he wanted food. We explained to him how unhelpful it would be to encounter another bullet at close range, so could he please shut up. Finally we heard farewells, the front door slamming and the beep of the downstairs alarm being switched on.

Fyffe opened the door. 'That's that! They've gone for the day. Lanya!' She hugged Lanya and slipped easily into Breken. 'And who's this?' She looked down at our patient and turned the sheet back to get a better look at his bandaged side. 'What happened?'

'It's a long story,' I said.

'Okay,' she said slowly. 'Tell me over breakfast.'

Sandor complained about being moved but the promise of food was a powerful painkiller. He lay on a couch in the main room, and Fyffe and I made breakfast.

Lanya leaned on the breakfast bar and gave him a running commentary: 'Pancakes, syrup, fresh eggs—none of your powdered stuff here—bacon, white bread, honey, berry jam made from, it looks like, actual berries. And real coffee.'

We ate until we weren't hungry anymore, and admitted under interrogation from Fyffe that we couldn't remember the last time we'd done that. Then we had more toast and answered her questions about the attack on Moldam. She listened like she was the hungry one and this was food at last. 'A lockdown! Why?'

'We don't know,' I said. 'It could be an operation with the codename Havoc. Does that mean anything to you?'

She shook her head and sighed. 'I've been up at Ettyn Hills, and all I heard was that there'd been a move against hostiles who were planning a strike on the city. It was a great success, apparently. God.' She put her head in her hands. 'I have to get back to this, to you, to something real, instead of sitting here stressing about what to wear to the Dry.'

'So you are leaving,' I said, looking round at the packing cases.

She nodded. 'Not for good, but for a good while.' She paused then went on, 'The place up at Ettyn Hills is… well, we buried Lou and Sol there, and it's so quiet and empty. Dad tried his best to cope with it but Mum couldn't cope at all. So then came this plan that we go away, to the Dry. There's a oasis hub there that's amazing, apparently. It's built over this huge acquifer and there are orchards and meadows and everything's built to handle the sun and the heat, and they say that the night sky there is—'

She stopped.

'Sorry. That's my dad talking—it's his spiel to get me excited about going. But it's all beside the point, isn't it. Here's me packing to go on a break and here you are in the middle of rocket attacks and some kind of stupid punish-ment. I want to help. That's why you're here, right? To look for help?'

I said, 'Kind of. It wasn't exactly our plan to come to you. But then Sandor got hurt—'

Sandor, who was dozing under the influence of pain-killers, lifted a hand and gave a pathetic wave.

'Shot,' he said. 'Let's be clear about that.'

'Shot!' Fyffe sat up straight.

'That's right,' he declared. 'Took a bullet for these two.'

'What?' said Fyffe. 'How? No, tell me later, we have to get him to a doctor.'

'At last,' he said. 'Somebody cares.'

'You're doing okay,' I said to him. 'Shut up for a second. He's okay, Fy, really. It's a graze.'

'Hey!' he protested.

'Quite a bad one,' I admitted. 'And seeing a medic would be a good idea, sometime soon, but not this instant.'

Sandor muttered, 'That's gratitude for you.' Soon after that he was snoring peacefully.

'Your trip to the desert?' I said to Fyffe.

'Oh, it's so pointless!' she said. 'We're going with some others: the Coultens, the Venables, the Mar—'

'The Marstersons, the Hallidays and the Tallins?'

She looked at me, startled. 'Yes, how do you know? It's supposed to be a secret.'

'When do you go?' I asked.

'Soon. We were meant to leave this weekend. I've had my vaccinations and everything, but there's a hold-up. Which is probably good, because as you can see, I'll never be done packing in time.'

She cast an eye over the boxes stacked against the walls: some were sealed, but most were half full and surrounded by odds and ends that hadn't found a home in one yet. They were very different odds and ends from the ones we'd seen at the market the day before: these were tall porcelain vases, antique wind-up clocks, a large polished chunk of obsidian and ornaments like the linked silver fish that used to sit on the table at the top of the stairs.

She saw me glance at it all and gave an apologetic smile. 'Sometimes I want to sell the lot of it. It's shiny and beautiful and useless and it will all be mine one day and I won't have a clue what to do with it.' She picked up the coffee pot and went to refill it. When she came back she said, 'How did you find out who's going to the Dry?'

I didn't answer. I was putting puzzle pieces together in my head.

'Don't go all classified on me.' She turned to Lanya. 'What's your plan? How did you get here? What do you need to do? How did your friend get shot? I want to know everything!'

'Hold on,' I said. 'This trip to the desert. Why are so many people going?'

She shook her head. 'I don't even want to talk about it, I'm so embarrassed.'

'Don't be. Just tell me.'

She shrugged. 'Business opportunities—that's the main thing, you know, "investing in the Dry". That's what they say at the dinners and receptions they're holding for the delegation of Dry-dwellers that's come here. Also, no one says it, but Southside supporters are kicking up around the city. There's this group called One City: they're running a campaign of street protests and messing with the traffic and the phone system and hacking into media channels with messages about the crackdown on Southside. Some of the families want to leave because they're fed up with all the disruption. My dad won't let me near any of it, of course. In fact, you're the closest I've got to anything Southside in six whole months.'

'And what's the hold-up?' I asked. 'You said there was a hold-up.'

'It's the delegation we're supposed to be going with. One of their people has gone missing.'

'Nomu,' said Lanya quietly. She was curled in one of the big leather chairs, watching us thoughtfully, like she was putting together her own puzzle pieces.

Fyffe turned to her. 'Yes, that's right. One minute she and her brother are all over the news and chat channels being famous for coming from the desert, and then she disappears. We don't know if she's run away or if something terrible has happened. Her people say they won't leave without her, so we might not be going so soon after all.'

Lanya and I looked at each other, and Fyffe said, 'What? What did I say?'

'We found her,' said Lanya. 'She washed up on the riverbank the night the bridge was bombed.'

'Oh, no!' said Fyffe. 'Drowned?'

'No,' said Lanya. 'She's alive.'

'Alive!' She gripped Lanya's arm. 'No way! That's fantastic! You must tell them!'

She jumped up and began pacing and planning, delighted at the fact that the world can sometimes deliver random good stuff. Then a thought occurred to her, and she stopped and looked at me. 'There won't be a ransom will there? Or an exchange? Nik? Say there won't be.'

I was gazing at her, not really seeing her at all. Seeing instead an unlooked-for chance to fold back the barbed wire and send the squads of soldiers packing. The girl under the bridge. Could we do that? Could we ransom her for an end to the lockdown? How would that work? Would there be a handover on a bridge? Of course there would be. And as I thought that, I swear I felt Sol's breath on the back of my neck.

Fyffe was watching me, waiting for me to say 'No, of course we wouldn't do that.'

I looked at her. 'What would you do? You've got a whole township that needs Cityside to come to the table, and the one card you have to play is a girl so important that they'll do almost anything—even talk to us—in order to get her back.'

'It won't work,' said Fyffe. 'They'll punish you for it.'

'They're punishing us now! We've run out of medical supplies and pretty soon we'll run out of food. People are gonna start dying. You want them to starve us into submission?'

'They'll march in and take her.'

'They might try.'

I thought of the mayhem and tear gas on Battleby Road.

'Moldam is angry, Fy. They might not succeed.'

Fyffe stared at me for a second then turned away and began to collect the breakfast things with an angry clatter. We'd done half of the dishes in silence before she said, 'You really would ransom her, even after Sol?'

I couldn't look at her. 'For this,' I said, 'I would.'

More silence. When we'd finished, she walked away and stared out the window. Beyond her, the black arch of Sentinel Bridge took your eye across the river to the concrete and bare dirt spread of Southside.

Fyffe said, 'You'd have to threaten to kill her for it to work.'

'I know,' I said quietly.

She turned back to me. 'It's not her fault she's landed in the middle of something that has nothing to do with her.'

'That's Sol you're talking about.'

She blinked and looked away. 'It's Nomu too.'

I nodded over her shoulder out the window. 'And the people over there? They landed in the middle of it too, just by being born in Moldam. Bad luck for them, but not a whole lot they can do about it.'

'Have you even met her?'

'Yes, I've met her.'

She was watching me with guilt-inducing intensity.

'It may never happen,' I said. 'I have to find my father. It's not up to me to put anyone in the firing line.'

'In the firing line!' she said. 'See! You know what a ransom could mean.'

'I know what the lockdown means too. Operation Havoc, Fy. Does that sound like peacekeeping to you?'

'I don't understand,' she came up to me and put her hands lightly on my arms. 'Six months ago, threatening someone's life like this would have been the last, the absolutely last, option for you and even then you would have argued against it. Now you're seizing on it like it's the answer to everything.'

'Fy—'

She turned away saying, 'I'm going to invite the Dry-dweller group for dinner tomorrow night. You should meet them before you make those sorts of decisions. And we should try some other options. Every other option. What about Dash? Do you think Dash knows what the lockdown's about?'

I thought about what Dash knew. About my mother working as a Cityside spook, for example. Hard to imagine that knowledge ever seeming irrelevant, but right then, it did.

'Nik?' said Fyffe.

'I don't know!' I said.

'What if I ask her?'

'She wouldn't tell you.'

'So that's it?' she demanded. 'You threaten Nomu's *life* when you haven't even tried anything else? Why would it be different from when they tried to exchange Sol? Why would it be any less risky?'

'Sol's not the only one who's dead.'

She turned and walked away. I watched her and thought, so this is it. This is how my last link with the Hendrys breaks. Not a clean break, either.

'We'll go,' I said.

'No,' she said, still with her back to me. 'Your friend has to see a doctor. I know one who won't ask questions. Can you wake him up and find some clothes of Lou's for you both? You can't go out in those things, they've got blood all over them.' She turned to Lanya. 'Come with me.'

I didn't want to do that, go picking through Lou's stuff. I wanted to get out, but it did make sense and it went okay until Sandor picked up the leather jacket that had been Lou's favourite piece of clothing.

'You're not taking that,' I said.

He ignored me and held it against his chest, admiring himself in the mirror.

'Are you deaf?' I said. 'No freakin' way are you taking that.'

'Why not?' He sat on the bed. 'The guy's dead, right?'

I nearly thumped him. I would have if he hadn't been stooped over with the gunshot wound. I grabbed the collar of the jacket and hissed in his ear, 'Put it down.'

'Hey! Take it easy—injured person here. Sorry and all that. I didn't know him, did I.' He dropped it on the bed and let it slide onto the floor, then he smoothed his hair in the mirror and gave me a cool stare.

'You know what they say about you over the river? Can't rile him, they say. Never loses it, they say. But look at you now.' He flicked open his fingers like a mini explosion.

'Shut up. Get dressed.'

I picked up the jacket and hung it up, then chucked a shirt at him. In the end, we settled on jeans, T-shirts and a couple of Lou's expensive cotton shirts. Also a dark jacket for me and a denim one for Sandor. We looked smart and unremarkable, which was exactly how we needed to look.

Lanya, on the other hand, looked amazing. Fyffe had given her some black jeans and a creamy white T-shirt with a wide neck. Also some silver beads and a short, bright green coat.

'There,' said Fyffe. 'That's better. No one's going to ask you for ID looking like that.'

Lanya gave Fyffe the small Southside bow. 'Thank you. So much.'

They both turned to Sandor and me. 'Tidy,' said Fyffe. 'You'll pass. Now, Sandor comes with me in the car.'

Sandor looked stunned. 'You have a car!'

She almost smiled. 'A small one.'

'A car!' he crowed.

We took the lift down to the garage where a little green two-seater gleamed in the shadows. Sandor was instantly in love.

'It's new,' I said.

Fyffe nodded. 'It's Dad, trying to say thank you for all the time I've spent looking after Mum up at the Hills.'

We eased Sandor into the front seat, and Fyffe said to me, 'If you're looking for your father, try Sentian. That's supposed to be where the One City people are. But there'll be soldiers there. If you're back here before five o'clock I can let you in before Dad gets home.'

I said, 'Do you want us to come back?'

She looked at me at last. 'I want a lot of things, and most of them I'm not going to get. Yes, I want you to come back.' She got in the car and drove off with Sandor.

Lanya and I walked across Clouden Street into the cool shadows of the alleyway opposite. Lanya said, 'You don't like to argue with your friends. Why didn't you tell her you saved Nomu's life?'

'What's she going to say? "Why did you bother?"'

'Why are you so sure an exchange would go wrong?'

'I'm not. It might go fantastically, perfectly right with happy endings all round.'

'Hey,' she stopped. 'Take a breath. This is me you're talking to.'

I kicked a tin can and watched it bounce to the end of the alley and out into bright sunshine.

'You're right,' I said. 'Arguing with friends is dire.'

We walked on, and she said, 'So, don't. Work out a better way.'

'What better way? Here's this gift that could break the lockdown, and all we have to do is threaten to kill someone to get it. Terrific. Do you trust any of the people in charge to manage an exchange without somebody getting killed? Even our lot? Especially our lot.'

'Then we don't ask them,' she said. 'We ask her.'

I stopped.

'She owes you, Nik. What if we go back and ask her to help us? To agree to come back but only once the lockdown is lifted.' She raised an eyebrow. 'What's the matter? I think it's a good idea.'

'A good idea?' I said. 'It's a freakin' genius idea. You are officially in charge from now on.'

She grinned and we walked on. She said, 'We can't exactly row back in broad daylight and talk to her, and we still need to find the One City people and tell them about Frieda's undercover agent. Let's go to Sentian.'

'Sentian it is,' I said.

'Good.' She slowed to inspect a line of *Break the Breken!* posters: someone had gone down the line turning *Breken* into *Banks* on every one. Beneath those was another set demanding that people *Report Breken Crimes!* but the people with paint had other ideas and most of those now said *Report Banking Crimes!* A few had been amended to *Support Breken Crimes!* and one at the end, inevitably, now said *Support Banking Crimes!*

Lanya ran her finger along them. 'Someone's had fun. Why are you so interested in the people who are leaving for the Dry?'

'Why do you think they're leaving?'

She raised an eyebrow. 'Not for business opportunities? You think Frieda's told them to get out while Operation Havoc creates some unpleasantness over the river?'

'Or they've told her that they're off for a bit and could she deal with the pest problem while they're away.'

I looked around, trying to work out where we were. The alleys were a lot grimier than I remembered: no one had emptied the overflowing skips and rubbish had blown about and ended up piled in stinking corners and soggy underfoot.

'Let's go this way,' I said.

We travelled a zigzag of alleyways and short streets until we came to an intersection leading into Sentinel Parade. To go further was to step into sunlight and scrutiny: even if the cc-eyes had been vandalised everywhere else, here they would be working. We had to cross the Parade to get to Sentian.

'Main Street, Cityside,' I said.

'Oh!' Lanya looked up and down the Parade. 'This is what I thought the city would be like.'

The Parade's tall glass-fronted buildings framed a strip of blue sky that stretched from Sentinel Bridge all the way to Watch Hill. At pavement level, sandwich bars and cafes, flower shops, chemists and discreet, up-market money lenders were busy with their Saturday customers. Above that, the buildings shone, not with sunlight, but with huge flickering advertisements. A ribbon of breaking news ran along the bottom of each one.

I pointed over the road to a dark little side street like the one we were standing in. 'That's where we're heading.'

'In a minute,' she said. 'I want to look.'

She was wide eyed, drinking it all in, and even I was feeling the strangeness of it, like this was a whole other planet from the one Moldam was on. Lanya nodded up at the ads moving on the buildings. 'What are they saying? They want you to buy things. What things? I don't understand them.'

'Drugs, mainly,' I said. 'Pills for everything. Pills for

being worried, pills for being fat, pills for getting old.'

She watched a few, engrossed. 'These pills have great side effects,' she said. 'They give you many friends and make you rich and beautiful.'

Just then, floating above the street noise, the bells of St John's struck two o'clock and every ad cut to a blue background followed by the fade-in of the silver crest of Security and Intelligence. It looked like a blue and silver banner being unfurled down each side of the Parade. People stopped and looked up at it, as though they had suddenly become robots waiting for instructions to be beamed at them from on high.

The first thing we saw was a two-storey tall picture of Nomu together with an announcement of a memorial service for her at St John's in three days time.

The next thing we saw was a picture of my father.

CHAPTER 17

I read the news ribbon running along the bottom of the image. Lanya nudged me. 'It's too fast. What does it say?'

'Wanted,' I said.

'Obviously.'

'Former—' I stopped and frowned at it.

'For what? For murder?'

'Close. Former army strategist—'

'Oh!'

'Former army strategist turned extremist, Nikolai Stais, is wanted for crimes against the City. Stais, the secretive head of extremist group One City, is believed to have ordered the destruction of Moldam Bridge—'

'What?'

'—in One City's latest attempt to destroy the peace process. Stais is armed and dangerous and should not be approached. Reward offered, et cetera…'

'Wow!' said Lanya. 'Some story!'

'Cityside remains committed to the peace process.'

'Oh, really?'

I stared up at my father's face until it was replaced by someone else on the wanted list. Where was he? And could any of that be true? Secretive! Tell me about it.

Lanya said, 'That makes no sense at all.'

I turned back to her. 'It doesn't have to make sense. But it means he's not going to be hanging around on some street corner in Sentian waiting for us to find him.'

No one was hanging around on any street corners in Sentian. The place was crawling with army. Trucks blocked Bridge Street so we navigated the sidestreets instead, hunting for signs of One City people and slipping sideways into alleys and doorways when soldiers marched by, which was often. There didn't seem much for them to do—most of the little shops and cafés were dark, with CLOSED signs on their doors—but I guess they were there to send a message: Sentian is occupied.

And not only occupied. Also under notice of demolition.

We stopped in front of Brown's and the Bard, a couple of antique bookshops nestled side by side in Caravall Lane off Bridge Street. My old home-away-from-school in the city. Inside each bookshop were three ramshackle storeys of tiny rooms and creaking staircases, dimly lit by narrow windows and yellow lamplight and lovingly packed with books: second-hand, third-hand, hundredth-hand books. The interiors of both shops were unlit now, and wide red stickers were plastered across their front windows announcing their imminent destruction. All the way up the lane it was the same story: the whole block was coming down.

The lane was empty of soldiers so I put my nose to the window of Brown's and squinted into the gloomy interior.

'These shops have been here for a hundred years,' I said. 'They can't just pull them down. I gotta see if he's in there. Wait here a sec.'

'Who? What are you doing? Nik!'

I shot round the side of Brown's, tried the gate but it was locked so I climbed up and over it. Lanya threw Fyffe's green coat over the top and followed.

I knocked on the back door, calling, 'Mr Corman? Are you in there? Mr Corman!'

There was movement inside. The sound of footsteps. The door was opened a crack and then wider by an old man: a very upright old man, with grey hair, immaculate, and a suit about fifty years out of date but immaculate also. Mr Corman, proprietor of Brown's and the Bard.

He opened the door wide and opened his arms too. 'Nikolai! Come in! Come in!'

A few minutes later, Lanya and I sat in his office among teetering stacks of paper—Mr Corman spurned electronic versions of almost everything—and while he made tar-black coffee on his little gas stove I told Lanya about his two shops.

'They're like church to some people,' I said. 'You attend at least once a week, you keep silence while you're here and you leave feeling like your soul is…I don't know…quiet, calm, something like that.'

'And would you be one of these people?' she asked.

'I have spent a few hours here.'

'Many hours,' said Mr Corman. 'Many hours, well spent. In better days.' He put tiny cups of coffee in front of us, 'But now—' He gestured out the office door towards the red-stickered front window. 'Now we are in harm's way, as you see.'

'Why are they doing this?' asked Lanya.

'A rats' nest of extremists, young woman. This is what they say. Sentian has become a rats' nest of extremists. And how have we earned this description? By asking for some basic rights. An end to the military rule of our city. Free elections of a civic authority. A news channel free from political interference. Peacetalks with Southside. This is all. But this is extremist in the eyes of the authorities.'

'Are you part of the group called One City?' she asked.

He sipped his coffee and didn't answer.

'Do you know where Nik's father is?'

He smiled and placed his cup carefully on its tiny

saucer. 'Ah, the notorious Commander Stais. I have met him. Some weeks—perhaps eight weeks—ago. He came here, scoping the terrain, I believe that's what it is called, and I said to him, I knew a boy once with your name.'

Lanya glanced at me.

'What did he say?' she asked.

Mr Corman gave that almost shrug of his that, like his accent, we used to make fun of at school but secretly wished we could perfect—a gesture of shoulders and eyebrows that was all world-weariness and sophistication.

'I think he did not know what to say. He asked me what books you read. I said, "But you must ask him yourself!"'

That didn't seem a wildly likely thing to happen.

'Have you seen him since then?' I asked.

He shook his head and held up a long, crooked finger. 'I will tell you this.' He looked at us with great seriousness. 'You should leave Sentian—'

Furious pounding on the front door startled us. Mr Corman stood up but motioned us to stay put. 'I will see. You must stay.'

More pounding.

'Stay!' he said again.

He went out and closed the office door, but I jumped up and opened it a crack to peer though. 'Soldiers,' I whispered to Lanya. 'Two of them.' Words were exchanged, then one of the soldiers marched in past Mr Corman, swept a whole lot of books off a table and planted a some kind of notice there. When they'd gone, with a mighty slam of the door, Mr Corman ripped the notice into tiny bits. We helped him pick up the books. 'They come most days,' he said. 'They wish to intimidate, that is all.'

'All!' said Lanya.

'But listen to me,' he said as he ushered us back into the office. 'Since they came to Sentian, young people have begun to disappear. One dozen, at least, in the last four weeks. Young people your age.' He paused. 'They are not the most cared-for young people—they are the ones who sit on the street corners singing or rattling a cup. One day there they are, the next—' he lifted a hand in dismay, '— gone. The soldiers blame One City.' He shook his head. 'It is not the work of One City.'

'You think the army is taking them?' I said. 'As conscripts?'

The head shake again. 'They are young people without homes, without shoes, and not healthy. They are not ready to be soldiers. I do not know. These are bad times.'

'In Moldam, too,' I said and told him about the rocket attack and the lockdown.

'Yes, I see,' he said. 'Do you know about the postings? No? These are attempts to spread the news, the real news: news of the army and the security service, news of protests and talks, arrests and hearings. The news on screens, we cannot trust, and all actions online are watched. So, with the ingenuity of the human race—' he smiled to himself, '—we have returned to the news on paper! Posted on walls and windows and lampposts. Posted on posts!'

'Where?' I asked.

'Every day at a different time and a different place, because they are no sooner posted than torn down or painted over. You see?'

I saw. 'But do you know where and when?'

'I like to read the news,' he said. 'People know this, so every day, through my door, comes a slip of paper with news of the news: a time, a place.'

'Every day?' I said. 'Today?'

'Today has been. The corner of Gilley Street and West Oaks Avenue at 11am.'

'Tomorrow then?' I said.

'I do not know until tomorrow. The slip of paper only comes a short time before.'

'Can we come back here early tomorrow and wait for it?'

He nodded. 'Surely.'

'Okay,' I sighed. A lead at last. If we could get to one of these postings, chances are we could make contact with One City.

The tall clock in the corner with its slow pendulum and antique face struck four.

'We have to go,' said Lanya.

Mr Corman told us to take care and walked us to his front door.

Back in the lane, Lanya said, 'We will come back, won't we? After all this is over. We'll come back and help him move the books before the 'dozers come?'

There were thousands of books in there, and Mr Corman probably knew every one of them. I thought about ripping the demolition notice off the window, but that would only bring him more grief from the army. He had enough grief.

'I don't think he'll be moving his books,' I said.

She looked from the bookshop to me, taking in what that meant. 'Or himself?' she said.

'Or himself.'

CHAPTER 18

Fyffe was on the lookout for us and hurried us up the stairs. 'Dad's due back in an hour. Then we're supposed to be going out somewhere for dinner, but I've told him I'd rather stay in.'

Lanya and I paused at the top of the stairs. The games room was still in its half-dressed state and looked forlorn in the slanting afternoon sunlight.

'You haven't done much packing,' I said, half joking, testing Fy's mood.

'I'm unpacking,' she said, flopping down on a couch and casting a glance around the mess.

'Oh,' I said. 'Why?'

'Because everyone is so keen for me to be leaving.' She looked at me defiantly. 'You have a problem with that?'

I held up both hands. 'No, of course not.'

She beckoned us in. 'Did you get to Sentian?'

Lanya sat on the edge of one of the leather armchairs, and I began a wander round the room, peering into half-packed boxes. We told her Lanya's idea, that we try winning Nomu herself over to Moldam's cause. It might at least put the lockdown front and centre on the news and force Frieda to back off.

Fyffe nodded. 'That could work. But how do we get to her with Moldam closed off?'

'We have a boat,' I said.

'Oh,' she said. 'Wait a minute.' She fired up the flatscreen on the wall and zipped through the day's archived news footage. 'Not that boat?'

There it was, our boat in an item with a Southside Smuggling Shock banner headline and a news reporter offering commentary as the battered old thing was lifted from the water and carted away. We watched, forlorn.

'Had a boat,' said Lanya.

'All right,' I said. 'We have to find the One City people. They must have links with Southside—comms links or tunnels or something. There'll be a way.'

'There's something else,' said Fyffe. 'I went to see Dash.'

That stopped me.

'I didn't say anything about Nomu,' she said. 'I wanted to know why the lockdown, but she's not letting on. She must know something. We'll have to push her.' She looked at me. 'Actually, you'll have to. She won't take me seriously.'

'And that would be fine,' I said, 'But last time I saw her she tried to arrest me.'

'She won't this time,' said Fyffe.

'This time?'

Fyffe looked down at her hands. 'I told her that I'd seen you. I know—I probably shouldn't have—I didn't tell her you were here, but I said that you'd seen the lockdown and that it was for real. She wants to hear about it from you. She'll be at the Inkwell tomorrow morning at eight. I made her promise to come alone.'

I looked at Lanya. We were going to the bookshop tomorrow morning. But suppose we found the One City people at the news posting, then we'd be swept off to do this deal with Nomu. I wanted to see Dash; I wanted to know if what she'd said at St John's the day before was true. That my mother had been an agent for the security services, in other words, she'd been working with Frieda against Southside, against my father, against all things Breken even though she was Breken herself.

This was off mission, as any good spook would say. It was a bad idea that could only go wrong. Why not leave my mother to be the person I'd imagined her to be? Why go digging? *Because*, the kid in me was shouting, *because I want to know!* And the me that was trying to be a grownup was saying *shut the hell up, it doesn't matter.* But it did.

'We're supposed to be going somewhere else tomorrow,' I said. 'To find us some One City people.'

'I can go,' said Lanya. 'We can meet up after.'

'You don't know the way,' I said. 'And it's—'

'Don't say it's dangerous! What isn't dangerous now?'

'Okay, but you still don't know the way.'

'I'll take you,' said Fyffe. She smiled a sunny smile at me as though she'd just suggested a picnic on the heath. 'You're not keeping me out of this. And don't look so worried!'

I looked at Lanya who nodded, and I felt a guilty relief.

Fyffe was saying, 'You go and find out what you can from Dash. She'll help, I know she will.'

Maybe, I thought. But Dash had changed. We all had.

We stayed the night, camped in the spare room. Thomas Hendry came home and went out again then Fyffe came in with a tray of ham sandwiches and chocolate cookies, and we sat on the bed and ate and talked about One City and fathers and old Mr Corman and school and Cityside food and what would it be like to leave all this and go somewhere new.

Late in the evening Fyffe went off to her room and came back holding out her hand. 'Look at this,' she said.

On her palm lay a finely crafted slip of silver, like an elongated S with as empty centre. The talisman of the Southside Charter: *Not crescent, not cross…each to their own god and their own Rule, but space at the heart of every Rule for mystery, for the unknown.* She said, 'I thought it might help us tomorrow in Sentian, if we need to prove who we are.' She looked at it doubtfully. 'It might not too, I suppose. I don't know.'

She handed it to Lanya, who took it and turned it in the light and asked, 'Where did you get it?'

'One of the nurses in the Moldam infirmary gave it to me,' said Fyffe. 'When she knew I was going back over the bridge with Sol. "A peace offering," she said.'

Lanya nodded. 'It's precious.'

She passed it to me. The talismans are supposed to be handed down, parent to child, but sometimes, too often, parents reclaim them from the bodies of their dead children. Sub-commander Levkova wore one for her daughter Pia. The one I usually wore had been given to me by my father, but I'd left it behind to come to Cityside.

I handed it back to Fy. 'Don't be caught with it by the wrong side.'

'No,' she said and closed her fingers on it.

We talked some more, and I asked Fyffe if she ever saw Jono. Back in school, Fyffe and Jono used to be together, the way Dash and I were, and Lou and Bella. Like Dash, Jono had graduated straight from school into the security services.

Fyffe shrugged. 'Not so much. We had a—' she searched for the word '—a falling out. A disagreement. I guess I came back from Southside a different person. He didn't like that. He wanted me to be quiet and scared, like before. And I am still, quite quiet and quite scared, but I don't need him to be rescuing me or protecting me, you know? I told him that, but he wasn't happy about it. He thinks we should still be together. But I do see Dash whenever I come to town. She doesn't mean any harm to you, Nik. She thinks you've been brainwashed. As far as Dash and Jono are concerned, everything Breken is hostile, and all Breken are the enemy.'

She stacked the dishes and stood up. 'I'd better go. I'll see you both tomorrow.'

'Fy?' I said as she reached the door. 'Thank you. I mean...' I looked for more words, but I couldn't find any big enough. 'Thank you.'

Lanya took the bed and I took the couch. We turned out the light, telling each other how tired we were and how great it was to have somewhere safe to spend the night, but sleep deserted me completely. Her too, because after a while she said, 'Nik?'

'Mm?'

'You asleep?'

'I wish.'

'What are you thinking about?'

Pause. 'You. Me. You and me. Your family. Mine. Dash and Lou and Sol and Fyffe. Moldam and the Marsh, revenge and the end of the world. You?'

She laughed softly, low and throaty. I loved that laugh.

'And did you come to any conclusions about any of that?'

'Nope. Not a one.'

We were whispering in case the Hendry bodyguard on the floor below us had robo-hearing. She said, 'I keep thinking, what if we're too late? What if that Kelleran woman has ordered some kind of hit. I mean: Havoc. It means war and plunder and destruction…' She rolled over and looked in my direction. 'Are you afraid?'

'Usually.'

She snorted a laugh. 'You know why I like you?'

'Wait. You like me?'

'Shut up. You know *why* I like you?'

'Is it for my extremely cool good looks and my amazing brain?'

She laughed again, into her pillow.

'C'mon, humour me,' I said.

'Okay. Those—'

'Thank you and good night.'

'But.'

'Oh.'

'Actually I like you most for something you're no good at.'

'Terrific.'

'I like that you're no good at pretending. You don't pretend you're not afraid. You don't pretend you know the answers. Even when you first came to Southside, you didn't try and tell people you were a Breken scavenger, you just let us assume that's what you were.'

'But you told me I was a different person over here.'

'That's not you pretending, though. It's what the city does to you when you're here. You slot back into it because this is where you grew up. You know it, and you know how to work it.'

I thought about that for a while. Then the fact that it was too dark to see each other and the other fact that tomorrow we'd be walking in different directions into enemy territory made me brave.

I said, 'How about pretending it doesn't matter that you might go off and be a Pathmaker. How am I doing at that?'

There was a little silence. Then she said, 'Um…'

'Um?'

'Okay. Not…badly, exactly….'

'But not great?'

'You give me space to think.'

I hesitated, unsure how to ask the next question. 'How's it going, that thinking?'

'It's got a little… derailed recently. I've had that plan my whole life. Derailing doesn't come easy.'

'So you feel like you're in a train wreck, then?'

I could hear the smile in her voice. 'No. I don't,' she said. 'Not even a little bit. We'd better try and sleep.'

As if. But then I heard her breathing slide into a deep, easy rhythm. I lay there listening to her, but it was a long time before I slept.

In the morning, Fyffe came in, closing the door carefully behind her. We were up and dressed and waiting. She said, half whispering, 'My medic friend just called. Sandor's gone.'

'Gone?' said Lanya. 'As in dead?'

'No, no. Gone as in disappeared from his bed some time in the night. It's crazy—it makes no sense.'

'It makes perfect sense,' I said. 'He knows where Nomu is. I'd bet any money he's after the reward.'

We were about to lose our one chance to bring pressure on Cityside.

'What do we do?' asked Fyffe.

'We carry on,' said Lanya. 'Find One City. Pressure Dash. And hope that we get to Nomu before the Kelleran woman does.'

The Inkwell, known as the Drinkwell by Tornmoor seniors, was a café-bar down a narrow lane in the old student quarter in St Clare. It was just big and dark and busy enough that you could bunk study periods in there and not be easily spotted by a passing teacher.

Dash was waiting for me. The place was busy with the breakfast crowd but everyone made a small clear space around her. That's the power of that uniform. I squeezed my way through to her booth and sat down opposite her. Her eyebrows rose and she smiled at me with so much confidence I felt like getting up and leaving.

She said, 'I didn't know whether to expect you or not after your disappearing act on Friday.'

'You had a gun. You were trying to arrest me.'

'Rescue you.'

'I don't need rescuing.'

One of the staff appeared with a platter of fresh bread and small curls of yellow butter. 'With our compliments,' he said, almost bowing at her. 'Would you like breakfast, ma'am?'

Dash shooed him away, hardly looking at him. He did the almost-bowing thing once more and left.

I watched him go.

'Times change, huh? Remember when they'd just about X-ray our money to make sure it was real before doling out the food? And now, look. Free food and service with a squirm.'

'Don't be like that.'

She glanced across the tables, sharp eyed, with the kind of look that went with the uniform: it said, I'm in charge and I'm watching. 'We provide a service, too. And they're grateful for it. Why shouldn't they be? We keep them safe.' She pushed the bread to one side and put a small reader in front of me. 'Take a look.'

'I'm here about Moldam,' I said.

'Just one look, it'll only take a second.'

'I want to talk about Moldam and Operation Havoc.'

'I don't know what that is.' She nodded at the reader. 'Take a look first.'

I tapped the screen. A photo: Frieda Kelleran, half turned away, and with her a younger woman facing almost full on to the camera. She had dark brown skin, wide black eyes, a gentle mouth, a braided rope of black hair trailing over her shoulder, a long orange scarf and a thread of gold across her throat. My breath stalled in my lungs. I widened the photo until there was only her face filling the screen, smiling at me.

Dash said, 'Well? What do you think?'

I tried to keep my face blank, but I didn't trust my voice. Finally I managed, 'How…how do I know it's her? I was four the last time I saw her.'

Dash smiled. 'You know. I can see it.' She reached out and touched the corner of my eye, 'Here,' and the corner of my mouth, 'And here. You know.' I pulled away. 'There are more,' she said.

I scrolled to the next photo: the same woman in a garden, smiling broadly straight at the camera. There were six more: of her with Frieda, and with other people I didn't recognise. She looked relaxed in all of them—no signs of fear or compulsion. I stared at her hard, trying to read her expression, trying to hear what she was saying across all those years. Why was she smiling at Frieda? Because Frieda was telling her lies that she wanted to hear? Or because she and Frieda shared a secret? I went back through them again. It was her. I did know it—something in her eyes, or her smile. Something in me wanted badly to reach out and climb into the photo.

I put a hand over the screen. 'Okay,' I said, 'She's talking to Frieda, but I don't know what they're talking about. It could be anything. I already know that they knew each other—this doesn't prove she was an agent.'

Dash's smile was still all confidence and superior knowledge. She said, like she was reciting from some official file, 'Elena Osei worked as an interpreter at the Marsh before the uprising in '87. Mrs Kelleran recruited her to work as an asset because she was everything they needed: very bright, beautiful, Breken—and loyal to the city. Perfect.' She leaned forward. 'She joined a group of Breken sympathisers here on Cityside and got together with your father and when the time came she did what was required and took him out of the picture.'

'No,' I said. 'Get your story straight. The line your bosses are running at the moment is that he was army.'

She nodded. 'That's right, army with a dishonourable discharge. He took his revenge by joining the hostiles on Southside.'

'What was he dishonourably discharged for?'

Why was I even asking—no way would the official record be the truth.

'I don't know,' she said. 'That was years ago. The point is, why would you trust someone with that on his record?'

'Why would I believe you about any of this? About his so-called record or about Elena?'

'You think those pictures are lying?'

I picked up the reader and stared at the photo of Elena looking straight at me.

'Probably. They're Frieda's pictures.'

She sat back with an exasperated sigh. 'Explain to me then, how you ended up in Tornmoor and your father ended up in the Marsh. It was Elena's doing, Nik: she arranged to send you to Tornmoor because she knew that if what she was really doing was discovered by the Breken, they would probably kill her but that you would be safe.'

She stopped and watched me. When I didn't say anything, she said, 'They killed her, Nik. Not us.'

She held out her hand for the reader and saw my fingers tighten around it. 'See?' she said. 'You know it's her. Now you have to decide whether you want to know more.'

Of course I wanted to know more, but more of what? Which was better: knowing something through a Cityside lens that was at best spin and possibly complete fabrication, or knowing nothing at all? At least I'd seen her now. That, I would remember, and maybe that was enough.

'That's not why I'm here,' I said.

'You don't know your mother at all. Yet.' Dash took the reader from me and waggled it in my face. 'Mrs Kelleran knows. You can ask her if you like.'

'That's not why I'm here. I'm here about Moldam.'

Dash turned the reader off and pocketed it. 'So talk.'

Lanya and Fyffe and I had decided that I needed to call Frieda's bluff in this conversation so I told Dash that we knew that an attack on Moldam was imminent and that if she didn't want to be party to mass murder she could help us by finding out when it was likely to start and how.

She studied me, blank faced. 'Who told you this?'

'Doesn't matter. Is it true?'

'I need to know who told you.'

'Why? So you people can work out how to shut them up?'

'You know we could take you in and haul that information out of you? There are people at the Marsh who would happily do that. You have no idea how gentle we're being with you—and that's because of me. I'm telling them that your brain is worth saving, but I don't know how much longer they'll listen to me. You don't want that drug, Nik. They say it's harmless, but it's not. If they use it on you too often it fries your brain.'

I looked around the café. It had emptied. A waiter wiped a table, and another one stood at the till gazing into space.

'All right,' I said. 'Nobody told me. I put two and two together: Frieda makes an unspecified threat, Moldam gets locked down. That means something's in the wind. What is Operation Havoc? You must have some idea.'

Dash shook her head. 'I can't help you.'

'What do you think the lockdown is for?' I demanded.

'To stabilise the situation.'

'A ceasefire and talks would stabilise the situation.'

'Well,' she said. 'One City put paid to that when they

blew up the bridge.'

I almost laughed. 'You can't believe they did that. That's crazy.'

'You think they're not crazy? You don't know them like we do. I can't help you. And I have to go.'

She slid out of the booth, glancing at one of the waiters as she went.

I got half way to the back door before two agents came through it. Two more came in the front door.

Dash brushed past me saying, 'Rescued you. Did I mention?'

CHAPTER 20

They shoved me into the back of their van and cuffed one of my wrists to a bar beside the window into the driver's compartment. I couldn't see through it because it was covered in wire mesh; the back window was too. The air stank of disinfectant, hot and thick and sick-making. Dash climbed in after me and the door was slammed and locked. She sat down in the corner by the door, out of my reach, holding her gun in both hands.

Stupid, I thought to myself. Stupid, stupid, stupid, to trust a promise from a security agent, even if she used to be a friend, more than a friend. I wiped the sweat off my face.

'You promised Fy you'd come alone,' I said.

She looked up at me, clear eyed and guilt free. 'Some things are too important.'

The engine started up and I grabbed for a strap hanging from the roof and stood swaying as the van moved off. No prizes for guessing where we were going. I'd never been there; even though Security and Intelligence ran Pitkerrin Marsh, as well as Tornmoor, they didn't exactly go in for guided tours. To us at school the place was always out there on the edge of the city: it was the Pit, the Mad Marsh, where dangerously insane people—criminals and politicals both—were locked away and got the help they needed or the punishment they deserved.

Dash spoke above the sound of the engine. 'You haven't been to the Marsh, have you. It's nothing to be afraid of. Like I said, they need you. They won't hurt you.'

Over the river, people told a different story. Everyone there knew someone who'd gone into the Marsh and come out broken or not come out at all.

'Your father was there,' she said. 'He seems to have survived okay.'

Survived, yes, I thought. But okay? That might be pushing it. I didn't know what he was like before he went there. I'd searched my memory for him and found nothing. I'd only known him after, in these last six months. Maybe he was always grim and silent, always turning away to the next thing he had to do. He never spoke about his time in the Marsh or, for that matter, about the time before that with my mother. All he'd said was that at the Marsh they specialised in so-called 'therapeutic interrogation', a process that had nothing to do with therapy and every-thing to do with interrogation.

We jolted and swayed through the streets. Dash didn't put her gun away. Maybe that was regulation, but maybe she really would shoot if she had to. I wondered if she'd ever used it. She caught me looking and changed her grip on it.

'If you're genuinely keen on a ceasefire,' she said, 'Why not work with us?'

I looked away and wondered how Lanya and Fyffe were doing. It was early yet. They might not have even got to the posting, wherever it was—a long way, I hoped, from Sentian and its wall-to-wall army.

Dash said, 'We know you've been to Sentian.'

I stared at the floor, careful not to look at her in case she read the alarm on my face.

'We caught you on a cam,' she said. 'You and a girl crossing Sentinel Parade yesterday afternoon, and then heading back a couple of hours later. Did you find what you were after?'

I started counting the tiny indentations on the rubber mat under my feet.

'Is Fyffe hiding you?' she asked. 'She must be. Does her father know? I wish you'd leave her out of this. She's got enough worries.'

Like friends lying to her, I thought.

'Okay, don't talk to me,' she said at last. 'You can talk to Mrs Kelleran.'

The van stopped. Voices called out, and then we

rumbled on a short way and stopped again. The back door swung wide. We'd stopped in a stone-paved courtyard surrounded by the high walls of a grey concrete building with barred windows. In the distance behind us was a ring of fencing but it was so far away I could only guess at the loops of barbed wire that topped it and the sentry boxes that watched over it.

They took me into the building, down a narrow, brightly lit hallway, then down some stairs and along another hallway into a windowless room where they took my wallet, my watch and my boots. My wallet, I didn't care about, but I knew I'd miss my watch and my boots.

When they'd gone I tried the door but it was metal and solid. I looked around for something else. A single fluro tube glowed pale and faint above me: everything else was blank, grey concrete—ceiling, walls and floor— all radiating cold and the stink of stale sweat and urine. I walked around the walls, and arrived back at the door. Nothing. It was a concrete box with a hole in the floor in one corner. I thought about yelling at Frieda that she was wasting her time because I didn't know anything, and that's when I realised that there were no cameras. Not a single cc-eye. That meant that whatever happened in this room was deniable. More than that—it wasn't a room for gathering evidence, it was a room for scaring the shit out of people. It was doing a good job on me, and no one had even arrived yet.

It might have been summer outside, but it was ice cold in that room. The floor was too cold to sit on, so I wandered around the edge of it trying and failing to keep warm while I waited. And waited. And waited. On Southside you get used to waiting because there you wait for everything, especially if it's coming from Cityside: food, medicine, permits for traveling to Cityside as well as for who can work there and under what conditions. I had no clue how much time was going by: it was long enough for me to get very cold, and plenty long enough to get me thinking about the people who'd been in the room before me, and wondering what had happened to them. I didn't have to wonder too hard; I had many Breken stories of the Marsh to keep me company. And of course, the one closest to home—the one my father hadn't told me.

Minutes then hours of freezing in the semi-dark ticked by, and I thought, what if these minutes and hours turned into days and weeks and months, years even. How would I cope? How would anyone? What if the only people you ever saw were the ones bringing the occasional tray of food, and syringes packed with 'truth-telling' drugs? You could be fairly sure that you'd betray your friends under the hammer of those drugs. And what if you found out while you were here that you'd not only betrayed your friends, but you'd lost your wife and your kid? You would be completely alone. You'd despair, wouldn't you? What could possibly keep you going?

Revenge might. Hope for revenge. But that's not what I'd seen in my father. Strategic, determined and utterly single-minded, he was all those, but I'd never seen him vengeful. What then? A promise. Suppose you made a promise to yourself here in the dark, that if you ever got out you would pour everything you had into the cause they'd made you betray.

Suddenly the lights blazed up and left me flinching. When I could see again, a light metal table and two chairs had appeared. Frieda was standing inside the door with Jono at her shoulder. He held out a chair for her and she sat down. Jono was in the black uniform now, same as Dash, and he looked huge and solid, as if he ate often and worked out even more. His eyes flicked over me then returned to a blank, straight-ahead stare.

Frieda pointed to the chair opposite her and said, 'Sit down, please.'

I thought about retreating and refusing to talk to her, but Jono would have other ideas. Some things are worth a useless act of defiance, but this wasn't one of them. Besides, there were things I wanted to know. I sat.

Frieda smiled her thin smile and placed her hands, one on top of the other, on the table. 'Nikolai Stais,' she said.

'Here,' I said. 'Still alive, no thanks to you. Do you know how many people died in your latest attack?'

'Time of war,' she said smoothly. 'How did you get out of Moldam?'

'Twenty-eight people,' I said. 'At least. Twenty-eight on the night, probably more by the time I left.'

'When you left,' she said, musing. 'And how did you leave?'

'I flew.'

She tutted and shook her head. 'I shall have to punish someone for their failure to maintain a simple cordon.'

'What's it for?' I asked, because anything was worth a try.

She considered for a moment then said, 'Since you ask, I'll tell you. It's going to end this seemingly endless war. I intend to bring it all to a close within a matter of days.'

Days. Not good. I said, 'A ceasefire could have brought it to a close a week ago.'

She gave a little shake of her head. 'I intend to bring it to a close on my terms.'

'How?' I asked.

But that she didn't answer. There was a knock on the door, and Dash came in and whispered in her ear. Frieda nodded, murmured, 'Oh, good,' and looked even more pleased with herself than usual. Dash left without looking at me.

'What's the point of bringing me here?' I asked. 'I don't know anything.'

'I'm less interested in what you know than in what you can find out,' she said.

Whatever that meant. I didn't ask.

I said, 'Don't expect my father to come for me. He won't.'

Her eyebrows rose. 'Actually, I think you're wrong about that. But I have a quicker way of getting what I want than tracking down your father, who is proving, I must say, to be rather elusive.'

'Good,' I said.

'I think he would come for you, but he knows our ways here and has built up, shall we say, some measure of resistance to them.'

Unlike me, I thought. Not reassuring.

'But in fact,' she sat back, 'I don't want to trade you for your father. I want to persuade you to join us. I'm a fair person. I'm giving you a chance. You'll save yourself a lot of grief if you take it.' The eyebrows went up, the mouth tried to smile again, but that wasn't its natural state and the attempt was short lived. 'What do you say?' she said. 'Now that you know the facts about your mother, you've no reason to oppose us.'

'I don't know the facts about my mother, and I have twenty-eight reasons to oppose you,' I said. 'And that's just in the last week.'

'Oh, please. That's no argument. Southside has plenty of blood on its hands.'

'Southside is prepared to talk.'

'Only because it's losing. And it is going to lose, make

no mistake. Why tether yourself to a losing side that you only encountered a few months ago? So your mother was Breken—so what? She made the right choice. Listen, Nikolai, your mother—'

'Don't talk to me about my mother!' I said, louder than was maybe wise.

Jono made a move towards me.

But Frieda said, 'Now, now. Calm down. Thank you, Agent.'

Jono returned to his post behind her shoulder, but now he was staring at me as though he was sizing me up for dismemberment.

I pushed my chair back and walked to the far wall.

Frieda said, 'Loyalty is admirable, but you cannot be loyal to both your father and your mother. You must choose.'

But I wasn't thinking about loyalty right then. Standing against that wall, feeling its cold seep into me, I was thinking about the people who'd been in this room before me, including, possibly, my father. People whose sweat was ingrained in the walls and floor, people who'd cried here and bargained and bled. Some must have died here: we held memorials on Southside for those who went into the Marsh and never came out. And I knew, too, from half-heard conversations, that some people left and died later, unable to live with the bargains they made here. Who would be next? Mr Corman, if he stood in the doorway of his bookshop and defied the bulldozers? Those behind the posters, who were trying to get the real news out?

'Well?' said Frieda. 'I don't have time to waste. What do you think?'

I said, 'I think that if you need a room like this to run your city, you can count me out.'

She shook her head. 'You are naive and foolish. It's time you saw the world for what it is.'

'Sure,' I said. 'Like all those people who are deserting the city so they don't have to watch what happens next? They're not so keen on seeing the world for what it is, even though they're the ones who could change it.'

She looked at me impatiently, 'I'm not getting anywhere, am I? Time for a new approach.'

She nodded at Jono who took a step back and knocked on the door.

It opened and Dash came in. And with her, Lanya.

CHAPTER 21

My heart lurched and all the breath leaked out of me. Lanya looked around, defiant. She didn't even come up to Jono's shoulder but she was ready for a fight. Her eyes locked on mine and she mouthed, 'I'm okay.'

No, I thought. Neither of us is okay.

Frieda said, 'How are those ideals now? Let's see if you can hold onto them in the real world.'

I barely heard. My heart was hammering too loud.

Dash moved back to stand guard by the door and Lanya came across the room holding out her hand. I grasped it, held it tight.

'Now,' said Frieda. 'Let's talk, seriously this time, about what you want. What you both want. Southside is beaten, you know this to be true. But you want a future, perhaps together, worthwhile work, food, money, a place to live. I can give you that.'

Sure you can, I thought. But not for nothing. 'For what?' I said. 'What do you get?'

'Something very simple. We need to locate the Breken sympathisers here on Cityside. They call themselves One City. They aren't Breken, they're misguided Citysiders, clinging to an old cause while the world moves on. We are going to rebuild and revitalise the city. You can help with that. The bridges will open. People from Southside will move freely: they'll work here, even live here. A new start.' She held up a hand. 'Don't answer yet. Think for a minute. Imagine how it might be.'

Lanya spoke, in halting Anglo. 'You sent rockets to our town.'

Frieda inclined her head. 'That was regrettable, but necessary. A message to an old generation of leaders. I'm offering this to you, a new generation.'

Lanya nodded.

'So you understand?' said Frieda. 'You see what's possible?'

'I do,' said Lanya. 'Will you tear down the wire around Moldam?'

'In time.'

'Tell us what it's for,' I said.

Lanya said, 'Why not tear it down now?'

Frieda shook her head. 'I said, in time. You must answer on the information you have.'

'Then my answer is no,' said Lanya. Her hand

tightened in mine. 'I do not speak for Nik.'

Frieda raised her eyebrows at me and I said, 'What do you think? No, of course.'

She said, 'You are foolish, both of you.' She spoke to Jono. 'Take the girl to Ward 23.'

'*Wait!*' I said. 'I can give you something else.'

Frieda held up a hand, and Jono paused halfway to Lanya. 'Indeed?' she said. 'What would that be.'

'I know where Nomu is,' I said.

I was watching Jono about to plant his hands on Lanya so I barely registered that Frieda gave a little start and moved her hands off the table out of sight to her lap. Several seconds went by. Then she said, 'That's irrelevant for our purposes—'

'But not for her people,' I said.

She stood up abruptly. 'Don't interrupt me! You don't get to bargain.' She nodded to Jono. 'Get on then.'

'No!'

I moved between Lanya and Jono. He slammed his fist into my gut. I doubled up and he drove his knee into my temple, and then I was breathing floor dust.

He said something like 'Pathetic' and stepped around me. Through a blur I saw him grab Lanya's arm, and they were out of the room before I could see clearly or stop gasping.

I climbed onto my hands and knees, pulling in air. I heard Frieda say, 'So like your father.' She stood and watched me until I was breathing evenly again. I was fairly sure that if I stood up I'd fall over, so I sat on the ground and looked at her.

She sighed. 'I did try. You are my witness that I tried. How like your father you are. So stubborn. Uselessly, stupidly stubborn. You have forced my hand. Here's what you will do now. You will find a way into the network of One City sympathisers and report back to me on the whereabouts of their leadership. For every day that you fail to locate these subversives, we will inject that young woman with a cocktail of sodium pentothal and other useful drugs. Sadly it's not as reliable as we would like; it can take time to get a result, so we'll be starting immediately. Even so, perhaps she will be unreceptive. I rather think she will.' Frieda paused, watching me, to check she was making an impact. She was.

She went on, 'That means we'll have to escalate the drug regime day by day. On the third day—Friday—she'll start to hallucinate. By Saturday she'll no longer be able to tell dreams from reality and her personality will begin to change, permanently, in unfortunate ways. Shall I go on? No, I can see that you understand. I'm going to send you out now, into the city, and the sooner you return with information—reliable information—of the One City network, the sooner we'll stop the injections and you and your friend will be free to go. You have until Friday at about midnight before the irreparable harm begins.

Sooner would be better for her, obviously.'

I thought about grabbing her and breaking her neck.

'Why—' I stopped and got my breath under control. 'Why should I believe you—that you'll let us go if I do what you want?'

She frowned, impatient with me. 'Because you are living proof that I keep my word.'

I was staring at her like an idiot.

'You're here,' she said. 'Alive and well, and not a casualty of war.'

It was dawning on me, oh so slowly. I said, 'You promised my mother.'

She didn't answer.

'You promised my mother that if she turned in my father and his network, you'd let me live.'

She inclined her head and watched me.

My mother's choice was my choice now: betray the uprising and my father, or lose Lanya for good. I struggled to my feet and managed to stay there. I looked from Frieda's self-satisfied face to Dash's blank one.

I said to Dash, 'Is this what you wanted?'

She stared straight ahead and said nothing.

I turned to Frieda. 'Look, this is mad. You've got all those agents and the army at your back. If you can't find them why do you think I can? Don't you have a plant in there? You said you did.'

She smiled. 'I did say that. We don't, as it happens,

have a presence in One City at the moment. You are about to be it. Doors will open for you, you'll see. Take these.' She handed me a bag with my watch and wallet and boots. 'You're a fool, like your father, but that's your choice. Now you're wasting time.'

Jono came back, and she said to him, 'We're done. He can go.' She marched out the door.

I put my boots on, and when Jono came to grab me I swung an elbow and connected with his cheek. He yelled in surprise and in the nanosecond of advantage I had, I landed a fist on his face. It hurt like crazy, but was it ever gratifying. He staggered backwards and I put a boot in his belly. My advantage ended there. He grabbed my boot and wrenched me off balance. We landed on the floor and tore into each other, fists, feet, everything. It lasted longer than it would have once, but the short version is that he beat the shit out of me. Finally he had me pinned on the ground with his arm pressing on my throat. His nose was bloody and he was breathing hard, but he managed a sneer.

'Temper, temper.'

I tried to push him off me. I had no chance.

Somewhere behind us Dash said, 'Enough already. Get off him, Jono.'

Jono pressed harder on my throat till I was choking, and then he climbed off me. I sat up, my breath rasping, and watched him walk out the door. He was limping, but not much.

Dash said, 'Well that was wasted effort. Stupid, both of you. Come with me. You can't go out of here looking like that.'

I followed her to a sick bay where she gave me a towel and I splashed cold water on my face, washed off the blood.

'You betrayed us,' I said.

She handed me a bottle of antiseptic and didn't answer.

'So you owe us.'

I pressed on a cut lip and a grazed cheek and held a cold flannel to my left eye which was starting to swell. I glared at her with my working eye.

'It wasn't me that brought your friend in,' she said. 'You were both spotted yesterday on Sentinel Parade, so she was on a watch list.' She paused. 'We know she's more to you than a friend.'

How the hell could they know that? 'You're wrong,' I said. 'A friend is exactly what she is to me.'

'Well, I can't help her.'

I looked at the damage in the mirror. Not as bad as it could have been. Other damage was starting to make itself felt in my stomach and back, but there wasn't anything to do but wear it. I leaned on the bench feeling sick.

'Do you really not know that Frieda has plans for Moldam?'

'No. It's propaganda, Nik. Let it go.'

'It's not propaganda. Operation Havoc—go and look. Find out what it is.'

She sighed. 'I can drive you into town, if you want.'

'Yeah.'

'Why do you have to be like this?'

'Because.' I threw the towel on the floor.

We drove without exchanging a word and she let me off near St John's Square. She said, 'I'd say be careful, but you'd laugh.'

I said, 'You owe me. I won't forget.' I slammed the door.

CHAPTER 22

I went to Clouden Street. Its houses basked in the golden glow of the late afternoon sun, smug, beautiful and bristling with security cameras, bars and barbed wire. Inside, there'd be no sign of any of that heavy fortressing: chandeliers would be bright above marble floors and staircases, tall windows and wide glass doors would be opening onto river views to catch the breeze, and kitchens would be busy with prep for dinners that would last late into the night because these people would all have curfew exemptions.

I walked up the middle of the street. I got yelled at by drivers of sleek black cars that slid past me and disappeared into underground garages, and I got frowned at, then pointedly ignored, by pedestrians hurrying past on their way home from work. The only time they stopped was to punch secret codes into wrought-iron gates and multi-lock front doors that opened silently to let them in and closed silently behind them. It was like walking through a virtual game where people vanish as soon as you lay eyes on them and every door shuts just as you reach it. A few times I saw people peering from windows, watching me, and one person took a photo. I stopped and bowed at him and he stepped back into the shadows.

I reached Number 11 without being arrested, climbed the steps and punched the doorbell. I was past caring who answered. The guard, Alan, as it turned out. He barked, 'Yes?' into the intercom.

I'd thought about summoning up bright and cheery and a story about being an old school friend of Fyffe's but my battered face in the security camera would give the lie to that so I simply said, 'Can I see Fyffe, please?'

He said, 'Get lost,' and flicked off the intercom.

I pounded on the door until he came and wrenched it open.

'I said, get lost!' he demanded.

I stuck a hand on the door before he could close it. 'Please!' I said. 'It's important.'

Fyffe's voice came from the stairs behind him. 'Alan? Who is it?' Then her face peered around his bulk, and she said, 'Oh! Come in, come in!' and almost dragged me through the doorway.

The bodyguard wasn't happy. He frisked me, hit on a few Jono-inflicted bruises, then followed us to the doors of the pool room and planted himself there while we went inside. The room was stifling; Fyffe pushed open the riverside doors and we left the guard behind and went out onto the wide balcony. We leaned on the glass barrier, trying to catch some breeze but the air was still and heavy with the day's heat and the salt smell of decaying seaweed. To our right Fyffe's neighbours were having a small elegant party on their balcony; half a dozen people were dressed for dinner, each with a glass in hand, chatting and laughing to the clink of bottles in buckets of ice. One of the women waved at Fyffe and she waved back, but moved away to the far corner of the balcony. I followed.

She said, 'Lanya and I got to the posting but never got to talk to anyone because the army arrived. They rounded everyone up, even Mr Corman! Then they realised who I was and dropped me like I was poison, but they wouldn't let Lanya go. I tried to stop them, I really tried. I threatened all kinds of things but they piled everyone into their trucks and left me standing on the roadside. I've spent all afternoon trying to find out where Lanya is. I went out to the Marsh, but I couldn't get hold of Dash, so I left a message for her to call me.' She studied my face. 'She hasn't yet. You look terrible. Tell me everything.'

I did, and she swore with un-Fyffe-like explicitness. 'But Dash—'

'Yeah, Dash. Tell me about it.'

Fyffe shook her head in disbelief. 'She promised. She

promised *me*! They can't do this!'

'Yes, they can. They can do whatever the hell they want.'

'We'll see about that. What are you going to do?'

'I have no idea. None.'

'I mean—are you going to look for the One City people? You could try Sentian again, but the place is kind of a ghost town, except for the army.'

'Suppose I find them,' I said. 'What then? What am I supposed to do with that? I turn them in and they go to the Marsh. I don't turn them in and Lanya—' I stopped. Started again. 'Everywhere I go takes me to a deadend where somebody's hurt or killed.'

Glasses clinked next door and someone laughed long and high. Fyffe watched them for a moment and then said, 'I'll go and see Dash tomorrow and I'll ask to see Lanya. I'll demand to see her. I'll wear Dash down and make her help.' She looked at my bruises and said, 'You should stay here tonight.'

Tonight seemed a long way away, with a lot of thinking to do before I got there. 'Yeah, I don't know.'

'Please stay. And we'll…we'll…' She was casting about but, like me, coming up with nothing.

'We'll what?' I asked.

She screwed up her face. 'I want to say we'll work something out and it will be all right.'

I managed half a smile. 'Go on, then.'

She smiled ruefully back. She was dressed in something long and pale and floaty; the setting sun turned it a faint red-gold.

She said, 'I used to think there was always an answer, you know? Just do the right thing and the answer will pop up and be there for you.' Her eyes brightened with tears. 'But we did the right thing for Sol, didn't we. Every step along the way we did the best thing we could think of.'

'Do you think so?'

She looked surprised and blinked her tears away. 'Yes,' she said. 'I do. You did. I did. You don't doubt that?' She peered at me. 'You do. Look at you. Well please don't. It wasn't your fault and it wasn't mine either. We did the best we could, and we almost managed it.' She dabbed at her eyes. 'Not that that helps us now. We know the worst can happen, whatever we do. But, you know, maybe there are people along the way who can help and…and chances…there might be chances for us to take. We have to hope for that. Go forward a step at a time and watch for those people and those chances?' She grimaced. 'Best I can do. Sorry. It's not much help. I wish you'd stay, you need food and sleep.'

Being kind may seem small compared to being brave but it's not, and Fyffe was both of those.

I said, 'You are a huge help. Always.'

'Feeling pretty helpless right now. Still—' she glanced at her watch '—the people from the Dry are coming for dinner tonight. Should I tell them about Nomu being safe? They're expecting a memorial for her and it seems wrong to keep them in the dark. I don't think they'll go running to Frieda.'

'It won't matter if they do. Frieda knows.'

Fyffe's eyebrows shot up. 'Oh no. How? Did Sandor—'

'No. Nothing to do with Sandor.' I stared out over the river. 'I told her. Fy, I told her without a second thought. Our one chance to bargain for Moldam and I gave it away.'

All that time I'd spent thinking Sandor was a low-life and here I was giving away our one great secret at the first hint of pressure.

'You thought it would save Lanya?'

I nodded. 'And you know what? Frieda barely noticed. "Irrelevant," she said.'

Fyffe thought about that and shook her head. 'That's curious,' she said. 'It's been huge, here, Nomu's disappearance. It's been top of the news for days. Look at this.'

She went back into the pool room and turned on a wall screen. She found a news channel and sped through its archive until it showed a picture of Nomu. 'Look.'

She played though the footage: there was Nomu getting off the boat from the Dry, smiling shyly at the cameras and being hurried into one of those long black cars. She and her group were dressed in the loose, cream-coloured clothes of the Dry, but the next shots showed them arriving at some official function or other and this time her hair was curled and piled high, and she wore a bright flower-patterned dress and some very high-heeled red shoes that made her awkward on her feet. She waved nervously at the crowds as the group was ushered up some steps and inside someone's fancy house.

'We got invited to lots of these functions,' said Fyffe. 'Someone did a makeover on Nomu and her brother so she looks like one of us now, which is kind of a pity.'

Next came the distressed Dry-dwellers pleading for anyone who'd seen her to get in touch, and, finally, shots of plastic flowers and soft toys piled on the steps of an apartment building.

'Frieda's got to be interested in this, even if she pretends she's not,' Fyffe said. 'She'll be Ms Popularity if she finds Nomu and brings her back. We should pre-empt that if we can. Nomu's own people should be the ones to find her.'

I said, 'Feel free to be the bearer of good news. It's not as though we can use her to bargain with anymore.'

She turned to me, 'I think you should tell them.'

'No.' I shook my head. 'I need to go away and think about what to do next.'

Suddenly, all along the riverbank speakers wailed the first curfew siren: it began as a moan and climbed quickly into a shriek specifically designed to freeze your blood and send you scurrying inside.

Fyffe was watching me doubtfully. 'But you can't go now, can you.'

I watched the people next door pick up their glasses and wander off their balcony, still chatting and laughing.

Fyffe said, 'What are you thinking? That you're going to stay, yes?'

The front door buzzed.

'Oh!' she said. 'That's them.' She stood straighter and took a deep breath. 'Listen to me. If you go out into the curfew and get picked up you could lose a whole day in the cells and that's a day you could spend getting Lanya back. I'm going to take the guests upstairs. I'll tell everyone that you're here and that you've got important news.' She nodded and tried to look encouraging. 'It'll be okay.'

She hurried away.

Terrific, I thought. An ambush. That's what it would feel like to Thomas and Sarah Hendry. Plus, I was still wearing the dust and grime of the Marsh's basement floor, and I could feel my eye quietly swelling shut. Perfect for a reconciliation with the people who thought I had betrayed their friendship and was at least partly responsible for the death of their youngest son.

I watched the shadows creep across Southside and thought about Lanya. I had no good plan for getting her out. I knew that she wouldn't sink peacefully into drug-induced oblivion. Part of her training as a Pathmaker was meditation and exercises for mental discipline. She was tough. Maybe that would help her resist the effect of the drugs. And maybe peace would come and everyone would live happily ever after. The adrenaline rush from the fight with Jono had long worn off. I felt like I'd run into a wall at speed.

I decided to leave, hole up in a corner somewhere and think things through. I didn't want to meet the Hendrys, and I was certain they wouldn't want to meet me.

Fyffe reappeared beside me. 'It's all settled. They're waiting for you. Come on.'

I shook my head. 'You tell them. I'm gonna go.'

She hooked her arm through mine. 'I'm not arguing. They know you're here, and they want to see you. I promise.'

She marched me towards the stairs.

CHAPTER 23

I stood in the doorway to the dining room and looked at a memory: the long table set for dinner, candles in tall shining holders, crystal glasses and the family silver, the starched white tablecloth, bowls and platters of roasted meats and vegetables. But in the shadows beyond the candlelight the packing cases were piled high, the kitchen was dark and there were no waiting staff. Fyffe's mother, Sarah, had cooked this meal and now she sat at the table with her guests and the remains of her family in a tiny oasis of candlelight, like an echo of family dinners that used to be.

Sarah Hendry had lines on her face that never used to be there, and her shoulders were rounded as though she spent her days curled into herself. The candlelight made shadows of her eyes. She looked at me, and I knew she was looking for Lou to be standing in the doorway instead. Fyffe jumped into the pause.

'Nik, come in. Sit down.'

Once, months ago, I'd had this fanciful idea that one day I'd visit the Hendrys and tell them how brave Fyffe had been in trying to rescue Sol. And they'd listen and nod, and then I could say thank you for the way they'd been kind to me over the last however-many years and things would be right again between us.

I said to Fyffe, 'No. I'll just…I'll just tell you what there is to tell and then…and then I'll go.'

'Where?' said Fyffe. 'You'll break curfew.'

Fyffe's mother stopped staring at me, sat up straighter and brushed some imaginary crumbs from the tablecloth. When she looked up again it was like she had pulled on a mask and become, for the evening, unbreakable. Everybody looked at her and waited.

She said, 'Fyffe, take Nik to get cleaned up, and find him some clothes that are presentable for the dinner table.' She looked at me and I couldn't tell if it was her or the mask that said, 'Go on. Dinner's getting cold.'

When I came back, showered and acutely aware that everything I was wearing had once been Lou's, Sarah Hendry said, 'Now, Nik, eat something and then tell us whatever it is you have to say.'

I looked at the heaped dishes on the table and my brain said, *You haven't eaten in twelve hours,* but my stomach said, *No way.* I put some roast potatoes and slices of meat onto my plate and hoped she wouldn't notice that I couldn't eat any of it.

The four guests from the Dry looked just like they had in the screen footage: an older guy, lean, weathered and brown, with short grey hair and beard; a younger man and woman, both with black curling hair and sharp, wary eyes; and a boy about my age with copper-coloured hair and a thin, brown face. Fyffe introduced them, but their names went right over my head, until she said, 'And this is Nomu's brother, Raffael.'

'Oh!' I said and looked at Fyffe. 'Raffael?' And my brain, playing stupid tricks on me, thought, I have to tell Lanya, she'll laugh.

'Yes,' said Fyffe. 'Why?'

'Because,' I said, 'That's the first word I heard Nomu say. Almost the only word.'

The boy just about jumped over the table at me. 'She's alive? You've seen her?'

'Yes,' I said. 'She's alive and I've seen her.'

But that explosion of relief was followed by a tight, careful conversation where the things that weren't said were much more interesting than the things that were. At first, I thought the delicate tiptoeing around Nomu was all about the problem of being over-the-moon happy at finding someone who's been lost when you're with people whose grief for their own loss is as real as the empty chairs at the table. But then something happened that made me think there was more going on than that.

I told them that as well as calling for Raffael, she had said something to me about Pitkerrin Marsh. 'I don't know what she meant,' I said, 'but I wonder if she's been in the Marsh?'

They all nodded, totally unsurprised.

Raffael said, 'Yes, we have been working in a laboratory there.'

That earned him a sharp whisper in desert language that sounded like a telling off and he scowled and shut up.

When it came to the question about what to do next the older guy was all action. 'We will go across the river. We will find her and bring her back.' He even stood up, gripping the back of the chair, and looked like he was about to head out the door straight away.

'Wait.' Thomas Hendry held up both hands. 'Please. You must tell the security services. They'll help you. You can't go off into hostile terr—into Southside without help.'

The guy rubbed his forehead like he had a headache and sat down again. 'Yes, I see, yes. Forgive me. We are not courteous. We have been preparing ourselves for the worst news. But now—' he opened his arms towards me and smiled, '—now we have hope. Of course we should ask the Security.'

Glances were exchanged among the Dry-dwellers,

which, if you had a suspicious mind, you could interpret as unhappy.

'But—' Fyffe began.

'Fyffe,' said her mother.

The man smiled at her. 'Then, when Nomu is found and safe, we will go to the Dry, all of us together.'

A wave of his hand encompassed the whole table. Mr Hendry poured more wine to cover the awkward pause that followed.

It didn't worry me not to be included in their adventure south, but I did think that the Dry-dwellers were not looking entirely thrilled at the prospect of taking the city's elite home with them.

When the visitors left, Fyffe and I did the dishes. In the kitchen, away from scrutiny, I put a big slab of roast beef between two even bigger slabs of bread and ate at last. Fyffe clattered the dishes to cover our conversation.

'That was news to me,' she said. 'That they've been working in the Marsh. I don't know if that makes them friends or enemies.'

'What are they doing there?' I said. 'What are they doing in the city at all?'

'People are allowed to visit.'

'The Marsh? This isn't a business delegation or a fact-finding mission. They've come here to work in the Marsh and to escort a lot of—'

I stopped in time, but Fyffe said, 'Go on, say it. A lot of rich people.'

'A lot of rich people out of here just when the security services and the army are planning some kind of surge to put down the uprising. They don't sound like friends to me.'

'Shh,' said Fyffe. 'Not so loud.'

I peered out the door. Fyffe's mother was standing in the dining room staring down into one of the open packing cases. I turned back to Fyffe and said quietly, 'I have an idea about what to do next.'

'About Lanya?' she whispered.

I nodded, but then her mother appeared in the doorway saying, 'Just stack them on the table out here when you're done. There's no point putting them back in cupboards. Shall I help?'

She looked so forlorn standing there that I said, 'Sure,' and handed her the plate I'd just dried. We finished the dishes over small talk about the sight-seeing opportunities in the Dry.

Sarah Hendry sent her daughter to bed with a kiss on the forehead as though she was six years old. Then she looked at the bruises on my face and asked me if I was able to help her move some boxes downstairs. I said, 'Sure.' The bodyguard helped too, and we worked for a hour or so; we hardly spoke, but that was okay. At midnight she thanked the bodyguard and he went off to his own quarters. I started to climb the stairs, but she said, 'Nik. Stay a minute.'

Almost. I'd almost got away without this talk. I came back down and perched on the edge of a box. She sat on another nearby and looked at me levelly. She said, 'I want you to tell me about what happened to Sol in Southside, and on the bridge.'

'Oh,' I said. I hesitated, thinking, you really don't want to hear this. I know I didn't want to tell it. But she was sitting there waiting, and she of all people deserved to know.

I couldn't look at her. I stared down at my hands clasped in front of me and I told her everything straight, with all the detail I could remember. I had to tell her that we'd almost made it. That he'd been okay—a bit thin, a bit scared—but mostly okay once one of Commander Vega's squads had rescued him from the traffickers.

'A Breken squad?' she said.

'That's right. There are factions over there. One faction rescued him, the other—'

'Shot him. On the bridge.'

I nodded. 'He was so happy to be going home. To be seeing you. He didn't know anything when it happened. It killed him outright.'

I glanced at her; she was sitting tall with her hands in her lap and tears streaming down her face.

'I'm so sorry,' I whispered. I stared at my hands and

couldn't say another thing.

Her own voice was low and unbearably sad. 'Thank you. That was a hard thing to tell. I'm grateful.' She stood up and walked over to me, but I still couldn't look at her. She put her hand lightly on the top of my head, said, 'Good night, Nik,' and left.

Sometime later, I climbed the stairs. They'd given me my old room to sleep in, where Sandor had been just the day before—that felt like weeks ago. On the bedside table Fyffe had left me her silver talisman of the Southside charter.

I lay awake a long time thinking about the idea I'd had that I hadn't had a chance to tell Fyffe. I was going to find the one Southsider I knew who'd been at home in the city long enough to have connections with Southside allies and who would trust me enough to help me find them. I was going to find Mace.

George Macey was a Southsider and had been a security guard at my old school. Mace was the reason I still spoke Breken—in his godawful Gilgate accent. He'd spoken it to me from the moment I'd arrived at school, though never in anyone else's hearing. He knew who I was and who my parents were, but he never said so, and I didn't twig that he knew any of that until the night the school was bombed when he'd told me to get out before anyone official found me.

I had one or two clues about where Mace might

be found—more than I had about any of the One City people—and he knew me, so I wasn't going to have to prove who I was to get what I wanted.

What I wanted. Names. Hiding places. For Frieda. For Lanya. I couldn't even think in sentences about what I wanted.

I dozed until around dawn then got up and dressed in the semi-dark, wanting to leave before Fyffe or anyone else was up. I put the talisman round my neck—which felt like signing up again to being Breken—and sent a mental thank you to Fyffe. Then I went out into the games room, boots in hand, hoping I wouldn't meet the bodyguard on my way downstairs.

Thomas Hendry was sitting in one of the big leather chairs. I stopped, decided he was asleep and tiptoed past him.

'Nik.'

Damn. 'Sir? Sorry. Thought you were asleep.'

'You're leaving?'

'Yes.'

He saw me glance towards Fyffe's room and nodded. 'I was going to ask you—'

'To leave Fyffe out of it?' I said. 'Yeah, I think so too.'

He nodded again then sat up straighter and rubbed his hands over his face. I thought how old he looked now. Too old to be spending the night in an armchair but, I guess, never too old to be trying to protect his daughter.

I said, 'Sir? I wanted to thank you, and Mrs Hendry, for the bed and…everything.' That sounded pathetic. 'I mean—'

He smiled. 'I know what you mean. You're welcome, Nik. You were good for Lou, and Sol.'

But I'm not good for Fy, I thought.

He pulled his wallet from a pocket. 'Here.' He held out a wad of cash. 'Take it.'

I hesitated, and he said, 'I can't help you, except like this. I'm taking my family away. I don't know what you're doing back in the city. You must have reasons and they may be good reasons, but I don't want to know what they are. How you go now is up to you, but money can't hurt.'

'Thank you.' I took it. It was a lot of money. 'I'll go. Goodbye.'

'Good luck, Nik.'

I closed the door gently and looked up and down Clouden Street. It was early-morning empty. Out towards Port the sun was barely up and the sky was hazy over-head. Already the air was warm and still; it was going to be another one of those hot, close days when all you want to do is chase the breeze—maybe climb on the heath and arrive up there soaked with sweat feeling like you've earned the wind cooling your skin.

But that's not what I was going to do today.

Today I'd said the last of my goodbyes to the Hendrys: Fyffe and her mother, then her father. Like a player in the game I'd imagined yesterday, I had tokens from them: the talisman from Fyffe, the cash from Thomas Hendry, and from Sarah Hendry, I didn't really know what—it had felt like a blessing, so I decided that's what I'd take it for. Also there were Fyffe's words: 'Watch for people, watch for chances'. Maybe all of this would help. But it was Freida's game, and she had stacked the rules in her favour. She had only to sit and wait. I had to run, and Lanya had to fight.

I wondered if Lanya was awake yet. She would be calm. She wouldn't be letting thoughts run riot in her head in useless, panicky circles: she would be finding a still, quiet place and staying there.

But the drugs would beat her down, hammering her defences and invading that space. I sent determined thoughts in her direction.

Today I would find Mace, and make a plan. By tonight it would be in play. Soon she would be out of there. Soon. The clock was ticking down. Thursday already. Far too fast, it would be Friday midnight, and she would be lost.

I hurried down the steps and across the road into the alleyway with the *Break the* ~~*Broken*~~ *Banks* posters. I was halfway down it when footsteps pounded behind me. I swung round and came face to face with Raffael.

'I was waiting, on the street, for you,' he said. 'Hiding. Since last night. Many hours.'

'All night?'

He nodded.

'What for?'

'My sister. You can help us find her.'

He was watching me with this expectant look on his face, as though I was about to conjure his sister out of the morning air.

I shook my head. 'No. I've got something else I have to do. Ask the Hendrys. Ask your friends at the Marsh.'

He gazed at me, processing what I'd said and realising it wasn't the answer he needed. He looked up at the sky and took a breath.

I said, 'Sorry,' and turned away, but he called after me.

'You do not know what is coming.'

That stopped me. I turned back to him. 'What did you say?'

He came up to me, close and dead serious. He was as tall as me so he could stare me straight in the eye. He said quietly, 'You do not know what is coming.'

As a veiled threat, it was a show stopper. 'What do you mean?' I said.

He stepped back. 'Help me. Then I help you.'

But he wasn't very good at threatening trade-offs because then he resorted to, 'Please! Please help us. We cannot ask the Security.'

'Why not? You've been working right next to them.'

'We…we do not trust them.'

Fair enough, I thought. Trust is in short supply and I really don't trust you.

'Then why are you working in the Marsh?' I said.

His stare narrowed. 'This is not our choice. You do not know.'

'That's right,' I said. 'I don't. Tell me.'

'It is…complicated,' he said. 'I could tell you.' The pause. The expectant look.

'If I help you.'

He nodded.

I so did not need this. I stared at the scrawled-on *Break the Breken* posters and listened to the city waking up around us: a gate slammed across the road, an underground garage door whined, and a car revved up a ramp and out onto the street. Time was in a hurry. I was too, but it was still early for Mace to be about. I sighed.

'All right. Come with me. I'm looking for a friend who's a Southsider. If we find him he might know someone who can help you get across a bridge and into Moldam.'

Raffael's face lit up. 'Yes! Yes! Thank you!'

'But,' I said, 'You have to tell me what the hell is going on.'

He nodded, serious again. 'I will do that.'

'Okay,' I said. 'Let's find my friend. You can tell me on the way.'

The Inkwell was just opening its doors. I got a coffee for us both and asked the guy who brought it if he'd seen George Macey about.

'Macey? Nah, man, we don't serve shanty scum in here no more. Since they bombed the shit out of Tornmoor? Hell, no. Why are you after him? Owe you money or something?'

I shrugged.

'Try the Stag,' he said. 'That's where they hang out, the leftovers, if they haven't run back over the river. Only place that'll serve 'em now.'

The Stag and Poacher, he meant—a seedy little bar over Torrens Hill way. 'Sure,' I said. 'Thanks.'

'Watch your back, though,' he said helpfully. 'Stab you as soon as look at you, that lot.' He went off to serve Citysiders.

Raffael watched this conversation, frowning slightly as he concentrated on the Anglo. 'Tell me about Nomu,' he said. 'Is she all right? Are you sure?'

'Yes,' I said. 'She's okay. Wherever she's been, it hasn't been great, but she's being looked after in Moldam. She'll be fine.' I hoped that was true. 'Now, tell me what's going on in the Marsh.'

But he was still thinking about Nomu. 'I should have looked after her better. We had never been outside the Dry before we came here. She is a—' he searched for a word '—a fierce person. Clever and fierce.' He spread his arms in a wide grasping motion. 'She wanted to do everything and see everything. There were dinners and parties. And our minders said we must have new clothes and new hair styles and, for Nomu, face paint, to look like the city women.' He shrugged mournfully. 'I was the big brother. I was too…' he dragged his hands down his cheeks and pulled a sour face. 'You know? And the more I was like this, the more she became wild. As though she wished to take it all in, all the food and wine and richness, and then to—' he made a violent motion with his hands, as though he was spewing it all out. 'She stopped coming to work with us in the laboratory. Then one day we came home and she was gone.'

This wasn't telling me what I needed to know. I finished my coffee and stood up. 'Keep talking,' I said. 'But let's go.'

He gazed around the cafe with a thoughtful look on his face. 'I do not understand. You speak Anglo, you know the city, you went to school with Fyffe. To me you are a Citysider.'

'I lived here once.'

'But you found Nomu over the water, among the savages.'

'I live there now.'

He gave me half a smile. 'You do not seem to be a savage.'

'There's time.'

'Explain to me,' he stared into his empty cup, 'There is a war. You must choose a side, yes?'

'No,' I said. 'I've told you about Nomu. Now you tell me what's coming.'

The city morning was bright and busy. Shopkeepers were swinging open their doors and stacking crates of food outside to entice customers inside: potatoes with the dirt still clinging to them, apples that looked like they'd been individually polished and bunches of carrots with their green leafy tops. It still surprised me, the amount of food on view here.

'This way,' I said, and we headed for the rundown, rat-infested squats of Torrens Hill by way of the back lanes that were too narrow for army vehicles.

'A fold in a hub in the Dry,' Raffael told me. 'That is our home.'

'A fold?' I asked.

'Like the tents of our ancestors,' he closed his palms together. 'Folded when it was time to move on.'

'Okay. Go on.'

'Thirty folds make our hub. One hundred families in each fold. We do not move on. We have water, so there is no need. It is in the rocks deep under the desert. We are careful with it, and our science is strong, so we can manage the water and also the heat and light of the Dry to grow food and keep animals—for ourselves and to trade with towns far away—and we trade our knowledge too, our science. We have a good life: perhaps…narrow, you would say? But there is safety in the hub and there is adventure outside it in the Dry for those who wish it.

'Three months ago a traveller came to our fold. We welcomed him—travellers bring news and we're glad to see them. After he had stayed two weeks, our people began to fall sick. A fever caught them and they bled inside, under their skin.' He rubbed the back of his hand. 'In their chests, even in their eyes. Death came quickly, in three days or four. Six people in one week, thirteen in two.'

He spread his hands in front of him and stared at them as though he wanted more fingers to count the number of his dead. 'It was nothing we had seen before.' He closed his fists. 'We had no answer, so we sent out word for help. And help came. From here. From this city. Men came with a drug that stopped the deaths, and with a vaccine. They promised it would make our people safe. For this we were very grateful. But then they said, "There is a price."'

'There's a surprise. What price?'

'Space in our hub. An *entire* fold of their own. They are escaping a war, they said. We said that we have no room for them, and yet they demand it in return for giving us knowledge of the drug and the vaccine. What could we say? We said, yes. And here we are, working in Pitkerrin Marsh, learning how to make the drugs and vaccine that will save our people. And soon, twenty-five of your families will come to the Dry and take our fold. And we must make way: one hundred families must find another place to live because your people—'

'They're not *my* people.'

'Because these people are greedy. More than greedy. The sickness was no mistake. The man who brought it knew he brought it, and the city men knew too. They pretended to be strangers to each other, but Nomu saw them together. She was outside climbing an old watchtower; she saw them laughing.'

I walked and thought: a virus deployed as blackmail by a bunch of Cityside's most powerful people. Why? What were they so desperate to grab out in the Dry? Or, looked at another way, what were they desperate to leave behind here?'

The closer we got to the Stag and Poacher the seedier things became: rows of tiny shops sat cramped together, dingy with neglect. The Hotel Grande was grand no more and looked like it had become a squat for people who couldn't afford a room next door in the creepy Best

Boarding House, or Beast Boarding House as the sign now had it. Pawn shops displayed people's treasures in their barred windows, and chipped, badly painted signs were wired to streetlamps or hung from doorways, offering to buy (no questions asked) and quick money, a way out of your troubles. People lounged on the steps and in doorways, smoking and watching us with drugged-out blandness. Raffael got the jitters and kept turning in circles trying to look behind us and ahead at the same time. I was more worried about the stares from cc-eyes and was glad to see that a lot of them had been knocked off their perches and dangled blind in mid air.

Raffael stopped and turned to me. 'They think they have defeated us, but once we have the vaccine we will fight back. When these people come to the Dry there may not be the welcome they expect.' He gave a little nod, as though this was the end of his story, and walked on.

'Hold up!' I jogged after him. 'What does that mean—there may not be the welcome they expect?'

He glanced at me. 'People of ours are dead—friends, family—and our fold is taken from us. Should there not be a reckoning?'

'What kind of reckoning?'

'I cannot say. It is not for me to decide.'

I thought about Fyffe walking into that.

'Wait,' I stopped.

He turned back, eyebrows raised.

'Fyffe was kind to you,' I said. 'If it wasn't for her you wouldn't know about Nomu. You wouldn't be here now.'

'That's true. But—'

He shrugged.

'No, no, no,' I said. 'You can't just shrug that off. D'you still want my help?'

His shoulders sagged. 'Yes, of course. But it's not for me—'

'To decide. Yeah, you said.' I looked up the alley and pointed. 'See that?'

'What?'

I picked up a stone and hurled it hard. It clattered off the cc-eye. 'That,' I said. 'That is a camera. There's probably one of those for every five or six people living here. Oh shit, it's not dead.'

The camera was swivelling towards us.

'Come on!'

We sprinted into the next alley. Two cameras there were also on the move, as though the buildings had alien eyestalks and were coming to life. We kept running till we got to Mercers Lane where all the cameras had been yanked from their roosts.

We slowed to a walk, and I said, 'The people who put those cameras up—the Security that you don't trust anymore—they don't trust you either. They're watching and waiting; they're always ready for anyone who wants to fight back. They are not the kind of people who are going to bow to your so-called reckoning. They're not going to say, "Oops, sorry, won't happen again and by the way here's your fold back." It doesn't end like that. There'll be a basement in the Marsh where they're working right now on a different version of the sickness and a new vaccine because they know you'll want revenge and they will be a step ahead of you. Then what happens? It goes on and on and it gets bigger and bloodier every time. And before you know it, you might as well be here firing rockets at each other over the river. Forever.'

I stopped. Raffael did too—I didn't know if he'd followed the rant, but we'd arrived at the Stag and Poacher so I didn't care right then. The little pub looked very shut. I tried to get my head back around the reason I was here: find Macey, and through Macey find One City, and then? But then the path diverged depending on what I decided to do with that knowledge. I was carefully not thinking about that.

Raffael stood at my shoulder and said, 'The sickness is a weapon more accurate and powerful than any rocket. Whoever has control of it and its vaccine does not need rockets because they can decide who gets sick and who does not. The Security has spent all this time making it. Do you think they will use it only on us?'

Pieces of the puzzle were slotting together fast now. Frieda had a bioweapon on a leash. Alongside that, City-side's powerful families were desperate to get out of town, and Moldam was effectively under quarantine. I said to Raffael, 'Do you know what disease it is? Does it have a name?'

He shrugged. 'It is a hemorrhagic virus. We call it HV–C6.'

HVC. Havoc. I felt cold to my bones. Frieda was planning to end the war by ending Moldam. She'd set it up perfectly: inside the lockdown, Moldam's medics were stretched, food was short, and people were camping on the street. What better way for a virus to spread unchecked?

And the deserters were sufficiently worried about it all going wrong that they were getting out.

My choice was starkly simple. I could work with

One City to save Moldam from a deadly epidemic, or I could betray them to save Lanya. Whatever I decided, I had practically no time to do it. If the disease wasn't in Moldam yet it must be only days away. And days is all I had to get Lanya out: two days and counting down.

Macey was my gatekeeper. I had to find him first, and soon. Now would be best. I crossed the road to the Stag and Poacher.

Round the back we found an open door and this huge guy lugging out armfuls of empty bottles and dropping them with a crash into a bin.

The Stag is a place where the ambiance rears up and grabs you by the throat as soon as you walk in. The stink of old beer and cigarette smoke has soaked into every surface: the stained lino, the brown walls, the yellow-brown lampshades, the faded black-and-white photos of old horseraces and even older ball games. The glory days of the Stag and Poacher are long, long gone.

Inside, we found a solitary person at a corner table with half a bottle of whisky at his elbow and some papers in front of him. He folded them away fast when he saw us. He had pale skin and greasy grey hair pulled back in a tight ponytail.

He turned a narrow stare on us. 'We're not open yet! Scram!'

I pulled up a chair and sat down opposite him. 'We're looking for George Macey. Has he been about?'

He sat back, still with the stare. 'Who?'

'George Macey. You know. Security guard. Used to work at Tornmoor.'

'Who's asking?'

'Nik Stais,' I said.

His face was unreadable. 'That so?'

'Have you seen him? Recently?'

'Nope.'

'When did you see him last?'

'Couldn't say.'

'C'mon. Really?'

'Really. Scoot, kid. You're not old enough to be in here.'

'I'm not moving till you tell me where he is. I know he used come here and I know you know him. I just want to find him. Look.' I opened my jacket and arms wide. 'I'm harmless. I want to talk to him, that's all.'

'That's too bad. Can't help you.' He raised his voice, 'Salvatore!'

The guy who'd been clearing the bottles lumbered into the room. 'These kids are done here.'

Salvatore was gigantic, and he did not look open to persuasion.

I said, 'Wait a second! Listen—'

But we were out of there with our feet hardly touching the floor before I could finish that sentence. The giant slammed the door behind us and we heard the locks turn. We stood in the rubbish-strewn backyard of the Stag, emptyhanded.

So, doors would open for me! That's what Frieda had said. Like hell they would. After the Inkwell, the Stag had been my lead. My best, last, only lead. This wasn't how it was meant to go. I picked up an empty bottle and hurled it at the brick wall opposite. Someone inside shouted, 'Hey! Watch it!' I picked up another bottle and turned towards the door.

'No!' said Raffael. He pulled on my arm. 'We go.'

He dragged me down Mercers Lane and around the corner out of sight of the Stag.

'Stop,' he said. 'Be calm. Think.'

I leaned on a wall, closed my eyes and tried to make my brain work.

Raffael stood beside me, not talking. After a while he said, 'Tell me. This matters very much to you. Why?'

'Because,' I said, 'A good friend will die soon—as good as die—by Friday night, if I do not find Macey and if Macey does not help me.'

He nodded. 'So, now what do you do? We. What do we do?'

'Now, I don't know.' My voice was hardly working.

'You can work it out. How to find him.'

'Yeah.'

That's supposed to be what I'm good at, working

things out, but I couldn't think straight. Friday midnight was thirty-nine hours away. Thirty-nine measly, pathetic, short little hours.

Raffael said, 'Give me your watch.'

I frowned. 'Why?'

He held out his hand. I took it off and gave it to him and he put it in his pocket.

'Hey!' I said. 'I need that!'

He shook his head. 'You look at it every minute. How can you think when you look at your watch every minute? You give yourself no time for thought. Now. Questions. Where does the man live?'

'I don't know. I thought he was here. His family's in Gilgate somewhere.'

'Over the river?'

'Yeah.'

'Then we go over the river.'

I looked at him. 'You can't just walk over a bridge.'

'Because of the guards?'

'Armed guards. That's right.'

'I have this.' He held out his VIP ID card.

I shook my head. 'Not enough.'

'What would be enough?'

Nothing, I thought. Nothing is ever enough over here. I remembered saying something like that to Lanya: the city wants and wants and wants. Its soldiers, badly paid and in the line of fire, wouldn't be any different. My brain started to clear at last. 'I have money,' I said. 'A lot of money.'

The bridge to Gilgate is at Torrens Hill, not far from the Stag. Two soldiers in green fatigues and sunglasses paced in front of the bridge gate. They turned bored faces towards us; I could see our reflections in their dark glasses. I held up my fake ID and Raffael's VIP one, put on my best Ettyn Hills accent and said that my friend, visiting from the Dry, would like to walk on the bridge to look at the river because he'd never seen a river up close before. The guards laughed like I knew they would and waved us away.

'No,' I said. 'You don't understand. We *really* want to.' I showed them a handful of notes.

Eyebrows shot up above the glasses. One of them said, 'I guess you really do. It's going to cost you more than that though.'

I put the money away. 'You know what? There are other bridges. We might take a walk to them.'

They glanced at each other. 'Okay, wait,' said one. 'We can let you through. Don't do anything stupid, right? Walk to halfway and come straight back.'

'Sure,' I said. 'Thanks.'

I handed over the notes. Easy as that. We walked through the gate and onto the bridge. When we got to the middle we stopped and leaned over the side looking down to the grey water flowing around the bridge supports.

Raffael whistled. He shaded his eyes, looking upriver towards Westwall and down towards Port then kicked the side rail with the toe of his boot. 'This took a lot of making. It would be hard to destroy.'

'For sure,' I said. 'You'd have to really want to.'

I was watching the guards. As soon as they stopped looking our way, I said, 'Let's go.' We took off fast for the other side. The bridge gate on Southside was locked but unguarded. We climbed over it and dropped down into Gilgate.

Raffael grinned at me. 'This far, so good!'

'Yes,' I said. 'This far, so good.'

We dived into the Gilgate market crowd. Finally my much reviled accent came into its own—people took me for a local. I talked to stall owners, kids, streetsweepers, vagrants, shoppers, anyone who would stop and talk to me. Macey, I asked, did anyone know him? First name George, short guy, sturdy, kind, has—or had—a wife and two daughters.

By midday we had a lead and with the sun high over-head baking the streets and people retreating to any place shady, we made it to the old part of Gilgate. This part of town was built and long lived in before the division, before the bridges were controlled and the river laced with mines, when the city was just a city with a river flowing through it. We arrived in a road of tenement houses at a house that looked like any other. Windows above us reflected the sunlight; doors up and down the street were closed against the heat. Raffael waited while I climbed the steps and knocked.

My heart was pounding. I knocked again, and this time the door opened. A young woman stood there, all dark-eyed frowning suspicion, with a hand on the door about to close it in my face. I racked my brain for the names of Mace's daughters.

'Jenna?' I said. 'Louisa? I'm Nik Stais. I'm looking for George Macey.'

She shook her head. 'No. Not here.'

She started to close the door, but her eyes had flickered when I said her name.

'Louisa,' I said. I put a hand on the door, not pushing but holding it. 'Please? It's important.'

'No,' she said. 'No strangers.'

'I'm not a stranger,' I said. 'Look,' I took the silver talisman from around my neck and handed it to her.

'Show him this. Tell him my name. Nik Stais.'

Louisa took the talisman and closed the door. I turned to Raffael and he gave me an encouraging smile. We waited. The sun beat down on us. I thought about why I was there and then couldn't bear to think about why I was there. I stared at the door. Hurry, I thought. Hurry so I don't have to think about what I'm doing.

The door opened. Same woman. She said, 'This way.'

We went down a dark hallway, through a small, basic kitchen and out the back into a tiny garden with carefully hoed rows of vegetables. Under a ragged awning a figure sat in a cane chair. I had to look twice to see it was him, he was so bent and old.

He put both hands on the arms of the chair and tried to straighten up. The lines in his face were etched deep, his brows were set in a grimace and his mouth was a thin line.

'He has bad pain,' said Louisa behind me. She didn't need to tell me. I felt like I was towering over him, so I crouched down.

'Mace?'

He held out a hand and I gripped it. Tears filled his eyes.

'It is you,' he said. 'Nik, lad. Well, well.'

Louisa had brought out other chairs and a tray with a teapot, a fragile china thing that looked ancient, and some little matching cups the colour of old cream. We sat down and she sat beside Mace and held his hand while he told us what had happened the night of the Tornmoor bombing.

'They found me fast that night,' he said. 'Couple of agents. Didn't waste time. Broke my knees.'

'Jesus,' I said. 'Why?'

'Southsider on campus. Easy target.'

'Didn't they take you in? Question you?'

He shook his head. 'In a hurry, weren't they? A truncheon's a quick way to do what their drugs'll do slow. Besides, they were more interested in doing damage right then, than in findin' out where the troubles were stemmin' from. Thing is, I had nothing to tell 'em.'

'Nothing? Really?'

He smiled faintly. 'See? You don't believe me either.'

Louisa poured black tea into the cups, and Mace sipped from his and put it down. 'Listen, I got a job there 'fore you was ever born. Wanted to earn enough to take my family over there, away from this.' He nodded up to the high walls of the flats looming over the little bit of garden that was his. 'You could do that in those days. So I'd been there a few years, earning my money, counting it up, saving it, and one day this scrap of a kid turns up, and I've heard his name before, and I know about his parents, and now I got two good reasons to be there.'

I bowed my head.

'Well,' he said, 'Who else was gonna look out for you? Scrawny, you were.' He peered at me. 'Still are. Anyways, I knew about that hidden backdoor in the gatehouse, sure I did. And I knew some folk came and went through there over the years. But, y'know, they played it down. They said you was just a bunch of kids and some retired agents. They planted bugs but I never knew if those were any much use. So when they blew the damn place to kingdom come it was a helluva surprise to me.'

'You came looking for me,' I said. 'That night. You should've got out soon as you could.'

'Ah well. I knew that, and I knew you didn't. So least I could do was find you and send you on your way.'

I nodded.

He smiled at me, a crooked, weary smile. 'Find out who you are yet?'

I nodded again and his smile widened. 'Good. That's good. Used to watch you. Wanted to tell you. All those years. Couldn't of course. Less you knew the better for you. Hope you know now how important they were, your mum and dad.'

He settled back like he was about to tell me just how important they were and I knew I couldn't listen. With what I was about to ask, I couldn't bear to hear.

'Mace, I need help.'

He patted his legs. 'Not much I can do for you, lad. Not now.' He looked from Raffael to me and saw something on our faces that made him pause.

'What kind of help?'

'I need to find the One City network on Cityside. I need to find it now. Today.'

He leaned forward, interested. 'Why's that?' Not suspicious. Curious. Helpful.

I said, 'It's a long story and I'll tell you one day but I can't now. Can you give me a name or an address— anything that will get me in?'

'Well,' he said. 'Passwords change, of course. But I've heard one or two things since I've been back over here. I can give you a trail to follow. Should get you somewhere today.'

I nodded and heard myself say, 'That would be great. Thanks.'

He gave me two names, a password and two places to go looking back on Cityside.

'Now don't go writin' those down,' he said. 'But you won't need to, smart lad like you.'

He smiled and I felt sick. This is it, I thought. This is what you do: you want something bad enough, you decide who and what you'll sacrifice to get it. I stood up. Truth is, I couldn't bear to look at him anymore, sitting there with his smashed knees, and me contemplating pointing Frieda towards more people like him.

'Here,' he held out the talisman that I'd given to Louisa, the one Fyffe had given me for luck.

I shook my head. I couldn't wear it now. 'No,' I said. 'You keep it. I'll come back for it one day.'

He smiled. 'I will, then. Take care of y'self now. Come and see me again soon.'

'Yeah,' I said. 'Sure.'

We went out into the sunbaked town. I went down the steps, across the road into the shadow of the tenement block and threw up.

Raffael stood at my shoulder looking alarmed. 'You are sick. You need help?'

I leaned back on the cool concrete wall, dragged the back of my hand over my mouth and closed my eyes. Lanya would be deeply drugged by now. As far as I knew she'd never taken any kind of drug—she didn't smoke, she didn't drink, she didn't do any of the adulterated crap that did the rounds over here, knocking people out of their grim reality into some kind of fantasy world for a while. You saw them sitting outside the shacks in the shantytown, out of their skulls, escaping. The Marsh drugs would hit

Lanya hard. Tomorrow midnight, Frieda had said, irreparable harm begins. Maybe it had already begun.

I had something to give Frieda now, in exchange for Lanya: a couple of safe houses, a password, the names of two people.

I had made my mother's choice.

I could tell myself that those people had signed up for this in a way that Lanya never had, but that didn't make it any easier. And it wouldn't just be two people, would it? It would be everyone connected to those people in the network. Including my father. Is this what had happened once my mother had turned him in? Had he talked in the Marsh under the influence of their drugs, delivering his allies into their hands?

How do you live knowing you've done that?

I was about to find out.

Raffael was watching me. 'You *are* sick.'

Mace and I had spoken Breken. Raffael couldn't know what I'd just done.

I pushed myself off the wall. 'I'm not sick. We need to go back to the city.'

I headed towards the river and got half way down the road before I realised that Raffael hadn't moved. I looked back and called, 'Come on!'

He jogged up to me. 'I do not go with you this time.'

I frowned. 'Why not?'

'Nomu,' he said. 'She is here, on this side of the river.

I will go and find her. I thank you for helping me, truly.'
He turned away.

'No! Wait!' I grabbed his arm. 'You can't do that. You don't know where to look. You don't know Breken, and if you speak Anglo here people will think you're the enemy. And Moldam is quarantined. You'll never get through. If you wait a day—just one day, until I've done this…this thing I have to do, then I'll help you.'

He hesitated. 'But she is here and I am here. I will find a way to ask. Tell me the direction.'

I said, 'It's a long way, and I don't know what you'll find when you get there.'

He didn't care, of course. He was going whatever I said. He'd be picked up by a squad in no time, and then what would happen to him? Nothing good. He was a complication I didn't need. What I needed was to concentrate on whether to try and save Lanya by selling out a whole bunch of people who'd end up like Mace, or worse. I knew Lanya would be appalled to be rescued like that. But leaving her in the Marsh meant she would be lost, not just to me, but to herself.

There were no right answers. I needed a miracle. I didn't believe in miracles.

Raffael was watching me, impatient to leave. I decided to go with the problem standing in front of me: the one that I could solve.

'I'll take you,' I said. 'But we have to hurry.'

CHAPTER 28

Following the river took us to Moldam in as direct a line as there was, through Ohlerton, Blackbyre and Curswall. We jogged down the riverwall road, stopping once at a roadside stall to buy two cups of water from a woman who seemed needlessly cheerful. Those townships were new territory to me, but I didn't see them. I was inside my head the whole way, trying to find a way through, one that didn't lead to a deadend and someone's execution.

What if I went to the people Mace had pointed me towards and told them what Frieda's deal was? Would they feel honour bound to storm the Marsh and get Lanya out? Unlikely, because even if they wanted to, the odds made no sense. A whole lot of people could lose their freedom, at the very least, to rescue a girl they'd never met who wasn't even under threat of death—just some mind-altering drugs. Just.

Besides, if I told them what the deal was with Frieda I'd lose control of anything that happened. They'd stop me selling them out, and so they should.

I ran and thought and thought and ran. At least running felt like doing something. We stopped on the outskirts of Moldam and eyed a patrol guarding the barbed wire looped across the River Road intersection. A bribe might work for getting us in, but getting out would be harder.

I went up to one of the soldiers and told him in Anglo what I wanted to do. He laughed at first, then I explained that if he didn't let me in now and out again in an hour, he would be making Security Director Kelleran a very unhappy person. There was confusion. Then consultation with the rest of the patrol. Then more consultation up the line of command via a comms unit. I don't know how high they went, but finally they arrived at bemused agreement and one of them clipped away some barbed wire and let us in.

It was late afternoon. I wanted to deliver Raffael to Levkova and get back over the river before curfew. Part of me hoped she'd be out and I could leave him on the doorstep with a message explaining who he was. I didn't want to see her, because I figured she'd look right through me and know straight away that something was badly wrong.

Levkova answered the door and let us in without a word but with quick pressure on my arm, which was as

0227

close to an expression of affection as she ever got. 'This is Raffael,' I said and started to explain who he was, but she was nodding already.

'Nomu was here,' she said. 'She's gone over the river with your father. You've only missed them by a few hours.'

Raffael was delighted. 'She is well then? She is safe!'

Levkova inclined her head. 'She is well, but not safe. No one is safe right now. Please sit down.'

She gave me the long appraising gaze I'd been dreading and I couldn't meet her eye, but whatever she thought about that she kept to herself.

She said to Raffael, 'Your sister knows things that are dangerous to know. But thanks to her, we know them now too. A Cityside squad has been here looking for her. I don't know how they found out she was here, but, fortunately, they came too late. You know that they do not mean to simply reunite her with your people?'

He looked at me. 'I do not understand. Why not?'

Levkova clasped her hands on the table and began to explain. I liked Levkova, I respected her and I owed her a lot, but looking at her now, I thought of Frieda and the way the two of them wove their web of strategy and counter strategy from one side of the river to the other. They had been playing this game, fighting this battle, for years. It was impossible for me to grasp hold of a thread of it and not get hopelessly entangled in all of it.

Levkova was saying, 'They are experimenting at the

Marsh on a virus. Nomu has seen these experiments and seen people die because of them.'

'Operation Havoc,' I said. 'You know what it is now?'

Levkova nodded, 'And we know that it's not only punishment for the uprising. It's also a lesson to the rest of Southside from Cityside. Behave or else.'

I said, 'Do you think it's here yet?'

She shook her head. 'Hard to know. No one's been reported sick, but that doesn't mean it's not here. I think, though, that there has been a delay in its release in order to accommodate the departure of certain of Cityside's families to the Dry.'

She gave Raffael a small smile. 'Your people have done us a favour in refusing to leave without Nomu.'

'They're not going to wait much longer,' I said. 'They're arranging a memorial service for her.' I stood up. 'I'm going back over the river. Do we have a plan?'

'Nomu is our key,' she said. 'She's agreed to help us make an alliance with the Dry-dwellers and to expose what's going on. You must find her and your father. I can tell you where they've gone.'

She hunted for a pen and paper and wrote down the address for me. She said, in Breken, 'Read it. Burn it. Tell no one, not even—' she smiled at Raffael '—your companion.'

The note gave me a familiar name and address. Of course it did. It was one of the addresses Mace had given me: the very people I was supposed to be handing over to Frieda. I found some matches on the mantelpiece, lit one and burned the scrap of paper, dropping it into the fireplace, where it turned to glowing ash and smoked out. I watched it and imagined the Moldam settlement burning to the ground as people tried to cleanse it of a plague: terror and chaos as people tried to leave and weren't allowed to. Piles of infected bodies. The rest of Southside watching and learning.

Something flickered at the corner of my brain— something about learning lessons. Who was this lesson for, exactly? Southside, obviously. But even with Moldam quarantined, everyone in Cityside and Southside was potentially at risk and would think themselves at risk. Frieda was offering disaster and reprieve: here's a virus, with a vaccine if you behave, minus the vaccine if you don't.

And then I realised I might have my chance after all. A small chance. Born, it's true, out of disaster and terrible danger. And small, very, very small, but a chance nonetheless. What I realised was this: I had a way to change the rules of Frieda's game. She worked by picking on people one at a time, identifying their breaking point—most likely, the people that they loved—and applying intolerable pressure by threatening the lives and sanity of those people. That's what she'd done to my mother: choose between your husband and your son. That's what she'd done to me: choose between this person who is precious to you and your father and his people. And it worked because you couldn't, by the nature of the deals she struck, tell anyone that this was happening. The very people that you'd look to for help were the ones you had to betray.

But whoever had decided to use this virus—maybe Frieda, maybe her superiors—had sown seeds that made its release everyone's urgent problem, not mine alone.

I turned around. Levkova and Raffael were watching me. She said, 'Do you want to tell the rest of us now?'

I nodded. 'Yes, I guess I do. You wanted to know how a Cityside squad could turn up here looking for Nomu. It's my fault. I told Frieda Kelleran yesterday—as good as told her—that Nomu was here.'

'You told her!' Shocking Levkova wasn't something you did every day. 'Why?'

'Lanya's in the Marsh,' I said. 'I have until tomorrow night to get her out. Frieda will let her go for—you can guess what.'

Her gaze narrowed. 'The name I just gave you.'

'I had it already. And another one.'

'I see.' She was quiet for a moment, watching me. 'What are you going to do?'

I managed to look her straight in the eye for the first time since we'd arrived. 'I'm going to find my father,' I said. 'And Nomu, and whoever else is over there who can help, and we are going to break Frieda's rules.'

CHAPTER 29

Raffael and I got back over the river as the first siren for curfew was sounding. Once the guards on the City-side bridge had searched us for weapons and taken the money I offered, they told us to hotfoot it indoors before the second siren, and that was that. We took off.

It was dark by the time we arrived in a rundown street at the back of Bethun, close to the heath. No light shone in any window. I tapped on a door, and after a nerve-racking minute it was opened by a tall woman with a lined face, white hair and dark brown eyes.

I said, 'Are you Anna? Tasia Levkova sent us. I'm Nik Stais. This is Raffael.'

She studied my face and a smile bloomed on hers. 'Nik Stais,' she said, nodding. 'Yes. Yes, you are. Come in.'

She closed out the night. 'This way!'

She led us down the unlit hallway and opened a door

with a flourish and a cry of 'Good news! Look who's here!'

We walked in to a candlelit room crowded with antique furniture, paintings on the walls and a piano in one corner with sheet music strewn over it.

My father was there talking to an older man, and Nomu was there too, sitting on a rocking chair. She cried, 'Raff!' and flew past me to her brother. She seized him in a hug and burst into tears on his shoulder. They spoke in a rush of their own language, then stood each other at arm's length and made some kind of formal greeting with bows and quiet words and then that dissolved into laughter and tears and hugging again. It made us all smile.

I said, 'Hello,' to my father.

Got a nod and a handshake.

'Come and sit down,' he said. 'Meet Samuel.' I shook the older man's hand.

Raffael and Nomu sat on the couch with their heads together and ignored the rest of us.

One happy ending at least.

We ate a feast that night: a roasted chicken, carrots and green beans, potatoes tossed in butter, fresh bread, then figs and dates stuffed with walnuts, and we drank a lip-pursing dry white wine and then strong sweet coffee. Anna said we must celebrate every small victory, so we toasted peace and family reunions and then, over the crumbs of our meal, she said, 'Now, to work.'

Around the table we brought together everything

we knew about Operation Havoc: the virus, the vaccine, the quarantine of Moldam, the exodus to the Dry, and the people of ours in the Marsh.

Samuel sat back and whistled. 'Where to start?'

'With Lanya,' I said.

He had a wrinkled face with craggy white eyebrows overhanging dark brown eyes.

'You're very sure of that, young man.'

'By Friday midnight it will be too late for her.' I looked at the old clock on the mantelpiece. 'We've got twenty-six hours to get her out.'

Samuel's wrinkles grimaced. 'We can't bring down the Marsh in a single day, lad.'

'I think we can,' I said.

They exchanged looks. Then my father said, 'Frieda offered you a deal?'

I nodded.

'Which was?'

'You can guess.'

'I can. It's what she does. And you came here instead of going to her with this address.'

He looked at Samuel, who nodded slowly and said, 'Ah well, for that we're grateful. So we must try.'

By midnight we'd thrashed our ideas around and come up with something that looked like a workable plan. Anna took Nomu and Raffael to show them where they could sleep and returned for Samuel but he was deep in discussion with my father about the ethics of some political movement I'd never heard of and she raised her eyes to heaven and smiled at me. I helped her clear the table and as I piled the dishes by the kitchen sink I said, 'Thank you—that food was fantastic.'

She put her hands on my shoulders and looked me directly in the eye. 'Look at you,' she said. 'So like your mother. All evening I have been sitting at the table wishing she could see you now.'

Her eyes got misty and she turned away to run water.

I hunted for a teatowel—the kitchen was like the dining room, crowded with old stuff, all of it hard used, but beautiful too: a wooden dresser with blue-and-white plates and cups, a work table made of a great hunk of wood whose surface had worn unevenly, a solid, ancient-looking oven. It felt well lived in; it invited you to relax and tell the story of what you'd done with your day. I was trying to work out how to ask Anna about my parents, but she was way ahead of me.

'You should talk to your father,' she said before I'd opened my mouth. She looked at me with smiling dark eyes. 'About your mother. Why not? Are you afraid to?'

'No, of course not.' I dried a plate and put it up on a shelf. 'A bit…maybe.'

'Talk to him. You both deserve that conversation.'

When we went back to the dining room Anna

hooked her arm through Samuel's and said, 'Come, old man.' He grumbled but he stood up, grunted goodnight and they left.

My father hunted in his pockets for a cigarette, found one, stared at it and put it away unlit. He saw me watching and said, 'Saving it for when I really need it.'

I sat down opposite him at the table and said, 'Tell me about Elena and the security services.'

He took the cigarette out again.

'Funny,' I said.

He snorted a laugh, then grew serious. 'Elena. Your mother was Breken, you know that. She grew up on City-side in the days when that was still allowed. She was a gifted linguist—she spoke five languages fluently and could handle another two or three, no trouble. And, yes, she worked for the security services.'

He lit the cigarette, waved out the match and drew long squinting at me through the smoke.

'So did I.'

A bunch of things went 'click' in my head.

He waited for me to say something, and when I didn't he looked at me closely and said, 'You're not surprised.'

'I guess not,' I said. 'Frieda hates you. She *hates* you. Where does that come from except from you turning your back on something you believed in together.' I thought of Dash's scorn, Jono's contempt. Not so different. 'What happened?' I asked.

'I grew up on Cityside,' he said. 'I went into the army when I was about your age, but after a few years I applied to be a security agent and went to the Marsh to learn how. That's where I met Elena. We were both working in the Marsh when you were born. But then Daniel Montier was captured and brought in. He'd been leading the Southside uprising at that time and I was assigned to follow his interrogation.'

He sighed and ran a hand through his short greying hair. 'Montier was a wise, intelligent, committed man with a gift for leadership and a desire for peace and we slowly destroyed his mind. Elena was the interpreter for his interrogation. In the end she and I conspired to get him out. Not soon enough though.' He paused and looked at me. 'He was never again the man who went into the Marsh. We lost a leader we sorely needed. Your mother and I were found out soon enough and we had to get out.'

'Why didn't Elena go over the river then?' I asked. 'Why did she stay here?'

'She didn't stay here. But Southside was being shelled every day and it was too dangerous to take you there, so she took you west to a safehouse.'

'Oh. What happened?'

He smoked the last of the cigarette and pitched it into the fireplace. 'It wasn't safe enough,' he said. 'They found her and took you.'

I shook my head. 'I don't remember.'

His smile was grim. 'I do.'

'Why don't I remember? I remember being with her when someone raided our rooms. I remember standing with Frieda at the gates of Tornmoor. I don't remember anything in between.'

'You know what they're good at. Work it out.'

'They drugged me? They drugged a four year old?'

'That would be my guess.'

I put the pieces together. 'So Frieda makes a deal with Elena and Elena hands you over. For me. To get me back.'

He nodded. 'We talked about it and that's what we came to.'

'You knew!'

'Of course. I told them I'd come in, alone, but no, they had to send someone to bring me in. They sent De Faux.'

The man who'd tried to assassinate Commander Vega in the winter just gone. I remembered Levkova telling me about him.

'He killed Daniel Montier,' I said.

My father nodded. 'May he roast in his own private corner of hell.'

'And Elena?' I asked. 'What happened to her?'

'I never found out. And, believe me, I tried.'

'Do you think she's dead?'

He glanced at me. 'I do.'

Silence fell between us. I said, 'I'm sorry.' It came out as a whisper.

'I am too,' he said. 'I'm sorry you didn't know her better, or for longer. She was remarkable.'

I said, '"Your dead stay with you." That's what you said to me on the Mol last winter. "They pitch camp in your mind."' I looked at him. 'She has stayed with me.'

He smiled a genuine smile. 'And me.'

'Tomorrow,' I said. 'We get Lanya out.'

'Yes,' he said. 'Yes, we do.'

CHAPTER 30

I left Anna and Samuel's house early on Friday morning and walked to the Marsh. Fog hovered at ground level across its flat fields and the sun was just up in a pale, clear sky—I figured it was light enough that they wouldn't shoot me without asking a question or two first. The air was cool and damp and it would have been a good time to be out and walking if my heart hadn't been hammering so loud and I didn't feel queasy with fear.

I stopped at the guardhouse by one of the vehicle barriers and told the guy inside that I had a message for Director Kelleran. I handed him a sealed envelope and said I'd wait there for her reply. He called in a minion who beetled off with it to the main cluster of buildings. I imagined him knocking tentatively on a basement door where Frieda slept hanging upsidedown from a rafter with her wings wrapped around her.

My note said: *I have what you want. Bring Lanya to St John's at midday.*

Her reply came back fast: *Yes.*

This far, so good, as Raffael would say.

St John's was cool inside and marble quiet. My father sat on the steps leading up to the altar, and I walked up and down the aisle until he told me to stop, I was making him nervous.

'*I'm* making you nervous?' I said.

'Fair point. The likelihood of the army descending on us is making me nervous, but you're not helping.'

'I don't think you should be here,' I said. 'What if the army does descend on us?'

'Then we'll cope. We're bringing down the Marsh today, remember?'

I sat down beside him and tried to act as calm as he looked. As the bells began to strike noon over our heads the latch on the big double doors clacked and they swung open.

'Ah, Frieda,' he muttered. 'Always one for a fanfare.'

I jumped to my feet as she marched up the aisle. She was as grey and pale as usual, wearing dark glasses that hid her expression. She left two agents at the door and another two walked around the perimeter, hand guns drawn, peering into side chapels. Behind Frieda came Dash and Jono, pinpoint neat in black, and between them they marshalled a wrecked-looking Sandor. I looked past him for Lanya with a fleeting thought that he'd be bugged by how filthy his clothes had got.

Frieda took off her glasses and raised her eyebrows at my father. 'Well,' she said. 'The whole family.'

My father opened his hands. 'As you see.'

I said, 'Where's Lanya?'

But Frieda was still looking at my father. 'Why are you here?' she asked.

He smiled.

Her gaze darted around the church as though she was expecting hostiles to leap from the upper balcony and abseil to the attack.

Behind us someone opened a door and peered in. The minister—I recognised him from when we'd sheltered here after the Tornmoor bombing. He was a youngish guy with receding hair and sharp, intelligent eyes. He wasn't happy.

He pointed at the agent moving up the altar steps. 'No guns in here!'

The agent looked back to Frieda who gestured towards the crypt. 'Put him in there for now. Until we're done.'

The minister objected, loudly, but no one was listening.

When they'd shut the door on him Frieda turned back to me. 'So, you found your father. I should warn you, it won't be to your advantage. He worked for us, did you know that?'

'Where's Lanya?' I asked again.

'Hey!' called Sandor. 'Pleased to see me?'

I said in Breken, 'Sure, Sandor. You all right? You look terrible.' Serves you right for trading on Nomu.

'Yeah. Feel terrible.' He leaned on a pew.

'What about Lanya?' I asked.

'Not yet,' said Frieda. 'I brought you this one. You'll get the other one when I've verified your information.'

She nodded to Dash who marched up to me and said, 'I hope you've seen sense. Tell me you have.'

When I didn't immediately hand over anything that looked like information she glared at me and muttered, 'But what are the odds?'

I stepped around her and said to Frieda, 'This wasn't the deal.'

'Hey!' said Sandor. 'Remember me? I'm not here to be haggled over, you know.' He shuffled away from Jono, sat down in the front pew and wiped a hand over his face. 'I need a medic,' he said.

I said to Frieda, 'We had a deal!'

Behind me, my father said, 'Nothing changes.'

Her gaze slid past me to him. 'What did you expect?'

'This,' he said. 'How unoriginal of you.'

She shook her head. 'Why are you here? You're infecting your son with the same romantic revolutionary delusions you brainwashed Elena with. It will cost him the same way it cost her—'

'No, no,' said my father. 'Let me at least correct the record. Elena was a much more principled idealist than I ever was. She convinced me there was hope for peace because Southside had a leader who was prepared to negotiate. The problem was, they had that leader and we didn't. Some things don't change. Many things.'

'Good sense doesn't change,' said Frieda. 'Daniel Montier was a dead man the moment he walked into the Marsh. What was the point of getting him out? You had everything to lose and you lost it.'

'Not quite,' said my father.

'Nonsense. You lost the boy, you lost Elena, you lost the uprising. I think that counts as everything.'

My father looked at her for a moment then said, 'We're not here to reinvent the past. We're here to get Lanya back. And you haven't brought her.'

'I'm waiting for some genuine intelligence,' she said. 'And I mean that in both senses of the word.'

Her comms unit buzzed and she squinted at it, then said to me. 'Don't make the mistake your mother made.'

'I've already made it,' I said. 'I thought you'd keep your word.'

'And I will. As soon as you provide the information and it's been verified. Your mother's fate, for the record—' she glared at my father '—had nothing to do with me.

I would have kept her on as an agent but my superiors decided she was too compromised. They were probably right. Loose ends, you see. We don't like them.'

'What happened to her?' I asked.

She sighed impatiently. 'I don't have time for this.'

My father said, 'Yes, you do. You've got at least two spare minutes and all the guns. Tell him.'

Frieda looked from my father to me. Her eyebrows lifted slightly as if she was calculating the pros and cons. Then she relented.

'Elena discovered you were at Tornmoor. She went to get you back. Stapleton reported that she wouldn't leave until she'd seen you, so we were sent to take her away: myself, and two others.'

She hesitated and I thought I saw a shadow of regret pass over her face, but maybe I imagined it.

She went on, 'We persuaded her to come with us to the Marsh and in the car on the way one of the agents pressed a poisoned needle into her neck. Very simple. Very quick. Within an hour she was dead. I didn't know that was going to happen—you won't believe that, but it's true. At least it was quick and relatively painless. There's some mercy in that.'

Mercy. Everything this war was not.

'No,' I said. 'You do not get to use that word.'

I turned away and walked back towards my father.

'Wait!' she called. 'What about my information?

What about the girl?'

'Taking my chances on that,' I said.

'Her comms unit buzzed a second time.

I turned back to her. 'You should answer that. It's probably important.'

'Arrest them,' she said as she unhooked her comms unit and looked at its message.

Jono pulled his gun and yelled, 'Freeze!' in a voice that bounced all the way up to the roof and back.

'Cool it, Jono,' muttered Dash.

Dash, I trusted not to shoot me, but Jono, never, not even in a church. I retreated to the altar steps and sat down beside my father. Jono advanced up the aisle, gun still raised until he stood close enough that I could see the sweat on his upper lip and the glint in his eyes over the gun.

Dash came up beside him. 'I said, cool it. He's not going anywhere. Enough already.'

Jono lowered the gun, but he didn't holster it. I was getting his very best stare. I thought about asking him if he practised it in the mirror every morning. I said, 'Thanks,' to Dash instead.

'You're such an idiot,' she said to me.

'Hey,' wailed Sandor. 'What about me? I need a medic.'

I fished in a pocket and found the remains of Mr Hendry's cash, handed some of it to Dash. 'Give him this.'

He brightened immediately, pocketed it and gave me a nod then heaved himself upright and headed slowly for a door.

'It's for a medic,' I called after him.

Frieda was still on her comms unit talking ferociously and directing angry glances towards us.

'Do you know what's going on?' Dash asked Jono.

'I do,' I said.

They both looked at me as if to say 'Yeah, right.'

'It's Nomu,' I said. 'The lost girl from the Dry. She's been found, and right now she's appearing on Cityside News, telling everyone that the disease that came to her people in the Dry has come to town and if people here want the vaccine they can get it from the Marsh. But they'd better hurry because there's not enough for everyone.'

Dash looked puzzled. 'What are you talking about?'

I smiled at her and didn't answer.

Frieda had finished on her comms unit in time to hear the last of what I was saying.

'So this is your plan?' she said. 'You think a mob will descend on the Marsh and bring it down?'

'Something like that,' I said.

She looked at me like I was deluded. 'No mob will be taking the Marsh while its under my command.'

'Your command?' said my father. 'You do the bidding of people in the shadows who'll never admit to what happens in the Marsh. You do as you're told and that's all you do. The Marsh is not under your command.'

She advanced on him, eyes blazing. This was an old argument born of old enmity. She almost hissed at him.

'All I do? All? No. This is my time. *I'm* ending this war. You have failed, as usual. Moldam is finished. The virus is there now. Surrender of the South will follow because every other settlement will know that they could be next and that we hold the vaccine.'

My mouth went dry. My father swore.

'That's right,' said Frieda. 'The squad that went to Moldam looking for the Dry-dweller girl. They left it wherever they went.'

The Marsh was going up in flames. The fence on the western perimeter was down—a combination of the weight of numbers pushing on it and a judicious use of boltcutters. If the order to fire on the crowd had been given, it hadn't been obeyed; maybe the guards had abandoned their posts to be first in line to grab a box of the vaccine or, better, maybe they'd seen people they knew coming over the fence and couldn't face killing their own. Either way, the crowd was now going from building to building unopposed.

But the Marsh is big—almost a small town. And a lot of it is classified; you're supposed to know where you're going or you shouldn't be there, so there weren't any signs saying *HV–C6 Vaccines: Get them here!* There must have been people still in the grounds who knew where that storehouse was but they were lying low.

Frieda had brought my father and me back to the Marsh from St John's. She'd left us in different buildings to be processed separately and she'd gone off with Dash and Jono to pull the situation out of the fire—that was before any actual fires were lit. Now it was looking like she wouldn't be getting a performance bonus this year.

Meanwhile, I'd got away from the guy taking me to my cell by the fairly simple ploy of threatening to breathe on him. As we walked down a corridor I'd grabbed the comms device clipped to his belt and when he yelled, 'Hey!' and went to take it off me, I backed away and said, 'I was in Moldam yesterday. In a house where your special ops team planted that virus. Want me to breathe on you?'

He said 'Christ,' or words to that effect and stood there eyeing me and the device.

I waved it at him. 'Touched it now.'

Then I lunged towards him, and he bolted. The device was multifunctional and let me pull up a plan of the Marsh. I was looking for some reference to who was being held where. And yes, there she was: *Breken female, adolescent. Order: interrogation. Regime: sodium pentothal. Authorised by: Dir. Kelleran. Ward 23.*

Found a map. Went for it.

The first time I ever saw Lanya she was holding her own in a knife fight on a Moldam back street. The second time I saw her, a few hours later, ten thousand other people were watching her too as she and the other Moldam

Pathmakers danced with firesticks across a barren stretch of land near Moldam Bridge to honour six people killed in the uprising. She was barefoot and fierce, those braids and beads flying, and all of her, body and spirit moving to the needs of the fight and the beat of the drums and their song.

I remembered that as I ran through the corridors of the Marsh trying to find her and not knowing how she would be when I got there. I remembered it and told myself she would survive. I ran three flights of stairs, eight corridors, twenty-one sets of firedoors to get to Ward 23.

No one stopped me. Everyone else was going the other way, because the siren ordering the evacuation of the building was blasting in every corridor. The staff had taken off: computer monitors were blank, paper cups of tea sat half drunk on desks and empty ones rolled on the floor.

I yelled in Breken, 'Lanya! Are you here? Where are you?' I looked into every room off the main corridor—all of them empty. It looked like the staff had let the inmates go. 'Lanya!'

Then a figure came out of a room at the end of the corridor. A familiar figure and not in a good way.

Jono. My stomach did a flip.

'What are you doing here?' I said. 'Everyone's left, hadn't you noticed?'

He leaned in a doorway. 'Yeah, I noticed. I was waiting for you.'

'Where is she?'

'Gone.'

'Gone where?'

He smirked.

'I'm sick,' I said. 'Infected. I'll breathe on you if you don't tell me.'

The smirk widened. 'I've been vaccinated—one of the perks of being on Kelleran's team. You're no threat, never were.'

I turned away and yelled again. 'Lanya! You here?'

The sirens drowned me out; they were doing my head in. I went along the corridor looking again into every room. Jono watched me, and eventually I came back to him.

'Where is she?'

'She was here,' he said. 'Until a couple of hours ago. I took her away when we got back from St John's. I decided she should be with her own kind.'

His comms unit pinged. He glanced at it. 'Dash. Gone soft, has Dash.' He nodded up the corridor. 'I'll take you. Cos they're your kind too.'

We retraced my steps down to the ground floor until we were right back where I'd started but Jono kept going—outside, away from those ear-busting sirens. There was full scale looting going on now; some people seemed to have forgotten their quest for the vaccine and were carrying away computers and cc-eyes along with all kinds of other tech, and some were even clumsily lugging furniture away. The speed of the collapse was mind boggling: the most feared place in the city brought to its knees by fear. A reporter with a microphone and a cameraman in tow was trying to pull people together to organise a search for the vaccine storehouse. He was shouting, 'People! People! Listen to me! Let's divide into search groups!'

Jono headed east along an asphalt walkway lined with trees and bushes. I was so preoccupied with being scared for Lanya that when Jono swung round and punched me hard in the gut I didn't see it coming. I hit the ground. He stood over me and I thought I was going to get a boot in the face. I rolled away and stumbled up gasping, 'What the f—?'

'You turned Fy,' he said. 'I won't forgive that.'

I put my head down, hands on knees, and tried to breathe. When I had air enough I said, 'Wasn't me. It was all her.'

'Bullshit! She was never like that before.'

'Yeah, she was.' I found a tree to prop me up. 'We never noticed, that's all.' Before he could object I said, 'She's her own person, you moron. She's not gonna do what someone says just because they're in charge or they're giving the orders that day.'

'Had a nice cosy time over the river, did you?'

'Looking for Sol? Sure. It was a bundle of laughs.'

Then it dawned on me what he meant. I straightened up.

'Is that what you're aggro about? You think we got together over the river?'

He didn't say anything but his gaze slid away.

I said, 'Well, I'm sorry to set whatever mind you have at rest, but we didn't.'

His eyebrows went up, and then came the smirk again. 'Just friends, then.'

'As if that's a small thing. You know fuck-all. Can we get going?'

We arrived at last way out on the eastern fenceline, at a boring-looking building that I took to be a storehouse. But inside we went downstairs through a series of doors that Jono had the codes for, and two levels down the place opened up into a maze of corridors and labs. We stopped outside a double set of doors in an airlock arrangement so that you went through the first one and waited for it to close before you could open the second. There should have been biohazard suits hanging in there, but I guess they'd suddenly become valuable and someone had filched them.

Behind me Jono pressed an intercom switch. 'Visitor for you,' he said and opened the first door. I went in and peered through the window in the next door. Lanya came straight up to it, eyes wide, hands on the glass.

I punched the door button to go in. Nothing

happened. Pushed it again. Still nothing.

I turned round to Jono saying, 'You want me to go in or don't you?'

But the door back to him was shut. And locked. I yelled and pounded on it. He smiled at me, tapped the glass and went away. I found the intercom.

'Lanya? Can you hear me?'

She nodded.

'Can you open this door?'

She shook her head.

'Find the intercom switch,' I said.

She looked around and found something, pressed it and I heard her voice. 'Nik! Get me out of here!'

'I'm trying,' I said.

I levered the cover off the elock and peered at its insides. Then I realised something important and looked back at her.

'Hurry!' she said. 'What's the matter?'

I was looking into her eyes and she was looking right back with all the smarts I knew she had.

'You're supposed to be all drugged up.' I was starting to smile.

She shook her head. 'They gave me one injection early on and that's all. Hurry, Nik. There are bodies in cages.'

'Cages?'

'Hurry!'

'I'm trying, I'm trying. Don't touch anything.'

'I said a crossing prayer for them. They're just kids. Please hurry!'

I was looking at the elock innards, still puzzling over what she'd said.

'Did you say one injection?' Then I remembered what Jono had said about Dash. 'Did you see Dash?'

'Wasting your time,' said Jono's voice. I spun round to see where he was. 'Look up!' he said.

'Up?' I stared round my small airlock space. Then Lanya knocked on the glass and pointed. And there he was, in the observation window high in the wall of the room she was in.

His voice came through my intercom and presumably hers as well.

'Dash went soft, like I said. You won't open that door. There's a master control here that overrides it.'

'What are you doing?' I said.

'Justice,' he said. 'I'm doing justice. I lost Fyffe cos of you. Now you get to find out what that's like.'

I think my heart stopped, then it started again with a thump and went full-on like someone had rammed a lever up to maximum.

'Jono—'

'Shut up! Ever seen anyone die of a nerve agent?'

'Christ, Jono!'

'Thought not. Watch closely then.'

I switched off the intercom to Jono so he couldn't hear me and covered the cc-eye so he couldn't see me, then said to Lanya, 'Go find a biohazard suit. They must have an emergency one in there somewhere.'

'What are you doing?' she asked.

'Calling the cavalry.'

'The what?'

'Just go!'

I switched the intercom between Jono and me back on and heard him saying, 'Uncover that camera!'

I was hunting through the multi-device I'd taken earlier in the day searching for a comms contact for Dash. I could hear Jono clattering about, swearing under his breath. It sounded like he'd discovered that he couldn't simply plug a cannister of nerve gas into the relevant airvent and flick a switch. File that under hope: faint but real.

I found *Bannister, Ashleigh* at last and started to type a message to her. But where the hell were we? The Marsh and its stupid anonymous buildings.

I closed my eyes and went back to the path we'd walked down, saw the building as we came to it, saw the door that Jono opened: there was a number above it—a code instead of a sign for whatever happened in that building. Got it. Typed: *Store 36C–P1, Level G minus 2. Speed or death. Seriously. N.* Pressed SEND. Prayed.

'Uncover that camera,' yelled Jono.

Speed or death was a game we had played at Tornmoor—its real name was probably something like Tactical Training Exercise No. 48. But we didn't know then that the security services ran the school—all we knew was that they came every year to recruit the best of the senior students—Jono, for example, and Dash.

In fact, there was nothing tactical about that game; it was just brute speed over an impromptu obstacle course through the buildings and grounds of the school. If you didn't make it in time you were 'dead'. As the game went on the time for each run got shorter and shorter—everyone was 'dead' by the end.

I looked through the glass to see what Lanya was doing, but I couldn't see the whole room and I couldn't see her. I typed a second, longer message to Dash and talked to Jono.

'You want to burn your entire career on a single act

of revenge? Nothing happened between Fy and me. We helped each other out, that's all.'

Lanya appeared at my window. I turned off comms to Jono.

'I found a cupboard,' she said. 'It's got a symbol on it, could be a bio-suit, but it's locked.'

'Okay,' I said. 'I'll try and find a code for it.'

I dived into the multi-device again and switched Jono back on.

'Remember chemistry class?' he was saying. 'Remember nerve agents?'

Yes, I remembered nerve agents. But they were just fodder for assessment then.

'Remember what they do to people? Are you listening to me?'

'Yes, I'm listening.'

'I found them. The nerve agent cannisters. I found where they're stored, and I'm going to get one. Don't go away!'

I wasn't sure whether to believe him. I'd been hearing a lot of keyboard activity up there. With luck, he needed a code he didn't have to get what he wanted. Same as me.

I went back to the multi, trawling through layers of the Marsh: departments, operations, special projects. I shut out everything else: Jono crowing upstairs, Lanya standing staunch on the other side of the door, Dash running—please God, running—this way. I shut it all out and searched for this room on the multi. For the location of the emergency suit inside the cabinet inside the room. For the code that would unlock it. It had to be there. Every problem-solving, code-breaking, proof-finding effort I'd ever made I poured into the search for that code.

I couldn't find it.

As far as the multi was concerned the room Lanya was in didn't exist. The emergency cabinet didn't exist. The bio-suit inside it didn't exist. Lanya put a hand on the glass.

'Nik, I can't wait for you. I'm going up there.'

She'd pulled a fire extinguisher off the wall and was wrapping it in a sheet she'd found.

'What are you doing?' I said.

She stood up. 'Making a harness. Gonna climb a cage and smash that window.'

I looked up at the window, thought it would be reinforced glass, but didn't say so.

She hauled on her makeshift sheet harness and strapped the extinguisher to her back, adjusted it, tightened it.

'I know,' she said. 'It'll be reinforced, maybe even bullet proof. But d'you think he knows that? Even if he does, d'you think he'll risk it?' She looked at me—bright, fierce, so beautiful—and smiled. 'Wish me luck!'

I laughed, despite it all.

'Hey!' yelled Jono. 'I'm back! Look!' We both looked

up to see him holding a small cannister. 'Here it is!'

Lanya ran for the cage directly beneath the window and started to scramble up it. She was halfway there before Jono noticed what she was doing and then even he stopped to watch her. She reached the top, hauled herself onto it and crawled carefully across the mesh until she could stand up and almost look him in the eye. She took off the harness and tied the extinguisher into it so she could swing it at him.

The grin left Jono's face. They stood glaring at each other, daring each other.

'I'll do it,' he said.

'You'll die,' I said.

'So will she.'

Keep talking, I thought. Never my strong point.

'Did you calibrate the canister size to the room size?' I said.

No answer.

I bet you didn't, I thought. I had no idea if it mattered—probably the canister was easily big enough for a lethal contamination of the whole room, but I was chasing any nanosecond of doubt and delay I could catch.

'Fuck you,' he said. 'Say your prayers.'

CHAPTER 33

I yelled something wordless and desperate.

Jono yelled too, but not at me. Dash's voice came through the intercom.

'Stand down, Jono! Jono! Stand down or I will shoot you.'

'You're a joke,' he sneered.

'You think?' she said. The intercom blared a wild burst of static and Jono yelped a short, sharp scream.

I heard Dash again, crisp, all business.

'Nik? He's down. Are you there?'

I breathed. 'Yes,' my voice shaken loose in my throat.

'Speed or death! For real this time. You won't believe the obstacle course out there right now.' She paused and peered through the window. 'What is this place? What's going on?'

'Let me in there.'

'Hold on.'

'Now, Dash!'

'In a second. I'm looking for the door release.'

She was poring over what must have been a console and peering into the room.

'Did you shoot him?' I asked.

'No, tasered. I've cuffed him and he won't move for a while.'

Lanya had left the sheet and the fire extinguisher on the top of the cage and was climbing down.

I kicked the door. 'Dash! Hurry up.'

'All right, all right! There! Go!'

The lock clicked, the door slid and I ran into a wall of warm air so stale and stinking it made me gag. The room was a festering sore: lines of cages reached up to the level of the observation window whose white rectangle of light outshone the dim fluoro tubes way above our heads. The air was rank with disinfectant, sweat and sewage and something else: the sweet stink I'd known in Moldam—bodies decomposing in the heat.

Lanya had reached the floor and sagged into a crouch, head bowed. She was shaking and breathing hard. I crouched beside her, lifted the braids off her face. They were dripping with sweat.

She turned away. 'Gonna throw up.'

She took a deep breath, held it, blew it out, shuddering. She turned back to me.

'No. I'm all right.' She gave me a bleak almost-smile and started to get to her feet. I put out a hand to help but she turned away. 'No. Don't touch me.'

'Hey.'

'I'm okay, but…' Her eyes were dark and wide and dazed. Her face shone with sweat and she was clinging to the wire of the cage to stay upright. 'They're all dead. I called to them and none of them moved. I tried not to touch them, but I had to see. Their skin is all bruises and their eyes…their eyes are full of blood—'

She stopped to catch her breath.

'Take it easy,' I said. 'We're getting out of here now.'

'No, you don't understand.' Her voice was shaking. 'They've been shot.'

'Jesus. What?'

'A bullet to the head, every one of them. Someone must have panicked when the looting started, they couldn't let infected people get outside. They're sick with something terrible, or they were. This is what's coming to Moldam, Nik! That agent—the one who brought me here—that's what he told me.'

'Stop. Take my hand.'

She shook her head. 'I've been in here for hours— I've breathed the air and bent over bodies and touched that sheet. The sickness will be in me now. You can't touch me. You mustn't.'

'At least let's get out of here?'

She nodded and let go of the cage, but then swayed where she stood and began to fold.

I caught her as she fell and held her while she vomited a stream of something pale and thin; she spat the last of it out, gasping, and wiped her mouth. She was shivering in short spasms and breathing with effort. I turned her towards me, put her head on my shoulder and held her.

It was whole minutes before she stopped shaking. Then she lifted her head to look at me. I kissed her forehead and, lightly, her lips.

She pulled back and whispered, 'Why did you do that? What if I'm sick?'

'Why do you think? Can you stand?'

She nodded, and we left the room at last, but for a long time after that my skin crawled with the heat and stink of it.

Upstairs, the observation area was empty—Dash had taken Jono away. The room wasn't much wider than its window and only half a dozen paces deep; it seemed that its sole purpose was as a place to watch lab rats perform and/or die. A bank of screens and controls took up half the space beneath the window, a table with chairs the other half. There was also a large paper shredder at the back with a pile of shreds underneath it and its red light blinking. Someone had been busy. I sat down at the console: the computer was logged in—thank you, Jono—and gave me access to much more than I'd got from the multi-device.

I hunted through the system looking for anything that might point us in the direction of the vaccine, preferably roomfuls of the stuff that would be enough for us and all of Moldam. Lanya leaned against the desk beside me, watching my face.

'Suppose I'm infected,' she said. 'You could be too, now.'

'Like it was your fault you ended up in there?'

I went back to the screen. 'Look at this. It's a map of this place. But now what? Labs? Would they keep the vaccine in labs? Or storerooms? What about storerooms attached to labs? Or storerooms miles away from labs to hide them better? Or,' I sat back, 'none of the above because it's all so freakin' secret that only Frieda knows for sure?'

'What good's a vaccine if we're already sick?'

'If we get it early enough—Raffael told me—if we get it early enough, we stand a good chance of not dying.'

She studied me, not believing. 'Do you know anything about the symptoms?' She was back looking down at the bodies.

I shook my head. 'Don't look at them.'

I still couldn't find anything on the stupid system. I hunted round in the console drawer and found a pen and a scrappy notepad that looked like it had lost most of its pages to the shredder. I started jotting down the room codes, looking for patterns, but that gave me nothing. I tried tracking people who'd logged in to the observation room over the last seven days. Frieda had visited three days before. Had she then gone off to gloat in private over her store of vaccines? No, it looked like she'd gone back to her office. Who else had been in? Not that many people—half a dozen or so, including Jono who'd come with Frieda, but not Dash. Frieda's Operation Havoc was looking like a close-kept secret.

Lanya was watching over my shoulder. When I sat back, thinking I'd reached a dead end, she said, 'All right. At least we have something to work with.'

'We do? What?'

Her voice began to lighten and lift as she got into problem-solving mode. 'We—you and me—are now something that Frieda hasn't planned for. Havoc on the loose.'

I looked at her. 'That's true.'

Dash came through the door. 'All done. He's locked up. I'll go back and get him when he's good and quiet.' She peered out the observation window, frowning. 'What is this place?'

'You really don't know?' I said.

'Never been here.' She picked up the cannister Jono had been waving around and read the label on it. Her eyebrows shot up. 'This really is nerve gas. You weren't kidding.' She looked out the window again. 'What's in the cages?'

'You mean who,' I said.

'What?'

'Don't be dim,' I said. 'What do you think the Marsh is for?'

She darted me a look of alarm and disbelief and then walked along the window trying to get a better view below. 'Is that true? Are there people down there? I mean—'

'Yes,' said Lanya. 'People. And yes, they're dead.'

Dash had gone pale. 'What did they die of? Not nerve gas, or you'd be dead too.'

'They died,' said Lanya, 'of Frieda Kelleran's plan for Moldam.'

Dash turned her back on the window and gave us her full attention. 'From the top, please.'

'But you know this,' I said. 'You heard Frieda in St John's all of—I don't know—six hours ago? She said they'd released the virus in Moldam. What did you think she meant?'

'They what?' said Lanya. 'They've done it?'

I nodded. 'Dash?'

'I don't know!' she said. 'I heard and didn't hear. I thought she was trying to scare you. I didn't know what she meant.'

She looked around the room at all the tech, out the window at the cages, and finally at me. 'Tell me.'

She listened, grim-faced, until I got to the exodus by Cityside's most powerful, and the blackmailing of the

Dry-dwellers. She shook her head at that.

'I don't buy it,' she said. 'It has to be coincidence, that timing. Who told you?'

'Someone I believe.'

Dash's eyes narrowed. 'The Hendrys wouldn't be in on something like that.'

'Take a look around you!' I said. 'D'you think Frieda's on a power trip all her own to end the war? Someone's pulling the strings.'

'Yes, but not those families—'

'Why not? She has her own lackeys, the ones who do the poisoned needles into necks and truncheons smashing knees so that she can claim no knowlege of any of that. But she's a lackey too, and what she does is another version of the same thing.

'You want rid of the people who might crowd your space and your comfortable life? Sure you do, but you're not gonna do it yourself and you're not gonna do it by taking the long way round—sitting down and talking—because that would mean compromise and mess and your comfortable life might get fractionally less comfortable at the margins, and let's face it, you want it all, even at the margins. So you convince yourself that compromise means defeat, and you tell your lackey to deal with it, but you clear out while she does that because you can't actually bear to watch what you've set in train. No, you go off to impose yourself on some other second-class people who only really exist for your benefit anyway.'

Dash and Lanya were both staring at me.

I shrugged. 'End of rant. Except that Frieda didn't count on Jono throwing Lanya in that room.'

'No,' said Dash. 'I see that. How long were you in there?'

'Long enough,' I said.

'Then you need help,' said Dash, on firm ground now that she had something she could do. 'A doctor. We need to find some vaccine for the two of you. To get you out of danger.' She was at the door in two paces.

'No,' said Lanya. She'd been looking down into the cages below, listening. Now she turned round and said, 'It's not so easy.'

'I know,' said Dash. 'I've no idea where to look, but if I find a doctor—'

'I mean,' said Lanya, and she looked at me, 'all of Moldam gets the vaccine, or none of us gets it.'

She held my gaze to see how that settled on me, and I saw where she meant to go, and where I would have to go if I wanted to be with her.

'Forget it,' Dash was saying. 'You don't bargain with Frieda. Do you think she cares about you dying of some virus?'

'No,' said Lanya. 'But she will care about the whole city dying of it.'

'Which is not about to happen,' said Dash. 'How

could it?' She looked at me.

'Weaponised humans,' I said, finding my voice at last. 'Frieda made the virus into a weapon. But she thought it would be safely contained in Moldam. She didn't count on Moldam coming to town.'

Dash's blue eyes got wide. 'But you're not going into town. No way! I won't let you. And even if you could, Frieda will hunt you down.'

'Yes, she will,' I said. 'But only if she knows where to look.'

Dash shook her head. 'I can't be a part of this. I'm sworn to protect the city.'

'The whole city?' I asked.

Her comms unit buzzed.

'Hold on,' she said. She studied at its message, glanced at us, clipped it back on her belt.

'The army's here, upstairs, and—'

But before she could finish, an intercom buzzed and a voice blared in the corridor ordering everyone who was not authorised to be within the perimeter of the Marsh to leave now or face immediate arrest.

'I've been ordered to report for duty,' said Dash. 'The mob's being rounded up. It's over.'

CHAPTER 34

Lanya bowed her head to her knees, took a deep breath and came upright with a long breath out and a look on her face that I knew well—that blaze of energy she found when she was in the heart of a Pathmaker dance, all of her focused and burning bright.

'We're leaving,' she said.

Dash moved to the doorway. 'I won't let you do that.'

She unclipped her gun and hefted it in her palm.

'Then shoot us,' said Lanya. 'The Kelleran woman will, when she finds us here.'

'She won't find you,' said Dash. 'Let me hide you here while I go and find the vaccine.'

The corridor intercom blared again and made us all jump. It repeated the order for people to leave or be arrested. Any minute now the army would be charging down to this level searching for troublemakers.

I shook my head. 'They'll find us. You have to take us into town or hand us over.'

'You'll be putting the whole city at risk,' she said. 'I can't let you do that.'

'The whole city is already at risk,' I said. 'And Moldam's well past risk. The virus is there, Dash. Thousands of people are about to get sick and die!'

'But—'

'There is no but,' said Lanya. 'There is mass death of people who have done nothing to deserve it except be born on the wrong side of the river, or there is all of Cityside in fear for their lives crying at the Kelleran woman to release the Havoc vaccine for Moldam. Those are your choices.'

Long pause. Long, long pause.

Dash said, to me, 'You'd actually do this? Kill people?'

I said, 'We have to put pressure on Frieda to vaccinate Moldam. What do you suggest? We ask nicely? Or we make people realise that the quarantine on Moldam won't hold, because, look: here we are, from Moldam, infected, and in Cityside.'

Dash shook her head. 'But why do you have to be infected—just the rumour should be enough.'

'Do you know where the vaccines are?'

'No.'

'I was in Moldam yesterday and Lanya's been in that room down there. Chances are, we're infected.'

Another long pause.

'I'll take you to a med centre,' she said. 'It's that or nothing. Frieda won't find you, I promise. I'll give her a message from you—you can make it as threatening as you like, because, God knows, what she's done is so wrong, but I'm not taking you anywhere populated.'

Lanya and I looked at each other. I said, 'Deal.'

The intercom warning rattled us again; it wouldn't be long before this whole discussion became irrelevant. I grabbed back the pen, tore a page out of the notepad and wrote an ultimatum to Frieda. I showed it to Lanya who nodded and held it out to Dash.

'Wait,' I said. 'You've been vaccinated, right?'

Dash nodded. 'Routine protection against bio-terrorism. Which is what this is, by the way.'

'Tell that to Frieda,' I said.

Dash frowned at the message. 'This is in Breken.'

'I'm fairly sure Frieda can read Breken,' I said.

Dash shot me a glance. 'Yeah, that's not what I meant. You really are gone, aren't you.'

'Will you give it to her?'

She nodded, eyeing the signature at the bottom. 'Nikolai Stais. She won't know if it's you or your father.'

'Good. She's a lot more scared of him.'

'Maybe,' said Dash. 'How do I explain why I didn't shoot you on the spot?'

'Tell her we were gone by the time you got here.'

She thought about that, then hefted her gun again. 'Let's go.'

'Hold on,' I said. I scrawled another note, folded it and handed it to Dash. 'For Fyffe,' I said.

'What is it?'

'The whole point of this is no one dies, right? On her own, Frieda would do a deal with us on the quiet and then backtrack and we're dead. Simple. We need maximum exposure so that she can't finesse her way out. That means the whole of Cityside watching. Fyffe can make that happen.'

Dash shook her head. 'Two things. First, Frieda has the news channels under her thumb. They won't go near this without instructions from her. And secondly, Fyffe? Are you serious?'

'There you go, just like Jono. Give her the note, stand back and watch what happens.'

She shook her head again and pocketed the paper.

'You were never so organised in the old days.' She motioned us to the door. 'Don't breathe on anyone. Don't touch anything. And pray that we don't meet Frieda on the way out.'

In the corridor everything was blue lit, in power-saving mode, but ready to blaze up at any moment once the place was back under Frieda's control. We retraced our way along corridors and up stairs until we reached the door that we'd come through so very long ago.

So far, so deserted.

Outside it was dusk, still hot as hell, and the air was full of fury. In the grounds to the left of our building a battle surged and roared: lines of army in riot shields and gas masks were marching step by step into the swirling crowd, halting as volleys of stones clanged off their shields then advancing again. Tear gas canisters shot into the crowd and a water cannon arced through the billowing clouds of gas. The crowd was driven back and back. Then it surged forward again, charging in, hurling stuff and darting away.

They weren't your average Joe and Jo Public come to look for the vaccine. These people were dressed for battle in helmets and goggles, scarves wrapped round faces, and homemade shields cut from rubbish bins. Some of them picked up gas canisters with gloved hands and lobbed them back into the army ranks. Fires burned across the grounds adding smoke to the gas. Shouted orders came from both sides, as well as yells of outrage and abuse from the crowd. A megaphone blared at people to *Move Out, Move Out* and we heard shots fired—in the air, you hoped, but maybe not: we saw people with blood-streaked faces being dragged semi-conscious towards army trucks. By the time we'd gone a dozen paces our eyes were streaming and our lungs were burning.

'Be cool,' said Dash above the din. 'They want people to leave and we're leaving.'

Above us, above the smoke, the sky was glowing in the last light of a huge red sunset. Behind us the air rang with the echo of the megaphone, the explosion of gas canisters, the roar of the crowd and the clash of stone on riot shield. We reached the parking building where the vehicle fleet was kept. Dash waggled Jono's swipe card with a grin and used to it get us inside.

'Wait here,' she said. 'I'll get a car.'

Lanya and I retreated into the shadows of a stairwell. She leaned back on the wall and closed her eyes.

'Hey,' I said. 'How are you?'

'I am dead tired. And I stink.'

She plucked at her T-shirt in disgust. She was still wearing the black jeans and white T-shirt that Fyffe had given her but they were all kinds of filthy now.

'What's today?' she said. 'Friday? I haven't had a change of clothes in three days. Four! Nearly four days!'

She shivered and I wished I had a jacket to give her—I was in jeans and a T-shirt too and couldn't even remember what had happened to the jacket of Lou's that Fyffe had given me.

The minutes ticked by. Lanya said, 'I hope your friend hasn't changed her mind. Do you trust her?'

'I used to.'

'You were together, weren't you?' said Lanya. 'Once.'

'Yeah. There were six of us and we kind of paired up. People said we were good together.'

'Were you?'

'Mostly. Not always.'

'And now?'

'Now I don't know if I trust her at all, not after she landed me in this place. She said she was rescuing me. She's so sure of herself and her ideas about what's the right thing to do, it's pretty hard to convince her otherwise.'

Dash went everywhere with truckloads of confidence—always had. And that was great when you wanted to bask in the warm glow of infallibility while demolishing your opposition. Not so great when you were the opposition.

Lanya was quiet for a while but she shivered in little starts every half minute or so.

'Are you okay?' I asked.

'Are you going to ask me that every five minutes?'

'Probably.'

'Once every half hour, no more.'

'Raffael took my watch,' I said. 'I'll have to guess.'

A moment later Dash pulled up at the exit in a car with tinted windows. Lanya and I piled in the back.

Dash locked the doors. She was grim faced and unspeaking as she sped us towards the city, and I wondered what news she'd picked up when she went to get the car.

When we got to the parks and tree-lined streets of Bethun she said, 'There'll probably be roadblocks so keep quiet and let me do the talking.'

'Roadblocks?' I said. 'Why?'

'The unrest is spreading. People are ransacking warehouses in search of the vaccine, and One City has grabbed the chance to tip the whole city towards chaos. They've reoccupied Sentian, they're threatening to occupy Watch Hill and you've seen what they're doing at the Marsh. I guess they want a strong place to bargain from. And they hate the Marsh. Anyway, it means that the army will be stretched to get the city under control any time soon.'

Sure enough, when we turned into one of Bethun's wide avenues an army checkpoint pulled us up—young guy, gun, hand up, palm out, bright in front of a floodlight rigged on top of a truck.

Dash slid down her window and wielded her ID like a weapon. 'Soldier, I'm in a hurry.'

The kid on the receiving end jumped to attention, saluted and said, 'Ma'am! Thank you! You're free to go!'

His squadmates sniggered at him saluting a security agent and he tried to recover with a nonchalent wave of his hand and a grown-up 'Drive on.'

Dash pocketed the ID, put up the window and we drove away.

'Where are we going?' I asked.

'St Clare,' said Dash. 'Down near the bridge. There's a med centre there with someone I know on the staff. He'll help.'

We drove along empty streets past rows of darkened

buildings. Their windows were blank and black but I felt eyes on us, as though people were standing in the dark of doorways and windows watching us glide by.

We pulled up beside a concrete slab of a building with an unlit MED sign. Dash unlocked the door on Lanya's side and got out.

Lanya climbed out slowly, smiled at Dash, then bolted.

Dash yelled, 'Hey!' and pulled her gun. She shouted in Breken, 'Stop! Now!' and aimed at Lanya's back.

I launched myself out of the car and knocked her arm off target before she could fire, and by the time she'd regained her balance Lanya had disappeared into the darkness of the unlit street.

'No!' Dash wailed. 'No!' She turned the gun on me. 'You promised!'

'Whoa!' I held up both hands. 'Be cool, okay? Let me go after her.'

'No.' She shook her head, emphatic. 'You promised!'

'You have to let me. She won't know where it's safe to hide and she'll spread this thing without even meaning to.'

Dash flicked her glance despairingly from me to the street where Lanya had gone. 'Why are you doing this?' she demanded. 'You're risking your life, Nik. And it's not like they're even your people!'

I was watching her gun; it drew an unwavering bead on me. My breath was coming short and fast and I wondered if you could ever get used to staring down a gun barrel from the wrong end.

She said, 'The Hendrys are your people. And Fyffe. And me. And our friends from Tornmoor. Not Southsiders. You only met them six months ago.'

I looked away from her, towards the river. I wanted to slow things down, give Lanya time to run, let Dash's temper cool. The arch of the St Clare Bridge gleamed over the slow pulse of the water. I watched it for a few seconds then turned back to the metal gleam of the gun barrel and tried to speak without my voice shaking.

'It's not about who are my people. I don't have a tidy answer to that, anyway. It's about forty thousand innocent people and a war crime. You have to let me go after Lanya or she'll spread the disease whether she means to or not.'

The gun wavered. 'Where would you go?'

'I can't tell you that.'

'Let me come with you then.'

'In that uniform?'

'Okay, okay. At least come in and see if there's some vaccine here.'

I shook my head and her frown deepened.

'You don't trust me.'

I took two steps backwards still holding up both hands.

'I trust you not to shoot me.'

Three more steps back. Dash looked miserable.

Then I turned and ran after Lanya.

Dash yelled at me, but she didn't shoot.

Lanya was waiting in a darkened doorway two blocks away. She called out quietly as I jogged by and joined me on the road.

'You got away.'

I was still spooked. 'You nearly didn't.'

'She wouldn't have shot me?'

'I honestly don't know. If she thought it was the only way to stop you spreading a deadly disease through the whole of Cityside, then she might have.'

'Where are we going?'

'Sentian. To find a place to hide. And wait for Fyffe to make trouble.'

The lights were on in Sentian. Lamplight and bulb light and battery light and candlelight spilled out of the windows and doors of the tall houses wedged together along its alleyways, making the place seem inviting and homely. People were talking in little groups in their open doorways and there was plenty of foot traffic. So much for curfew and blackout, I thought. In fact, so much for the eviction of all those people whose houses were under notice of demolition; a sniff of victory and they'd come flooding back. They'd thrown a barricade across Bridge Street exactly where we'd seen the army trucks a few days before and people were milling about, still building it up, heaving torn mattresses across the skeltons of old cars, weighing them down with rubble from the beginnings of the demolition.

We went past slowly, avoiding attention, avoiding

people as much as we could.

Brown's and the Bard are in deepest, darkest Sentian, slumped together, their upper storeys leaning over the alley as though they're about to spill their books onto unsuspecting passers-by. That night they looked deserted.

'Dear Mr Corman,' I wrote on the notepad I'd taken from the Marsh. I explained that we were camping next door in the Bard and that he shouldn't come near us because of the virus. I signed the note with both our names and posted it through the door of Brown's, which was old enough to have a little slot in it for hard-copy mail.

'He'll be asleep,' I said to Lanya, as we explored the back door and peered in the windows of the Bard looking for a way to break in without making too much noise.

'Who can sleep when revolution is in the air?' Mr Corman leaned on his cane in the unlit doorway at the back of Brown's, and then came carefully down the steps. 'We sleep when we are dead,' he said as he reached us. 'Please use this key. I do not wish you to break the door.'

'Mr Corman! Read the note! You shouldn't—'

'Shouldn't, nonsense. Inside with you both. There is revolution about, but also—' he lifted his face and breathed in the night air '—other things. Unsavoury things, the unwelcome guests of revolution. In! In!'

He ushered us inside and up the stairs past doorways that opened into dusty booklined rooms. We climbed to the third floor—Cosmology & Quantum Physics, New

Urban AI, and Weird Fiction: 19th & 20th C—where Mr Corman took hold of a shelf lined with H. P. Lovecraft stories and hauled on it. The whole bookshelf pulled away from the wall, dragging with it a mass of cobwebs and exposing a low wooden door. He opened it and we stooped down to follow him into a cramped, stuffy room with a bed, a sofa, a few chairs, a kitchen area, and door to a tiny bathroom. He leaned on his stick and looked around.

'People hide here sometimes,' he said. 'Stay. For as long as you need.'

He walked about turning on lights and firing up a gas water heater and a gas cooker while we stood gaping with gratitude.

'Which is first?' he asked. 'Food? Hot water?'

'Food!' I said, just as Lanya said, 'Water!'

He nodded. 'I will return with coffee and bread.'

I wondered how many times he'd done this: the hidden room, people on the run, food, shelter. Safety and unquestioning kindness, with no fuss or heroics.

Lanya dived for the bathroom while I hunted around and discovered a functioning screen hidden away in a cupboard. I hauled it out, tuned it to the news channel and waited through a business report and a weather report before it came to what I wanted.

Back to the Marsh now, where quick action by the army is bringing the situation under control. Meanwhile concern is focusing on the township of Moldam where it's believed the viral outbreak began. We'll shortly be hearing from Dr Parrish of Pitkerrin Laboratories. Oh, we have him right now. Dr Parrish?

Dr Parrish was a tired-looking guy who kept smoothing down what little hair he had and fidgeting with the narrow glasses perched on his nose. He was nervy. Maybe Frieda was watching off-camera.

Welcome, Doctor. Tell us about this outbreak.

The man nodded and gazed solemnly out of the screen.

Thank you, yes. I can tell you that Moldam township on Southside has been placed under quarantine after a viral outbreak was confirmed there. This virus is no threat to City-side. The population here is perfectly safe.

He was moderately convincing, I supposed.

I see. It's dangerous though, this virus?

Well, uh, yes. Yes, somewhat.

Not so convincing.

We've heard there's a vaccine?

There is. That's right. Everyone will receive it in due course.

Good to hear, doctor. But what about this claim that there isn't enough vaccine for everyone?

There will be.

But there isn't right now? How much is there, doctor? What's the current stock?

We have plenty. Fifty thousand doses. More than enough

*to contain a limited outbreak here. But, as I said, we don't
need it. The disease is quarantined in Moldam.*

What about the people on Southside?

*Well, of course, we want to get it to those Southsiders who
are in danger, but until we have a guarantee of safe passage for
our medics, and that means an enduring ceasefire, I won't be
advising we send anyone over the river.*

'Fifty thousand.' Lanya came out of the bathroom
with a billow of steam and sat on the floor beside me.
'That's enough for everyone in Moldam.'

I glanced at her and did a double take. 'What are you
wearing?'

'Pyjamas. I found them in a cupboard in the bathroom. They were pressed flat and stiff as a board, and they
smell all right.' She sniffed at her sleeve and made a face
at me. 'I was desperate for something clean. Do I look
ridiculous?'

I laughed. 'No. You look stunning.'

She smiled and hugged her knees. 'What's the news?'

'Nothing we don't already know.'

*…Marsh, we have our reporter, Jasmine Fielding, on the
scene. Jas?*

*Thank you, Tim. I'm standing in the foyer of the admin-
istration block which, as you can see, is perfectly fine, but
there are fires burning in other buildings. A lot of people have
been cleared from the grounds, but there are still some thousands at the gates, and I can tell you they don't look like going*

home soon. With me is Director of Security, Frieda Kelleran. Director, thanks for joining us at this late hour. How much damage has been done to the facilities here?

Well, Jasmine, there has been some damage but it's minimal and will soon be put right.

You've made arrests?

We have certainly made arrests, and people will be dealt with speedily and appropriately, I can assure you.

'I bet,' I said.

Director, do you think there are professional protesters in the crowd out there?

We have no doubt that One City extremists are involved. In fact, we know that they've used this disturbance to effect the escape of some of their sympathisers who were in custody here. Two in particular we'd like to bring to the attention of the public…

'Oh, look,' said Lanya.

It was us. Mugshots they'd taken at the Marsh.

…armed and dangerous. We've launched a search, of course, and will be going door to door in places where they might be holed up. We're confident we'll find them.

Thanks, Director Kelleran. We'll keep those images on rotation. Remember, folks, armed and dangerous, do not approach. But on a brighter note, things look like returning to normal here at the Marsh very soon. Back to you, Tim.

Thank you, Jas. And now in other news, the on-going drought in the north is…

I muted it and we sat staring at the weather map on the screen.

'You did look dangerous,' I said. 'I wouldn't take you on.'

She grinned at me but that soon faded. 'She knows we're out and she knows we could be sick.'

'But she didn't say anything about the virus. And she probably won't—'

A clatter outside the door made us jump to our feet, but it was just Mr Corman with a small loaf of grainy bread, a hunk of cheese and a little bag of coffee from his precious store.

I tried one more time to ask him to stay away in case we were infectious, but I had no chance.

'Nikolai, I am old. I have seen off many epidemics and pandemics in my time. I do not think a new young buck of a virus will be interested in this ancient carcass. I will hear no more of this anxiety. No more.'

'They're looking for us,' I said.

'Yes, they will look. God willing, they will not find. Eat now. And sleep. I will leave you. Good night.'

We turned off the light and opened the window wide to let the room breathe in the warm night.

Lanya looked at the bread and cheese. 'Hungry?'

'Not very,' I said. 'You?'

She broke off a piece of bread. 'We should eat.' But she didn't.

'Nik, what if Frieda ignores us?'

'I know. She could. We have to hope that Fy will make such a noise that she has to do something. Besides, she doesn't know you at all. She doesn't know how much of a fanatic you are and how far you're prepared to go with this.' I glanced at her and tried to smile. 'I don't even know—how much of a fanatic are you?'

'You mean would I infect people on purpose?'

'Would you?'

'No. And you wouldn't either.'

'She'll have guessed that about me, but not you.'

'What if Fyffe's been sent away, or she's not allowed to go out while all the protests are going on?' Lanya started to pace around the room.

I sat on the couch and closed my eyes, wishing the dull ache in my head would go away. The buzz of the day's relentless action had leached out of me and all that was left was edge, and the bare fact that we were bargaining with our lives.

Lanya said, 'I've been thinking: why don't you go back and ask Dash to give you a vaccination shot?'

'I'm not doing that.'

'No, listen. It makes sense—and you're the one who's always wanting things to make sense and add up. It only needs one infected person to threaten the city.'

'Lanya. Don't do this.'

'But—'

'No.'

'Why not?' she asked.

When I didn't answer she came to sit on the couch with me. She hugged her knees; I could see her eyes glinting in the dark and smell the fresh cleanness of her pyjamas. 'Tell me why not,' she said in a matter-of-fact voice as though we were discussing why I didn't like swimming or cabbage.

In the street outside, a group of people was cheerfully breaking curfew. Laughter and chatter drifted in through the open window—they sounded confident, jubilant even, and why shouldn't they? They'd taken Sentian back. But inside in the dark we were a long way from confident or jubilant.

'I'm not leaving you,' I said.

Lanya watched me calmly. 'If you go back to that med centre and get vaccinated then you'll be able to go to the One City people and use their broadcasts to make a fuss about Moldam.'

'No.'

'Because? Give me a proper reason.'

'What does that mean?' I said. 'A proper reason.'

'It means a reason beyond being worried about me.'

'I call that a proper reason.'

'You need more.'

I have more, I thought. It's what my father had done. He left my mother and me because it was the strategic thing to do. It must have made sense to them both at the time, but then the security forces picked us off one by one.

I said, 'If I go and ask for the vaccine, they won't let me come back, and then you'll be alone. Alone is too hard.'

Lanya said nothing for a long time. Then she put out a hand and I took it. She said, 'Those people in the Marsh—they died blind and bleeding. This is a horrible disease.'

'We could both go back to Dash and ask to be vaccinated.'

'Is that what you want?'

'I don't know what I want. I want this not to be happening. What are we supposed to do?'

'Listen to me. You don't have to be loyal to Moldam. You don't owe it anything. It's not really home for you.'

The laughter outside receded down the street and faded to nothing. Now everything out there was quiet and waiting: the army licking its wounds, Frieda sharpening her claws, the activists inspecting their barricades.

'Home,' I said. 'Where is that?'

She turned my hand over in both of hers and studied my palm. 'If it's not here, and it's not there, it'll have to halfway between, Bridge-boy.'

'And you know what happened to the bridge.'

She smiled.

'My home's not a place,' I said. 'It's you, and Levkova and my father, I guess, and…all those people who make room in their lives for strays.'

The beads in her braids clacked as she shook her head.

'You're not a stray. But I get what you mean. We go back with the vaccine for everyone or we don't go back at all.'

We sat there, not wanting to move. At last she said, 'You know how they say that when you're about to die your whole life flashes before you?'

'Yeah.'

'I've discovered that it's not like that if you've got days to think about it. It's not your life up to now that you see, it's the life you won't get to live that unrolls in front of you.'

'And how does it look?'

'It looks sweet,' she said. 'So, so sweet. It's full of places to explore and opportunities to take and people that you love and who love you. It's impossibly full of amazing things that will probably never happen but they make you think to yourself, if only I get the chance, I won't waste a second of it.'

She looked at me with a smile then kissed my palm with featherlight lips.

CHAPTER 36

The pictures of the Marsh on the screen showed calm and clean, no protesters, no looters, no burning buildings. Old stock footage, I thought, which made me wonder what was actually going on there.

The voice-over was cheery and reassuring.

…and you're back with Cityside News, your official guide to the stories that matter. In reports just to hand, a spokesman for One City has conceded that yesterday's attempt on Pitkerrin Marsh was a failure—

A burst of static cut the picture and gave me a blank blue screen and a woman's voice.

Ha! No we haven't. Rumours eh? Are we on? Yes, we are ON. Good morning, everyone, this is your One City wake up call! We will be keeping you posted today with some real news about what's going on in your city. First up, the viral outbreak in Moldam. Yes, it could be as bad as it sounds.

Worried? You should be. Want to know the full story? Then stay with us. In the meantime, what should you look for? Fever, headaches, muscle pain, a sudden rash. But better yet, look for a warehouse full of vaccines. It's out there and just waiting to be—

Another static burst, then nothing but blue screen.

'Nik?' Lanya's voice croaked from the bed. 'What are you doing? What time is it?'

'Nearly six.'

She sat up, gazed at me blearily then flopped back on the pillow. 'What's going on?'

'One City's hacked the news channel. Not very successfully, though.' The Cityside News guy was back.

Sorry folks, some technical trouble there. Let's take a look at the weather. Another beautiful day...

Lanya peered at me from her nest of sheets. 'Have you been watching that thing all night?'

'No. A couple of hours, maybe.'

'Any news of Moldam?'

'Nope. We're on, though, you and me. Every hour with the headlines. They're still talking about searching door to door, but there's nothing about us being from Moldam or being infected with the virus.'

'She doesn't want to cause a panic.'

'No. We'll have to cause it instead. And we could, if One City can just get wind of us and get their hack sorted. D'you want some coffee?'

'I hear sirens.'

'Yeah. Not for us, though. When they come for us they'll be quiet. But stick your head out the window and take a look—sirens, smoke, alarms, the whole deal.'

Lanya got up and peered outside.

'Grief, what is going on?'

'I don't know. Maybe Dash was right? One City's grabbing the chance to make trouble.'

She turned back to me. 'They'll be far too busy to pay attention to us, won't they? Why would they even listen to someone like Fyffe?'

We sat and watched the news channel report inter-mittantly, with transmission getting cut and scrambled in a battle for signal between the official channel and the One City hackers.

You're with Morrison's Morning on Cityside News. Let's go to our reporters on the street. It's been one heck of a night, I can tell you. After failing to take the Marsh yesterday, One City extremists have hit out across the city bringing disruption and chaos. We'll go first to the Marsh. Carter, can you hear me? Carter? Are you there'

'Come in, Carter,' said Lanya. 'Concerned citizens want to know.'

It's still burning, Peter! I'm standing outside the perim-eter fence beside what used to be Gate 14, but nothing's left of the guardpost. The army regained control last night but the mob is back this morning, bigger than ever, and clashes continue. No one's available—

'I bet no one's available,' I said. 'Frieda, where are you now?'

We seem to have lost the link there. But I think we've got Megan in Sentinel Square. Megan?

Cut to a woman in a flak jacket pressing a hand to her earpiece and shouting at the camera over the sound of a crowd chanting and riot police banging truncheons in unison on their perspex shields.

It's tent city here in the square, Peter! Behind me, you can see about three hundred tents. They went up overnight. Police are covering the Sentinel Parade exit to Watch Hill, but people are still streaming in from Shale Street and they've hung a One City banner from the upper balcony of the Old Town Hall. It looks like they've occupied—

Blue screen.

'Quit doing that!' I threw a cushion at the screen. 'We want to see what's going on!'

Whoever was hacking must have thought so too because the picture came back a minute later.

…tent city here in St John's Square too, Peter. And much the same story—the mob is in control. And here's a strange development right out of the 'what the hey?' box: the minister of St John's claims to be offering sanctuary to known extremists, in fact to those two young hoodlums we've been warned about. Can you believe that? Can he even do that, Peter? I mean, is that still a thing? Sounds medieval to me…

'Hey,' said Lanya. 'That's kind. Do you know him?'

'The minister? No, well, sort of. He was at the church yesterday when we were supposed to be getting you back. Frieda locked him in the crypt to keep him out of the way.'

'Oh, look at that,' she nodded at the screen. 'That looks familiar. Isn't that just down the road?'

...strangely calm here in Sentian, a known hotbed of One City extremists and Breken sympathisers. A week ago this place was almost cleared and demolition of its slums had begun. You can see the bulldozers parked over there. But now it's been reoccupied. People have thrown barricades across the main thoroughfares, reigniting their campaign to bring down the Cityside administration and open the floodgates to a Breken takeover. Clearly, Peter, the sooner this place is levelled the safer we'll all be. Back to you in the studio.

More static and the blue screen again. Then a woman's voice.

No, let's not go back to the studio. One City here again, people. Telling you things you need to know. First up: what are we really after? In fact what we're after are ceasefire talks and negotiation...

Someone knocked on our door and we looked at each other and got to our feet.

'They won't knock either,' I said and went to open the door. It was Fyffe, looking relieved and hassled at the same time. She swung a pack from her back to the floor.

'Here are your clothes—the ones you came over the

river in. And here's some bread and eggs and chocolate—it was all I could grab in a hurry. Dash came last night with your note. How can I help?'

We explained what we needed—publicity and lots of it, via the One City hackers if possible.

'How did you get in here?' asked Lanya. 'There are barricades and—'

Fyffe shook her head. 'It's quiet out there right now. And people are quite friendly. I got a wave and a few "good mornings". And it's early so no one at home expects me to be up yet. But I need to get back before they know I'm gone. So, we need pressure on Frieda, right?'

'Right,' I said. 'We need to make sure that everyone knows the Moldam quarantine is broken and that Frieda is the only one who can release the vaccine. Also we need an actual stock of vaccine. And, we need Citysiders, including the security forces and the army, to agree to send the stuff over the river to the enemy. How likely is any of that?'

Fyffe was nodding as though she could actually deliver on all of it. She had that braced-and-ready look, like she was about to fly out the door and do battle.

'Anything else?' she said.

I smiled. 'That's not enough?'

She put the back of her hand against my forehead and on my cheek, the way I'd seen Lanya's mother test for fever.

'He's okay so far,' said Lanya. 'So am I.'

'I need to hurry though, don't I,' said Fyffe. She gave us a bright smile and was gone.

Lanya and I looked at each other and knew that we'd both rather be charging off with Fyffe to do something instead of hanging around waiting for the headache, the bruising, the fever to arrive; or for the crash of the front door being bashed in and the thump of boots charging up the stairs. It was hardly even morning and already the waiting seemed endless.

Early in the afternoon we heard boots taking the stairs two at a time. Then our book shelf door swung open. My father had arrived. He paused when he saw us, as though he was expecting us to be half dead already, then ducked under the doorframe.

'What do you think you're doing?'

'Hello,' I said. 'We're blackmailing Frieda, I guess that's what you mean?'

'So I've heard. Corman sent a runner with the news.' He looked at Lanya, then at me. 'Are you sick?'

'We don't know yet,' she said.

We told him what had happened with Jono in the underground room at the Marsh and Dash riding to the rescue. He listened, tight lipped, scowling at me the whole time, as though this was the worst idea anyone had ever had in many lifetimes of ideas, so I finished by saying,

'What would you have done?'

He walked over to the little window and stood there staring out at rooftops. When at last he turned back to us, he said, 'Frieda will call your bluff. She'll wait you out. You don't know her.'

I said, 'Do you know where the vaccines are?'

'No.'

'Me neither,' I said. 'So we've got no choice, short of making a private deal with Frieda for two doses of vaccine if we agree to go away and forget all this. Is that what you want?'

He gave me a grim smile and after a moment he said quietly, 'Of course that's what I want.' But then he looked away and walked around the room as though he was studying it for hidden dangers.

'All right,' he said. 'You've got two days. Meanwhile, we'll spread panic any way we know how. And I'm finding you a doctor.'

He turned and disappeared down the stairs.

We stood gazing at the empty doorway.

Lanya said, 'Did it ever occur to you that you might be wrong about your father?'

CHAPTER 37

It's News and Views! *Welcome to your midday round-up here on Cityside News with me, Jennifer Long. First up: there was controversy this morning in the midst of the continuing disorder as the delegation from the Dry weighed in to the fray. Our political expert David Hart is with me now. David, you've got more on this.*

I do, Jenny, thank you. The Dry delegation called a press conference this morning and this reporter was there. Now we at Cityside News are dedicated to truth in reporting, as you know, and I have to tell you that our guests from the Dry made some frankly outrageous and inflammatory statements at that conference. After careful thought, we have made an editorial decision not to give those claims any publicity. It was a difficult decision and we realise that it may not be popular, but we stand by it. Remember folks, it's in the interests of truth in rep—

Then came the static burst we were always waiting for: the blue screen, the woman's voice.

Twaddle! Does that, or does that not sound like sanctimonious twaddle to you? Yes, it's your One City friends back again. We were at that meeting too, and we've got the audio. Want to hear it? Good, because I'm going to play it for you. One thing first though: there are strong claims in this audio, and they do need to be verified. We're working on that. If they make you roll your eyes, well, roll away, but then hold onto your hat because at the end of this audio there's something you need to hear: hand on heart, people, I'm telling you, the safety of your family depends on you staying with it to the end. Listen up! Here it comes.

There were noises of the shuffling and banging of microphones, then quiet, and then Nomu's Anglo filled the room, soft, clipped, faintly rolling her 'r's in the back of her throat:

I know this disease. I will tell you how.

We heard her take a deep breath then she told the world what Raffael had told me: that a group of Citysiders had released HV–C6 on her people in the Dry; that they had demanded space in their settlement in return for the vaccine; that she had come to the city with her delegation to learn how to make the vaccine to take back to the Dry. And then we found out how she came to be under the bridge the night it was destroyed.

I gorged on the city—food and clothes and paint on my

face and paste in my hair—I gorged until I was sick. Home-sick. Heartsick. Sick of myself. So I ran away. I cut my hair, I took my old desert clothes, and I hid in Sentian where the rebels live. There were many of us who hid on the streets there, but one night the soldiers came and drove us like animals into a truck. They did not know who I was—they saw a brown face and a girl without a home, that was enough for them. They took us to the Marsh and put us in a room under the ground. Whitecoats watched us. They watched us sicken. They watched my friends die one by one. But I did not get sick. I was protected by the vaccine. The whitecoats looked closely at me then and saw who I was. When night came they put me on a boat and set it on the river and then a great explosion swamped the boat and tipped me into the water. I struggled to the shore on the south bank of the river. The people of Moldam took me in and cared for me, and two days ago they brought me back to my people here on Cityside.

More sounds of shuffling, then the audio clicked off and the broadcaster's voice came back.

Well, my friends, did you hear that? And you thought Moldam was under quarantine. This girl got from Moldam to here under the noses of whatever security is enforcing that quarantine. And she's not alone. No, indeed. Remember those two young extremists, so called, the security forces are chasing? They're from Moldam, and they've sent us a message. They're infected with this virus and they're not going home, or accepting vaccination, until they can go home with the vaccine

for all of Moldam. Sound like blackmail? Well, maybe it does.
Sounds like loyalty to me. What would you do in their place?

'Thank you, Fyffe!' I said.

The screen cut back to City News.

You're back with Jenny Long on your official news
channel. In breaking news: there's renewed chaos unfolding
across Cityside this afternoon as wild rumours circulate
that the Moldam quarantine has been breached. Assur-
ances from Security Director Kelleran have had no effect as
crowds surround warehouses, hospitals and medical centres
demanding the vaccine.

Lanya hugged her knees and rested her head on
them. 'Here we go at last,' she said.

The counterpunch came late that night. An explosion rocked us awake. Then another, and another. The
window and door rattled so hard they almost burst from
their frames and the building shook as though it was
trying to twist itself off its foundations. We raced to the
window, saw darkness, smelled smoke. We scrambled
into clothes and went out to the landing, unsure whether
to run or hide.

Run, as it turned out: my father came charging up
the stairs calling, 'Out, out, out! Now! The barricades are
blown, the army's here.'

We clattered down the stairs and out the back door,
and Lanya and I both turned towards Brown's, but my

father said, 'Don't worry about Corman. He'll brave it out.'

'How do you know?' I said.

'Because that's where I've been tonight. It's what he does. Come this way!'

We went along the back streets—Sentian is mostly back streets, and I knew them all. So, it transpired, did my father. People were spilling out back doors and climbing down fire escapes, running and yelling to each other, lighting fires in bins and handing out homemade contraptions of fuel and fuse. The air stank of smoke and turpentine and everyone looked like that was fueling them too: they were pumped.

'They're going to fight,' said my father, ushering us through the front door of a tiny grocery shop where two people were putting on protective masks. They greeted him by name and he nodded to them, then hurried us out into another lane.

'You have a different fight,' he said.

'Can they win?' asked Lanya.

He looked up and down the lane, and we listened for whether the fighting was close. It wasn't, and he relaxed a fraction.

'No,' he said. 'Not by themselves. We're outgunned. Sentian will go, but it won't go quietly and it will take much longer than it might have once, because it's not alone now. The army and the security forces are stretched.

We've been organised and waiting for this for years. We just needed the trigger.'

'Oh,' I said, understanding at last why the whole of Cityside had blown apart so fast.

'Yes,' he said. 'You, God help me, are the trigger. The two of you and this bioweapon of Frieda's. If we're going to save Moldam, we need to push hard now. We have to make Frieda declare her hand, and we have to win over the army.'

'Is that all,' said Lanya.

He almost smiled. 'Don't despair. Come on, this way.'

It was quieter now, and we seemed to have left the fighting behind.

'Where are we going?' I asked.

'St John's,' he said. 'The church is as good an isolation zone for you two as any.'

'And what's your plan?'

'It had been to dig in at St John's, Sentinel and other places around Cityside, hack the city's electronic systems— media, transport, finance, if possible—and bring the place to a grinding halt. We hadn't counted on our trigger coming with a deadline, and it's one hell of a deadline. Now we have to save Moldam any way we can, and that means bringing Frieda out of the shadows, exposing what she's done and hoping that most of Cityside doesn't want that much blood on their hands.'

We came to St John's, climbed the steps to the

darkened porch and looked back across the tent settlement that had sprung up in the square. The lights were the first thing that hit you—every tent glowed golden, and around the perimeter strings of lights swung from poles. Proper camping tents jostled for space with thrown-together tarps on tripods, all with their front covers thrown back to catch the breeze. But now the breeze brought a whiff of smoke from the battles raging elsewhere and people were moving, talking earnestly, starting to form a human barricade around the perimeter behind banners proclaiming *One City Is Possible* and *Speak Up, Stand Up!*

'Who are they?' asked Lanya.

My father gave a half shrug. 'They are many things. People who are tired of war. People who want a just peace, elections, a free media, commerce across the river. They don't all agree with each other about what they want and how to get it, but they do know what they don't want.'

We stood there a while, seeing what solidarity and hope for a bright new world looks like when it first kicks off. And I wondered whether it would extend to solidarity with Moldam.

'Sir?' said Lanya. 'I have an idea.'

My father turned to her.

'What if you go to Frieda and ask for a deal? Like the one you talked about: two doses of the vaccine for Nik and me if she'll look into helping Moldam. She'll think that will be the end of it and everyone will stop panicking.

But tell her to come here with the vaccines. Then you have your stage and your audience to expose what she's doing.'

My father looked across the square, thinking it through.

I said, 'But would she believe that was a real offer?'

Lanya drew me aside. 'Everyone has a breaking point, including your father. That's how Frieda works, isn't it. I don't think she'll have much trouble believing he'd do this to save you.'

CHAPTER 38

We slept in the crypt. Like old times.

The minister nodded to me saying, 'I remember you,' and gave me a pile of blankets and pillows. If he was freaking out because there were sick people in his church he didn't say so, but he had tried to throw out Frieda's armed agents a few days before, and he'd offered us safe haven in a news report, so I figured he must be an ally. He beckoned us over behind the slab of granite that was the crypt's altar and pulled back a wall-hanging to expose a small door.

'If you need to get out in a hurry, this takes you up some stairs and into the sanctuary, that's the room behind the main altar. You can get outside from there.'

My father went off to rally the troops or gather intel or make the deal with Frieda, or possibly all three. Lanya and I set up camp in a corner of the crypt. Lanya lit a candle in front of the altar icon and sat down beside me on our makeshift bed. We watched the light flicker on the gold leaf.

'How are you?' I asked.

'Okay. Tired. You?'

'Same.'

But I didn't really know. Was this headache just a headache? Were these muscle aches just a result of a few full-on days? For all we knew, the virus was hurtling towards us like a freight train, only we couldn't see it yet. Maybe we were conscious of the rumbling of its wheels in the distance, but soon, perhaps very soon, it might roar out of the darkness and run us down.

Lanya put her head on my shoulder and, with the world going insane above us, we fell asleep.

My father woke us. The candle had burned out and daylight fell through the doorway at the top of the stairs. Hard on the eyes. We surfaced slowly, trying to look bright eyed and ready.

'How are you both?' he asked. He was studying our faces carefully.

'Okay,' I said, and Lanya nodded.

He looked unconvinced.

'What's going on?' I asked.

'Frieda's agreed,' he said. 'She'll be here at noon with vaccine for both of you. We're getting the Dry-dwellers to verify that it's authentic.'

I rubbed sleep out of my eyes. 'She's not suspicious about meeting here?'

'Doesn't seem to be. There'll be a crowd in to watch, but she won't know that it's our crowd. We've put the word out for supporters to come in—we haven't told them what it's about, but we've set it up as well as we can to expose what she's doing to Moldam. It could all go wrong, of course—it's a big risk, to you in particular.'

'We've come this far,' said Lanya. 'We're not turning back now.'

He looked at me.

'It could all go right, too,' I said and tried to smile.

It must have looked like a win–win for Frieda, a great two-in-one deal: she could publicly defuse the explosive potential of HV–C6 roving the city unchecked, and she could show the One City crowd that their celebrated leader would sell out Moldam for his son. Accordingly, she turned up with a circus: a full media contingent from City-side News—a big-name reporter, three cameras, a bunch of tech people and their hangers-on; she also brought six agents, including Dash, Jono and two men who seemed to be medics. There was an army high-up too, with four of his underlings, as well as a thirty-strong division to patrol the outskirts of the square. There weren't enough of them to clear the square, they were there as a warning to the tent city: this is what's coming once you've had your fun—take note and, if you're wise, take off.

Frieda arrived in a bustle of busyness. She talked to the news team, she talked to the minister, she talked to her army chum.

Lanya and I sat on the altar steps and watched her make her way up the aisle, breezy with confidence. She led them all up past us to the wide space in front of the altar and said to the news team, 'Set up here.'

She looked around and noticed that people had started to drift in and occupy seats. She seemed slightly puzzled, as though she wasn't expecting an on-site audience as well as a city-wide one, but then she decided to capitalise on that.

She said to the news team, 'Make sure they'll be able to hear me too.'

Then she turned to Lanya and me. 'Here we are again. I told you the Marsh would stand.'

'It looked like it was burning to me,' I said.

She stared down her nose at us and walked away.

I looked across the crowd. Mr Corman had arrived, looking immaculate and in no way as if he'd just come from the street battle for Sentian. I saw Anna and Samuel, from the house in Bethun where I'd stayed when Lanya was in the Marsh. My father was talking to them. After a while he made his way up to the front. He stopped there, didn't look at Frieda, just stood with arms folded, watching, looking unhappy.

A minor commotion at the big front doors announced the arrival of the Dry-dwellers—Nomu and Raffael and the other three members of their team. They'd ditched their Cityside clothes and gone back to their own things: tunics, leggings and soft leather sandals. Nomu's tunic was a brilliant blue, Raffael's, almost white. They glided in a group through the crowd towards the front. People were curious and almost deferential towards them.

Lanya nudged me and nodded towards a side door: Fyffe had just come through it, all but dragging her parents inside. They look as nervous and out of place as she looked excited. Frieda couldn't hide that she was surprised to see them, and the newsman could barely contain his glee. He scurried down the steps, beckoning a camera operator to follow, and zeroed in on Sarah, who was more likely than her husband to deliver on the audience's appetite for grief.

The crowd cleared a space around them and the reporter said, 'Mrs Hendry, you've lost two sons to the hostiles. One of them shot by Moldam militants. Perhaps you're feeling that what's happening in Moldam right now is divine justice?'

He pushed a microphone at her, but she looked at him with cool intensity and said, 'I have nothing to say to you.'

The reporter looked surprised and disappointed that he had to abandon a heartfelt beginning to his coverage. He and his cameraman hurried back up the steps to where

Frieda and the minister were talking. The minister was asking for a chance to welcome the crowd and the wider city audience to his patch and she said, 'All right, but keep it short.'

By now the crowd had fallen quiet and watchful. The minister, wired up with a little lapel microphone, went to the top of the altar steps. He opened his arms wide and welcomed everyone to St John's, which, he said, was a place of peace and reconciliation, and he hoped that this would be an instance of exactly those things. He turned to Frieda and said, 'Director Kelleran, over to you,' and he went down into the crowd.

The reporter took his place and did his own piece about how we were all here to calm the spreading panic. Then he said to Frieda, 'Director. We've heard some alarming stories about these two young people here. Can you set our minds at rest?'

'Yes, Peter, I can. People seem to be concerned that the illness afflicting Moldam could jump the river. I can assure everyone that it is not an airborne virus. It will *not* jump the river. And we will be strengthening the quarantine around Moldam. Now, we don't know if these two individuals are infected or not, but I'm pleased to be able to dispense the vaccine to them here and now to put minds at rest.'

She beckoned to the medics and to Lanya and me. We stood up and moved front and centre. Frieda made a great show of taking a little black case from the leader of the Dry delegation and opening it. Inside were two syringes and two vials. She held up a vial to show the crowd and the cameras, then held out the box to the medics who took a syringe and vial each.

I looked at the vials and thought, here it is: rescue. No more speeding freight train. No more staring at a future that was short and full of horror. Both of us safe. Home, free.

'Ready?' said one of the medics to me. 'Hold out your arm.'

I looked at Lanya.

She was staring at her own vial of vaccine.

Then she gave a small nod and said, 'Now!'

She grabbed a vial. I grabbed a vial.

We dropped them on the floor and crunched them underfoot.

CHAPTER 39

The reporter swore loudly into his microphone. My father closed his eyes and bowed his head. I took the lapel mic the minister had given me earlier in the day out of my pocket and spoke into it.

My voice boomed through the sound system of the church. 'Do you want to know how we got infected?'

Frieda burst out, 'There's no evidence that you are infected!'

I pointed across to Nomu. 'That room that Nomu talked about at the news conference yesterday. Underground in the Marsh, where they've been testing this disease. We've been there. And we're not the only ones here who know about it.'

I turned towards Dash and held out the microphone.

Her eyes got wide and she mouthed, '*What?*'

'There is no such room!' Frieda cried. 'There

never was!'

People were starting to yell out. 'Tell the truth!' 'What are you hiding?'

Dash was staring at me. I kept holding out the mic, kept meeting her eye, willing her to move.

Frieda turned to the cameras. 'This is a fabrication! A girl from the Dry who's too ashamed to admit she's a runaway, and two Breken youths—*Breken,* let me remind you—who want to terrorise this city.'

The crowd was shouting at her, and she was starting to lose her cool and shout back, and the reporter was trying to break in, calling, 'Calm, everyone! If we can just calm down. Let the director speak—'

Then Dash moved.

She marched past her boss to me, took the mic and spoke.

'That room exists,' she said.

Everybody stopped and Dash spoke into the hush. 'I've been there. I've seen bodies there.' She pointed to the two medics. 'So have they.' She held out the mic to them.

After a brief, frozen moment one of them gave a little groan, set his mouth in a thin line and walked up to take it from her. He stared at it for a second then put it to his lips and said in a low, broken voice, 'Yes, God forgive me, I've been there too.'

Lanya prised the mic from the man's hand. 'The virus is a bioweapon,' she said in her careful Anglo. 'It has been released in Moldam to break us. But do you think it will stop there?'

'This is fantasy!' snapped Frieda. 'There is no secret room. There are no bioweapons. Moldam's problems are of its own making. If they agree to cease hostilities we will negotiate medical assistance for them. We've said it time and time again.'

She gestured to Jono and another of her agents. 'Take them out of here. All of them.'

Then she turned to the camera saying, 'This charade is over.'

She tore off her own lapel mic, dumped it into the hands of the dazed-looking reporter and turned for a side door.

But the crowd had other ideas. A ripple of movement, a step here, a shuffle there, and the doorways were blocked. Frieda paused, head high, imperious as ever.

She grabbed back the mic. 'I said, this is over.' And, to the army guy, 'Major? Clear the doorways.'

Someone yelled, 'It's not over till you tell us the truth!'

Then another, louder voice said, 'I'll tell you the truth.'

It was the minister, still wired up with a mic. He made his way out of the crowd and halfway up the steps.

Frieda was shaking her head at the reporter, but the cameras were still rolling and she was maybe wary of insulting a churchman. She walked down a couple of steps to be level with him and gave him a full-on stare as if to say, you can't see the gun I'm holding to your head, but do not doubt that it is there.

The minister looked across the crowd. 'We're tired of war,' he said.

The crowd stirred, some shrugged, tired of platitudes.

'We're hungry for peace.'

People murmured and a few shouted in agreement.

The minister turned to Frieda, 'Director, you have told us that Moldam does not want peace. That we cannot help them.' Then he turned back to the crowd, 'My friends, the director is lying. In fact, she is responsible for planting this virus in Moldam. I accuse Director Kelleran of a war crime.'

Uproar.

Frieda yelled at her two sidekicks to seize the minister, but he walked back into the crowd and to get to him the agents would have had to abandon Lanya and me and Dash and the turncoat medic.

The crowd was yelling for the army guy to arrest Frieda, and he was ordering his four underlings to take control, but they didn't have a chance unless they shot someone.

The cameras were still rolling.

Everyone who had a gun had drawn it and was aiming down into the crowd.

The minister tried calling for quiet but things just got louder so he shouted over the mayhem. 'Stop! Listen to me! Listen! Three days ago I heard the director say she had ordered the virus release in Moldam! I heard her say how it was done! Please! Please be quiet!'

People shut up at last.

'First things first,' he said. 'We must save Moldam!'

Someone started pushing towards the front of the crowd. Two people: Fyffe, who climbed the steps and came to stand with Lanya and Dash and me, and her mother, who held out her hand for the microphone that Lanya was holding. Sarah looked across the crowd, which was quiet, watching her, and then into the cameras and spoke to the city.

'People seem to think I want retribution for my sons. This is not true. What good would that do? What I want is a future for my daughter.' She looked at Fyffe and then at Thomas Hendry in the crowd. 'And that means taking the vaccine to Moldam. You understand why? The only way to stop this disease is to stop it in Moldam. There is enough vaccine to do that. So let's do that. We, all of us, have given too many of our children to this war.'

There was rustling and a rising tide of talk. Someone yelled, 'We don't know where it is—the vaccine!'

'I do,' said the turncoat medic.

Someone else yelled, 'It'll need an escort.'

And you knew, from the frisson in the air in that

church that every one of those people would walk the vaccine to Moldam, and so would everyone outside in the square, and in Sentinel Square and in Sentian. They'd all do it. But it wouldn't be enough.

Sarah Hendry knew that too. She turned to the army high-up who stood beside his soldiers, their guns still trained on the crowd. She didn't speak. She didn't need to.

He looked out at the crowd, then at all of us standing beside him, then at the cameras. And maybe he thought about the logic of what Sarah had said, and maybe he thought about the weight of numbers out there in the square and beyond, and maybe he thought about his own kids.

He gestured to his team and said, 'Stand down.'

There was total hush for a good ten seconds, as though everyone was astonished that we'd arrived at this moment. Then they all began talking at once. Fyffe flashed me a jubilant smile and went to her mother. Frieda turned back towards us with a look of utter disbelief on her face.

I breathed out shakily: all I could think was that no one had been shot.

Then Lanya's hand gripped mine and I realised, first, that she was breathing as shakily as I was and second, that something mighty had just happened.

Frieda marched across to the army commander. 'Major, what do you think you're doing? You have your orders and they are certainly not to—'

'My orders, Director, are to protect you and your team and to maintain order here.'

'That's right. And so—'

'I'm placing you in protective custody.' He looked around and called two of his people over.

'Take Director Kelleran and her team to the crypt.' He put a detaining hand on the shoulder of Frieda's turncoat medic. 'Except you,' he said. 'You, we need.'

Frieda drew herself up tall. 'You have no authority to do this, *Major*.'

The emphasis was to remind him, I guess, that he was middle ranking at best. But he wasn't subordinate to her, and she knew that.

He glanced across the crowd, which was still blocking all the doors and was starting to turn its attention from euphoric air punching and back slapping to what would happen next.

'Director,' he said. 'Right now I can't guarantee your safety in any other way.'

He nodded to his underlings and they swept her away, along with her five remaining agents, including Dash and Jono.

The major beckoned to my father. I wondered if the guy was itching to arrest this man who had been Cityside's most wanted for so long.

Turns out, he was.

He called his remaining two grunts over and said, 'Nikolai Stais, you're under arrest.'

I shouted, 'No!' and started to move, but my father shot me a warning look and I backed off.

The major glanced at me, then turned to the crowd, put thumb and finger to his mouth and whistled hard.

Everyone shut up and looked at him. By my count, there were over three hundred people in that church, and more behind pillars and in the foyer. The major had the complete attention of every one of them: they were focused, hard eyed, not trusting him at all, but wanting to trust what was happening right now, wanting to reach through the space he'd opened up and grab this chance.

'I'm clearing the church,' he announced. 'Everybody out!'

Nobody moved.

He drew breath, and I think he meant to say it again, louder, but he must have realised that these people weren't going to move, however loudly and often he issued the command. They weren't looking at the major now, anyway, they were looking at my father, who moved three steps to within quiet earshot of him. The armed grunts followed, like moons dragged along in the pull of a planet.

My father spoke in a low voice to the major, who stared at the ground at first, then lifted his head and looked slowly across the crowd. He was like a man advancing on new territory, knowing it was laced with mines but feeling compelled to explore. When my father finished talking, the major hesitated for a long moment, then gave a sharp nod.

My father turned to the crowd. 'Go,' he said.

And, simple as that, people headed out into the square. The news team followed, lugging cameras and audio kit and trying to grab interviews on the run.

The Dry-dwellers stayed, so did the Hendrys. Lanya and I did too, and I could see Anna and Samuel in the foyer keeping an eye on what was happening in both church and square.

Fyffe drew the turncoat medic aside in that gentle way of hers. She looked concerned for him and reassuring and wholly trustworthy. She told him her name and got his. Then she took him into the gathering of Dry-dwellers and her parents and began to introduce him.

The major watched the crowd leave and seemed surprised that they'd gone so calmly and completely at a single word from my father. He gave a slight shake of his head and said to him, 'You're still under arrest.'

But my father wasn't paying attention. He was listening to the others standing nearby. Fyffe had done good work with the turncoat medic: awed by the company he was suddenly keeping, he was spilling information about the location of the vaccines.

'How will you transport them?' called my father.

The medic looked around and stuttered, 'Ah…er…'

'A Hendry truck would do it,' said my father.

Thomas and Sarah looked alarmed, but Fyffe said, 'Yes! That's a great idea!'

'And an army escort would help,' my father added.

The major almost laughed. 'I'm not authorising that.'

Thomas Hendry looked at his daughter, who was lit up with excitement and commitment. He sighed.

'You don't have to, Major. We've decided what we're going to do. You can choose to help, or not.'

'With respect, sir, I can't let you do that without authorisation from—'

'Well, get it, man! We're not waiting.' Then the Hendrys and the Dry-dwellers, with the medic in tow, walked down the altar steps into the body of the church, and hurried away.

The major was in danger of being cut adrift; things were moving beyond his control, fast.

'You still have me,' said my father.

The major unclipped his comms unit and stared at it for a moment. I could see him wrestling with the bargain he was being offered: would the arrest of this wanted man be enough of a prize for his commanding officer to offset the action of escorting the vaccines across the river?

He clicked on the unit and walked away, talking into it urgently.

My father turned to Lanya and me. 'Go with the Hendrys.'

'No,' I said. 'I'm not leaving.' I knew what they did to their big-name hostages. They murdered them.

'Nik,' he said, 'You have to go. You're part of this bargain.'

I looked at the grunts with their guns standing beside him, and at the major, still talking but watching us now.

'What will you do?' I asked.

'What I can,' said my father. 'Don't despair. Now, go.'

It wasn't supposed to end like this. He was supposed to come over the river with us, Lanya and I would get the vaccine along with the rest of Moldam, and he would be the person who brokered the lasting peace.

Fyffe reappeared at the doors of the church to see, I guess, why we hadn't gone with her yet.

Lanya nudged me gently. 'They're waiting for us.'

'I know,' I tried to say but my voice wasn't working.

My father nodded and said, 'Go on!' but I was ambushed by the ache of losing him again. I couldn't move or speak. Lanya took my hand and walked a few steps, and at last I went with her, down the aisle and out into brilliant sunlight and the turbulent, crowd-filled square.

CHAPTER 41

We took the vaccine to Moldam.

We brought it across the river in a couple of Hendry trucks escorted by a crowd of twenty thousand plus, and the army. The major had decided, or been told, to support the bargain in play. And we did need the army. At the very least we needed them to stand aside and let us pass.

And that's what they did: they gave us safe passage over Curswall Bridge, although they did it in a stern-faced, we'll-only-do-this-once kind of way.

When we reached the barbed-wire barricades on the Curswall boundary road, the major gave the soldiers guarding them new orders: roll up the wire, let the trucks pass. And in we went. But once we were through, they rolled the wire back into place.

When we stopped outside the infirmary on the parkland west of the shantytown, I turned to Lanya.

'Made it. We actually made it.'

I jumped out and helped her down from the truck cab.

She swayed in my arms.

'Nik,' she said, 'I've got a fever.'

I sat at Levkova's kitchen table and listened to the house shift and creak as the day started to hot up outside. Slanting morning sunlight picked out the sunken armchairs by the fireplace as though it was inviting me to slump into one of them, but the grate was grey with old ash and behind me the stove was cold. I'd come in from sitting on the front steps where I'd been people watching: kids were sloping off to school, barefoot and cheerful, a hawker was hauling his cart up the street with a song-like yell, stopping as women came out of their houses to buy vegetables, a fix-it guy was going door to door offering to patch up broken stuff. Moldam was back to normal, almost, although there was the small matter of having no bridge.

We'd made it in time, mostly. People had flocked to the infirmaries and makeshift dispensaries and stood in long, patient queues. Two weeks later the barbed wire was rolled up and carted away and the quarantine was lifted. A few people did get sick—some very young, some old or not too healthy. A few people died.

Levkova.

Sub-commander Tasia Levkova. The virus attacked her lungs and she died within just three days. I couldn't get my head around it, how someone so staunch and fierce and downright commanding could succumb and be gone in a heartbeat.

Not all of those who died died fast. Some were dying slowly.

Lanya lay in an isolation ward fighting a raging fever, fighting the bruising that spread beneath her skin, fighting. They couldn't tell me if she was winning.

And me? I didn't get sick at all.

We buried Levkova in the hillside graveyard overlooking Moldam, the one where a rocket had gouged a trench in the earth the night they blew up the Mol.

We buried her with honour and great grief. I'd only known her half a year, but that was easily long enough to know what everyone standing at the graveside knew: that she was fearless and she was wise and, although she tried not to let on, she was kind too—why else was I now sitting in her house? When I'd first turned up in Moldam she could have looked right past me with a not-my-problem stare, and she could have turfed me out at any time since. Instead, she fed me and gave me a roof to sleep under and she treated me like I mattered. It was Levkova who told me that my father was not dead. It was Levkova who brought us, despite our mutual suspicion, back together.

Now she was gone, and I was sitting in her kitchen missing her no-nonsense presence: she would have told me to quit chasing down worst-case scenarios about Lanya and my father and to go and be useful to someone.

I thought about going to the infirmary, but I'd hung around that place for two weeks and the staff were sick of the sight of me. Only Lanya's parents were allowed in to see her. They were in a daze of anxiety—proud, but you could see them wondering why it had to be their daughter that turned hero.

I'd tried helping out on the hill; there was rubble to move and some half-destroyed buildings to demolish, but the organisers needed workers who could pay attention to bits of falling masonry and my brain was preoccupied, dealing 'what if' cards to myself. What if Lanya recovered but the disease blinded her? What if she was crippled and could never dance again? What if, what if.

What if she died?

And my father? We'd heard nothing.

I got up and went out into the little backyard in search of some sun on my back. Levkova's five chickens came running up, so I fed them and went looking for eggs while they pottered about chuckling to themselves. Then I fired up the stove and was heating water for breakfast tea when Fyffe came in from working a night shift in the infirmary.

She kissed my cheek. 'Hello.'

'Hi,' I said. 'How was it? How is she?'

She sank into a chair and rubbed her hands over her face. 'The same, the same. I wish I could tell you something different. Oh—but, in fact I can tell you this. Guess who turned up last night!'

I opened the firebox of the stove and stuck more kindling into it. 'Who?'

'Sandor! He came back over the river to lay claim to a vaccination shot.'

That did make me smile. 'Did he get one?'

'Sure. Why not.'

'What's he up to?'

'Schemes.'

'Naturally.'

'He looked like he was doing all right—smart clothes, good hair cut.'

'Also, naturally. What schemes?'

'He's found backers to set up a ferry service between here and Cityside. He said to say hello and to give you this.'

She handed me an envelope.

I peered inside. 'Cash? What?'

'Said he owed you. That you'd given him some a while ago?'

I laughed. 'I did. I should invest in his ferries.' I held it out to her. 'But actually it's your father's. You should give it back to him.'

She frowned in mock disapproval. 'Absolutely not. It's yours, yours and Lanya's.'

I thought about that. 'Okay. I'll keep it.'

After she'd gone up to bed I put it away in a drawer where it sat in the dark like Schrödinger's cat in its box, biding its time on the question of life or death.

Mid afternoon I was sitting at the table trying to reconstruct an old radio from bits I'd found in the shed. Someone came through the front door without yelling Hello!— which meant it was either an intruder or my father, who never announced his presence because he'd spent all those years on the run.

Since it was unlikely to be either of those, I got up and went to see.

I was wrong. My father came down the hall like he was home, in one piece and with a rare smile on his face. I stared for a second, then I met him halfway.

In the kitchen he studied me while I put water on to make tea.

'You're well?' he said.

'Yeah, I didn't get sick at all.'

He nodded, and wiped a hand over his face. 'I didn't know what had happened—about Tasia, about you—until I got here half an hour ago. I went to the infirmary. Thought you might be there.'

'Lanya's there.'

'I know. I had a word with her.'

I blinked at him. 'You *what*? She's awake? Since when?'

He laughed. 'Well, very recently, I suppose.'

Awake. My heart was thumping and my words rushed out. 'How was she? Is she okay? Can I see her?'

He held up both hands. 'Surely. I don't know. You can ask.'

I was locking the back door and heading for the front. I thought about waking Fyffe, but decided that could wait.

We walked to the infirmary; running would have been better, but walking I got to hear what had happened on the other side of the river.

'They're setting up the inquiry at last,' he said. 'There'll be a lot of talk before everything becomes clear. Your agent friend, for example…what's her name?'

'Dash.'

'She's accused of insubordination, but being insubordinate to a superior who's trying to perpetrate a war crime is, well, complicated.'

'And Jono?'

'That depends. He will face questions about his unauthorised access to nerve gas and threatening a civilian with it, but he could be a key witness against Frieda. Like I said, it's complicated.'

'What will happen to Frieda?'

'Once the inquiry is over, chances are she'll go to trial.'

'Alone?'

He nodded. 'Probably. She'll be loyal to the end. I don't know what that end will be but I don't think she'll be taking anyone with her. That's her way.'

'And all those people who were escaping to the Dry, what'll happen to them?'

He gave me a wry smile. 'What always happens. They're busy proving they knew nothing about any of this. I don't know if they'll get away with that; there'll be a trail to follow, but whether a judge will be dogged enough to pursue it, we'll have to wait and see. They're powerful people.'

'And peace talks?'

He smiled again. 'There will be peace talks. At last. We haven't talked yet, but we're setting up the conditions for talking. It's slow going, but it is going.'

'Better than shooting.'

'In every way, better than shooting.'

The medic on duty said, 'Five minutes, no more.'

I tiptoed in. Lanya's eyes were closed; her face was still. Her braids had been unplaited and her hair lay spread out on the pillow. The disease had done visible damage: her face was scarred, there were pale streaks on each cheek and across her forehead, and she was waif thin, even by Moldam standards. She opened her eyes, drowsy and heavy lidded.

'Hello,' I said.

'Nik,' she murmured. 'Hi.'

'How are you doing?'

She gave a small smile. 'Didn't die.'

'Nearly did.'

'Only nearly. You?'

'Didn't even get sick.'

Her smile widened. 'Cheat,' she said softly, and held out her hand for me to take.

About a month later we hitched a ride on the back of a truck trundling up the hill to the ruins of the HQ. The site was busy with workers deconstructing what was left of the big main building; thousands and thousands of bricks were piled high across the hilltop. The guys at work there stopped and said hello to us, but they looked at Lanya with nervous glances. Her beaded braids were back and so was her dancer's long-limbed, straight-backed stance, but the scars on her face made people look twice. They made me think of the warpaint a warrior puts on to go into battle or the bodypaint that shamans wear to make themselves safe when they go into their trances. They would fade, but never completely.

The day was still and grey with not even a breeze off the river—one of those days when the city and river and sky blend one into another and you see the whole land-scape together in all its shades of silver. The crashing and banging of the demolition retreated as we walked down to the graveyard.

Levkova's grave was six weeks old and there was no riverstone to mark it yet. Lanya knelt beside the mound of earth and was silent for minutes on end. At last she wiped her face on her sleeve, blew out a breath and scooped up a handful of soil. She whispered a prayer, then sprinkled it across the grave and chanted a Pathmaker's farewell, wishing Levkova a safe journey.

We walked back to the graveyard entrance, pausing by the old house to dip our fingers into the rainwater in the stone vases by the steps and shake our hands dry, the way we had on the night of the rocket attack when Lanya told me that's what you do when you're moving from the place of the dead back to be with the living.

We climbed up to the perspex map of the Cityside skyline and sat on the bench looking out over the river and the cityscape.

'Dammit,' said Lanya. 'I'll miss her.'

'Get in line,' I said.

'Do you think she'd want revenge?'

'Levkova?'

'Wasn't that your plan? That's what you told me, down by the river the night all this started.'

She gestured towards the demolition crews. 'Revenge for Sol, you said.'

I thought of Jono throwing her into the basement of the Marsh because he was convinced I'd taken Fyffe away from him.

I shook my head. 'I've seen revenge.'

She nodded. 'What's your plan, then?'

'Plan? Well, CommSec is in pieces over there and Levkova's gone, so I don't have a workplace or a boss.'

'You know what I think?' she said.

'Hardly ever.'

She laughed, then got serious again. 'All those weeks I had lying in bed, I made a plan. And I was thinking... you could come with me, if you want.' Her face was solemn but her eyes sparked.

My heart lifted and a smile burst out of me.

'Where are you going?' I asked.

She opened her arms wide. 'Moldam, Southside, the city. To rebuild!'

I looked across at the piles of bricks and rubble and down to the half-burned shantytown and the ruins of the bridge. 'That's big,' I said.

'Yes. I'll need help.'

'Count me in.'

She held out her hand. 'I will. I have.' Then she leaned over and kissed me—a gentle, warm, amazing kiss.

'We'll need other help though,' she said as we set off down the hill. 'Who else? Your father, obviously.'

'And Fyffe,' I said.

'Dash.'

'Commander Vega,' I said. 'When he's recovered.'

'Jeitan, too,' she said.

'Nomu,' I said. 'And Raff.'

'Do you think they'll stay around for a while?'

'I do.'

'Mr Corman?'

'Of course.'

'What about Sandor?' She was smiling.

'Good luck with that,' I said. 'But maybe. My father's friends, Anna and Samuel, in Bethun, definitely.'

'And Fyffe's parents—what about them?' she asked.

'Maybe.'

'Macey?'

'Or his daughters.'

'I have forty-six cousins,' she said. 'Let's count all of them in.'

'Then there's the twenty thousand people who walked the vaccine to Moldam with us,' I said.

'We don't know their names.'

'Yet.'

'The One City hackers.'

'The minister at St John's.'

We were still naming names as we reached the bottom of the hill and turned into the road west past the shanty towards Levkova's house. We stopped at our old spot on the riverwall and stood looking across the water.

Lanya leaned close. 'Are you humming?'

'You don't want to hear me sing.'

She laughed. 'What are you humming?'

'It's this old song about two people on the bank of a river they can't cross.'

'How does it go?'

'The water is wide, I cannot get over. And neither have I wings to fly…That's all I know.'

'Oh,' she said. 'What do you think happens to them?'

'I think they find a way.'

ACKNOWLEDGMENTS

I am indebted to everyone who helped this story take shape. I am especially grateful to my editor at Text, Jane Pearson, whose comments throughout have been clear-sighted and immensely helpful. Heartfelt thanks to Joanna Orwin, Kath Rushton, Barbara and Graeme Nicholas, members of the Hawkey D'Aeth and Campbell families, and to Niall Campbell, in particular, for his bright idea at just the right moment. Thanks, always, to Paul, who listened to many drafts and with whom plot conversations are a delight. This book is dedicated to my parents, with love and gratitude.